PRAISE FOR

THE MIDNIGHT CHILDREN

"A creepy, strange, and surprisingly sweet story of friendship and belonging. Equal parts Kate DiCamillo and Shirley Jackson, this book is unlike anything else I've ever read—you will love it."

—**JONATHAN AUXIER**, *New York Times*–bestselling author of *The Night Gardener* and *Sweep: The Story of a Girl and Her Monster*

"Somewhere swirled up in all the magic, adventure, and breath-catching suspense, there's a message here about true heart connections. And about the joy of belonging even in a place where you never quite fit. The midnight children might sneak into town quietly, but there's nothing quiet about this sparkling story. It felt like fireworks in my heart."

—**NATALIE LLOYD**, *New York Times*–bestselling author of *A Snicker of Magic*

"Sometimes a soul needs a story filled with intrigue, friendship, found family, and an enormous heart—a story to make a soul ache, a story to make a soul heal, a story to make a soul leap. *The Midnight Children* is that beautiful story."
—**DUSTI BOWLING**, award-winning author of *The Canyon's Edge*

"A magical and darkly humorous journey into a world of mysterious children, timeless villains, and the undeniable power of friendship."

—**MELANIE CONKLIN**, author of *A Perfect Mistake* and *Every Missing Piece*

"Distinctive narration and heart-pounding suspense will carry this kids-outwit-grown-ups tale deep into your heart to the place where courage is born."
—**ROSANNE PARRY**, bestselling author of *A Wolf Called Wander*

"*The Midnight Children* has a touch of Roald Dahl, a dash of the Boxcar children, and a whole lot of honesty and heart . . . Told in a riveting voice, this is Dan Gemeinhart's best yet—and that's saying something."

—**PADMA VENKATRAMAN**, Walter Award–winning author of *The Bridge Home*

THE MIDNIGHT CHILDREN

THE MIDNIGHT CHILDREN

Dan Gemeinhart

HENRY HOLT AND COMPANY
NEW YORK

Henry Holt and Company, *Publishers since 1866*
Henry Holt® is a registered trademark of Macmillan Publishing Group, LLC
120 Broadway, New York, NY 10271 • mackids.com

Our books may be purchased in bulk for promotional, educational, or business
use. Please contact your local bookseller or the Macmillan Corporate and
Premium Sales Department at (800) 221-7945 ext. 5442 or by email at
MacmillanSpecialMarkets@macmillan.com.

Library of Congress Cataloging-in-Publication Data is available.

First edition, 2022
Book design by Mallory Grigg
Printed in United States of America by Lakeside Book Company,
Harrisonburg, Virginia

ISBN 978-1-250-19672-9 (hardcover)
10   9   8   7   6   5   4   3

For all the souls that I call family,
whether by blood or by choosing;
and for all those souls still finding theirs.

ALSO BY
Dan Gemeinhart

~ ~ ~

The Remarkable Journey of Coyote Sunrise

Good Dog

Scar Island

Some Kind of Courage

The Honest Truth

PART ONE

EPIGRAPH

All souls, each and every one, deserve a home and a family. Even yours. Especially yours. Every soul deserves love, and friendship. Yes, even yours. Every soul deserves to find where it belongs. Each bird to a nest. Though it may take some seeking. Each bird to a nest, at last. That is, perhaps, what almost all stories are truly about.

This one is no different.

CHAPTER ONE

In Which a Wish Is Not Spoken, and a Secret Is Kept

Nearly all of Slaughterville was sleeping when the children came.

There was no sign welcoming visitors to Slaughterville, because most of the town's visitors were cows, and none of them were particularly happy to be there. They were even less happy when they left.

But, on this particular night, there *were* visitors. They arrived quietly, fingers crossed that they would not be noticed. And, for the most part, they weren't.

The town was dark, except for the silver of the moonlight.

In the little block of buildings on Skinister Street that Slaughterville called downtown, the sheriff was in her office. But her feet were up on her desk, her head thrown back, eyes closed and mouth open, dreaming along to the opera music soaring from the record player spinning beside her.

Next door, Mr. Chin the baker *was* awake. He could have seen the children pass by, but he was bent over, sliding yet another great round sourdough loaf into the oven, and missed them, just.

All the other shops and stores stood dark and empty. The bell watched silently from the church tower at the end of the block as the children rolled through town on Skinister Street and out the other side.

The windowless slaughterhouse that gave the town its name was still; its machinery quiet, its blades idle but waiting, the killing floor hosed clean and empty. Moonlight glinted on the steely points of the dangling meat hooks. Cows dozed behind the fences in the muddy stock pens, not wondering even a little bit about what awaited them the next day. Which was probably for the best.

Just past the slaughterhouse, the truck clattered over the narrow bridge that crossed Carcass Creek.

It took the first left turn after crossing the bridge, its headlights flashing for a second on a tilting sign marking Offal Road.

There were only two houses on Offal Road before it deadended into the woods. Both of them were dark, and only one of them held living souls. The house on the left was empty, at least for the moment. And across the street, in the house on the right, on the second story, a boy lay in bed. All around his window, which looked out on the street, were birdhouses. Dozens of them, all shapes and sizes and colors. The boy had made them all.

That boy is the hero of this story. Or, rather, *one* of the heroes. No one would have been more surprised to hear that than the boy himself. He was about as far from a hero as anything he could imagine.

Sometimes, though, a soul doesn't know how great it truly is. Until it has to find out.

The boy's name was Ravani Foster.

Ravani's mother and father were asleep. But he was not. He was staring at the ceiling. And he was crying.

He'd been woken, not by a sound or by a dream, but by a

feeling. A feeling so strong that it jolted him out of sleep and into darkness. The feeling that woke Ravani Foster on this moonlit night? It was loneliness.

I don't know if you've ever been so lonely that it woke you up. I hope not.

But isn't it interesting that this particular boy was woken on this particular night by that particular feeling, when that exact truck was turning onto that exact road? It seems more than coincidence.

It seems almost like *magic*, perhaps.

This boy, woken by loneliness, heard something. A low, growly sort of rumble.

He wiped the tears off his cheeks, got out of bed, and crept on quiet feet over to the window that looked down on Offal Road. A large white truck was parked in front of the empty house across the street.

Ravani rubbed his eyes, not quite believing them. The truck made no sense. No one had lived in that house since old Mr. Croward had broken his hip and moved to Ironburgh weeks before. And no one drove into Slaughterville at night, because nothing happened in Slaughterville at night.

But, nevertheless, there it was.

The engine kept rumbling as a large and lumpy man stepped down out of the cab. A fat cigar glowed between his lips. He looked up and down the street, puffing smoke like a dragon.

Satisfied with the silence, the man walked around to the back of the truck, undid a latch, and with a rattling clatter rolled the door up and open. Then he stepped aside and leaned against the truck, eyes back on Skinister Street.

Upstairs, Ravani watched, waiting. And then, slowly, his mouth dropped open.

Because out of the truck stepped children.

One. Two, three. Four. Five, six. Six children. The oldest, a dark-haired boy whose head swiveled to scan the moonlit street around them, looked to be sixteen or seventeen years old. The youngest, a yawning girl in a white dress, was only five or six. The others, two girls and two boys, were somewhere in between.

Six children. Stepping down into moonlight without making a sound. Each carried a suitcase. The youngest girl held a ragged stuffed giraffe in one hand. But they had no furniture, no lamps, no mattresses, no chairs.

Six children, appearing out of nowhere. Alone, together.

No. Wait.

As Ravani watched, one more child emerged from the blackness of the truck. A girl about his own age, twelve or thirteen. She stood for a moment in the back of the truck, looking around at Offal Road.

Her hair, which was tied back with black ribbon, looked silver in the moonlight. But Ravani thought that in sunlight it would look gold. She wore blue jeans and a white T-shirt. One hand held a suitcase, just like the other children, but the other held something else: a white umbrella. The lacy, pretty kind that fancy ladies carried at fancy events like horse races and country picnics.

"*A parasol,*" Ravani whispered, thinking that was the right word, and it was.

The girl twirled the parasol over her shoulder. She looked left, and then she looked right, and then she looked up.

For a breath, Ravani was sure she was looking straight at him, standing shirtless in his window. He gasped and stepped back, though he knew that if she *was* looking at his window, he'd already been seen.

But then her gaze dropped, and the older boy reached up to take her hand, and she stepped down onto the street.

The man closed the back of the truck and climbed into the cab, and then the truck lurched into motion and grumbled away into the night, leaving the seven soundless children behind.

Together, six of them walked up the path to the covered front porch of the empty house across the street. Only the girl with the parasol stayed behind.

Ravani watched her standing alone on the sidewalk. And as he watched, she set her suitcase down. And she wiped at her cheeks with the back of her hand. First one, then the other. Ravani bit his lip. He knew that motion well. It didn't matter that the girl was two stories down and a street away, or that the only light came from the moon, or that her back was turned to him: the girl with the silver hair was wiping away tears, and he didn't need to see them to know it.

The other six children climbed the porch steps and set their suitcases down, facing the front door. They reached out and grasped one another's hands.

The oldest boy said something. His voice didn't reach across the street and up to the window, but his mouth was moving, his head turning from side to side. The five children beside him lowered their heads, then said something as well.

Then they picked up their suitcases, opened the front door, and disappeared inside.

Ravani blinked. Then his eyes went back to the girl with the parasol, and his heart jolted.

She was standing in the moonlight, looking over her shoulder, directly up at him.

Ravani didn't know why he did what he did next. He wanted to hide, to duck behind his curtain.

But there was something about the girl, about her silence, about how alone she stood there in the night. About her private tears.

This story, like all stories, is about choices.

And Ravani, in that moment, chose to not hide.

Instead, he raised his hand in a silent wave.

Sometimes, when two lonely souls find each other, there is a reaching out.

The girl brought her own hand up. But not in a wave. She raised a single finger to her lips. She made no sound, but there was no mistaking what she was saying: *Sshhh.*

Ravani's skin tingled. The night had a new flavor. Danger.

The girl lowered her hand.

The older boy stalked out to the porch steps, his body tight and impatient. He cupped a hand around his mouth and a sound echoed out, a sound like the hoot of an owl. The girl reached down and picked up her suitcase and then strolled up the walkway, the parasol twirling on her shoulder. When she reached the porch, he grabbed her wrist and pulled her inside.

The door closed. And the street stood empty once more. Ravani Foster stood in his window, looking down on the moonlit street, his hand raised in a wave to a girl who came out of nowhere, and then disappeared.

The next morning, Ravani's mother stood in the brightness of the kitchen, drying dishes. Ravani smelled coffee and eggs and saw a plate waiting for him, but he walked past the table and into the dining room.

"Good morning," his mother said. "Did you sleep all right?"

"Yes," he said, looking out through the front window.

Through the glass, he eyed the house across the street. It looked empty, dark.

His stomach rumbled with hunger, but it was curiosity that gnawed at him. Had he really seen those midnight children arrive? Had it been a dream? Both seemed impossible.

"No bad dreams?"

He opened his mouth to answer his mother. To tell her about the truck, and the children, and the girl with the white umbrella. He remembered the ripple of danger he had felt. Surely he should tell his mother.

But he also remembered a girl, standing in the moonlight, asking him to keep a secret without saying a word. And he remembered her silent tears. His mouth went dry. His stomach clenched. But he made a choice.

"No, Mother," he said. "I slept sound all night."

Chapter Two

In Which There Is One Puddle of Blood,
and Two Escapes

Ravani Foster watched the house across the street while he ate breakfast. He watched it while he refilled his bird feeders around the yard. He watched it out the bathroom window while he brushed his teeth.

And all the while, the house stood silent. No doors opened. No curtains moved. No faces appeared. No voices rang out. The house looked as empty as it had every day since Mr. Croward had moved away.

Finally, Ravani's desperate curiosity could wait no longer.

He walked out his front door and across the sunlit street, stomach swirling. Took a bracing breath, and moved toward the shadows of the porch. He tiptoed, though he wasn't sure why. Creaked up the porch steps. Crept past the front door, to the big picture window. Choked down a dry swallow, then cupped his hands around his eyes and pressed them up against the glass.

The house looked lifeless and vacant. Mr. Croward's dingy furniture was still there, but it looked dusty and unused.

"*Are you in there?*" Ravani whispered. "*Or were you just a dream?*"

He was about to turn and leave when he saw it. Hanging on a closet doorknob.

A pretty white parasol.

Ravani's heart thumped. He smiled.

"What are you doing?"

The voice startled him, causing him to gasp and jerk away from the window.

It hadn't come from a mysterious child, though, but from a confused mother. His own mother, standing in his own yard.

"Nothing," he called quickly. He glanced one more time at the parasol, then trudged reluctantly down off the porch.

His mother held a metal lunch box out toward him. "Your father forgot his lunch again."

Ravani's mouth went dry. He hated going to his father's work. He opened his mouth to argue but didn't get the chance.

"Your father needs to eat, and I've got the laundry to do. Off you go."

Ravani groaned and took the lunch box.

His stomach rose to a nervous boil as he crossed the bridge over Carcass Creek. His heart beat a little faster with every step. He tried to lose himself by watching the birds that flew from tree to tree around him; he saw a brown nuthatch, a house finch, and plenty of crows. But far too soon he was there, looking up at the great steel building that was the Skinister Slaughterhouse. Ravani gulped.

The slaughterhouse growled and clanked with dark noises. Inside, the machinery of death whirred and cranked and hissed. Conveyor belts. Bolt guns. Pneumatic blades.

To one side stood the muddy fenced lots where the cows waited. Standing ankle-deep in the muck, staring out at him. He couldn't meet their eyes. One of them mooed hopelessly.

He wasn't sure what it was saying. *Help,* perhaps? At the back of the lot was a ramp leading into the building. A pair of brawny men shouted and waved their arms, herding the poor beasts in one by one. On the other side of the building, the trucks stood ready, SKINISTER QUALITY MEATS emblazoned on their sides, pallets of white-paper-wrapped packages being loaded into them. Packages stamped, Ravani knew, with grisly labels: GROUND CHUCK . . . SPARE RIBS . . . RUMP ROAST . . . BEEF TONGUE.

Ravani was glad it wasn't veal day.

He couldn't see inside the building—the only windows were small and very high up. But he knew what happened inside. Everyone did. The cows went in, breathing and thinking and feeling. And meat came out.

Ravani shuddered. And then he walked up toward the front door.

With each step, the noise grew louder and Ravani's stomach queasier. The sounds from inside got clearer: violent *whoosh*es and gruesome *ka-chunk*s and pitiable *mooo*s that made his hands break out in greasy sweat. A moist buzzing that could only be an electric saw blade cutting through bone. And beneath it all a dark pattern like a drumbeat: a hiss, then a startled moo that cut off abruptly with a meaty thud. *Hiss-moooTHUD! Hiss-moooTHUD! Hiss-moooTHUD!*

Ravani's feet stuttered to a stop on the gravel walkway. In the pen, now only a stone's throw away, a cow stood with its head sticking out through the fence. It looked at Ravani with pleading eyes.

"*I'm sorry,*" he whispered. *Hiss-moooTHUD!* The cow sighed.

Beside the door was a bulletin board papered with reminders and announcements for the workers. *Step Carefully . . . Floor May Be Slippery.* And, *It's Been 3 Days Since Our Last Accident.* And, *Support Our Town: Eat More Meat!*

And, in the middle, a flyer that Ravani had already seen posted all over town: *50th Annual Red River Raft Race! 4th of July at Sunset! Open to All Slaughtervillians 12 and Under! $100 Prize!* Beneath the words was a silhouette of two kids paddling a boat, mouths open wide in gleeful grins. Ravani frowned.

Then he pushed open the door and walked inside.

Before the killing floor, there was an office. In the office were some impressively full bookcases, several filing cabinets, a gigantic dark-wood desk, and the man who sat behind it, frowning at some papers in his hands: Mr. Sturgis Skinister himself, owner and operator of Skinister Quality Meats, as well as the local judge. The room Ravani stood in doubled as both slaughterhouse headquarters and occasional courtroom. On the wall behind the desk was a large framed painting of a black-suited, thick-necked man who looked almost identical to Mr. Skinister except for the grim sternness in his eyes. Ravani knew it was Strayhorn Skinister, founder of Skinister Quality Meats and grandfather of the man currently occupying the desk.

"Young Mr. Foster!" Mr. Skinister boomed in his deep baritone. "Father forget his lunch again?"

"Yes, sir. Sorry to bother you."

"No, no, don't be silly." As usual, Mr. Skinister seemed eager for an interruption to his work.

There was, thankfully, no window to the killing floor in the office. But the thin walls made the sounds within even louder and more immediate.

Hiss-moooTHUD!

Mr. Skinister grimaced, then looked to the lunch box in Ravani's hand. "What, er, did your mother pack today, if you don't mind me asking?"

Ravani set the lunch box on Mr. Skinister's desk and swung it open.

"Empanadas," he said, and at Mr. Skinister's squint, he explained, "They're like little pies with a savory stuffing." Ravani picked up one of the flaky-crusted pastries and handed it to Mr. Skinister. "She put one in for you."

Mr. Skinister, eyes shining, licked his lips and took it eagerly.

"Like a little calzone! What's inside?"

Ravani looked at the ceiling, trying to remember what his mother had told him.

"Um, leek and sweet potato, with garlic and . . . roasted jalapeño."

"No meat?"

"No meat."

Mr. Skinister shook his head, but more with wonder than disappointment.

"Imagine that, a meal with no meat. How curious . . . Tell her Thank you for me."

"Yes, sir. What did you bring?" Ravani asked, looking at Mr. Skinister's own lunch box, also sitting on his desk.

"Oh. Spaghetti. With meatballs, of course." His eyes dimmed a bit. "Eighty percent ground beef chuck, twenty percent ground pork."

Hiss-moooTHUD!

"But I made the marinara myself! Slow-simmered, with

tomatoes from our garden and plenty of basil and Parmesan. Old family recipe."

"Sounds great, Mr. Skinister."

Ravani clicked his father's lunch box closed, then eyed the door to the killing floor. He wasn't eager to go inside.

Hiss-moooTHUD!

Mr. Skinister saw Ravani's glum glance at the killing floor door. He tucked his lips in understanding, looking at the door with almost as much distaste as Ravani felt.

"I know, son. Just keep your head down and stay behind the yellow line. Try not to look anything in the eye."

Ravani sighed and was just turning toward the killing floor door when he was interrupted by the main door slamming open behind him.

His blood ran cold when he saw who had come in. Ravani's face went pale as the other boy sneered.

"Hey, Ravioli." The boy's voice was greasy with great globs of gloat.

"Bringing your father's lunch as well, Mr. Carter?" Mr. Skinister asked with a small frown.

Donnie Carter nodded, still smirking at Ravani.

On the other side of the wall, the horrid sounds fell silent.

"Ah, perfect. Lunch break," Mr. Skinister said, with a little nod to Ravani. "You're much less likely to be splattered. Go on, then. I'm sure your fathers are hungry."

Ravani shot nervous eyes at Donnie, who flashed a shark's smile back at him.

"After you, Ravioli."

Ravani turned miserably and pushed open the wooden door

to the killing floor. He could practically feel Donnie's hot breath on the back of his neck.

Ravani kept his head down and his eyes pasted to the cement floor at his feet. There was a yellow line on the floor that ran along the brick wall, marking the path that was out of the reach of swinging carcasses and slashing blades. Ravani walked quickly beside the line.

He took quick, shallow breaths through his mouth. He wasn't sure whether the stench of the killing floor was blood, or guts, or just the smell of death, but he *was* sure that it was revolting.

He scurried quickly, trying to stay ahead of Donnie Carter, but it was no use. The brute was right at his back, close enough to hiss foul words into Ravani's ears.

"*Whatsa mattow, Waviowi? Too much bwood for you? Too scawy? Make you wanna cwy for the widdle cows?*" He poked Ravani's shoulder with a rough finger. "*Ooh! Look at that one! It looks like it got turned inside out!*"

Ravani did not look at that one, or at anything other than the floor at his feet. He grimaced and stepped over a glistening crimson puddle that had spread across the yellow line.

He was nearly to the corner of the building; he'd take a left there, and then the lunch benches would be in the little alcove straight ahead, and freedom within grasp. He allowed a flicker of hope to kindle in his hammering heart.

Alas.

"*Watch your step!*" Donnie growled, and then kicked at Ravani's hurrying legs.

One foot tangled behind the other. A more athletic child

might have been able to recover, to regain their balance and shoot Donnie a dirty look.

But Ravani Foster was *not* a more athletic child. In all of Slaughterville, in fact, it would be hard to find a *less* athletic child.

He went sprawling to the floor. His breath flew out of him with a grunt, and he slid on the slick cement, across the yellow line. He felt a warm moistness on his chest. His right hand still clutched the handle of the lunch tin, but his left hand was gripping something . . . furry.

Ravani screwed one eye shut and slowly raised his forehead from the floor. And immediately wished he hadn't.

His fingers were closed around the leg of a cow. Or, rather, around *most* of the leg of a cow. A hoof, a length of scratchy brown fur, and then a rather abrupt and meaty ending.

Ravani gagged and jumped to his feet, gasping.

Donnie had already walked past him, chortling and snorting.

"Ooops. You got a little something on your shirt, Ravioli."

Ravani looked down. The front of his shirt was stained with a smear of dark red blood. Well, mostly blood. There was also a few brown bits that he tried not to focus on. *I hope it's brains*, he thought miserably, considering the other options. He stood for a moment, focused on keeping his breakfast in his belly.

It wasn't the first time an encounter with Donnie had left him gasping and bloodied. At least this time it wasn't his own blood. He blinked away the tears that had sprung to his eyes, and then continued walking.

As he came around the corner, he saw the slaughterhouse

crew gathered on the benches in the little side room at the back. Bloody coveralls, and chewing mouths, and slouched shoulders, and a low hubbub of gruff talk.

Ravani spotted the muscly bulk of his father, sitting with a few others on the nearest bench. The floor foreman—Karl Carter, Donnie Carter's dad—sat next to him, and Donnie was already strutting up to them.

Ravani saw his father's eyes look past Donnie and find him, saw them drop down to the mess on his shirt. He looked quick to Donnie, then back to Ravani. Ravani wanted to meet his gaze, to be as strong as his father for once. But shame filled his eyes again, and he looked away.

As Ravani walked up, he heard Mr. Carter's deep wheeze of a voice.

"You're late, Donnie. Been working on your boat, yeah?"

"Yes, sir," Donnie answered, all the smirk gone from his voice. He was a considerably smaller person when he was around his father, Ravani had noticed.

"You gonna win again this year, Donnie?" another worker called out.

"'Course he is," Mr. Carter said. "Three in a row, just like his old man. And he knows if he don't, he's sleeping in the henhouse!" He said it like a joke and it was met with the roar of expected laughter from his crew, but Donnie's smile looked strained.

Mr. Carter noticed Ravani standing there. A glint came to his eye.

"Ah, your boy's here, too, Foster. He gonna be racing this year?" Karl Carter never seemed to speak to Ravani directly.

Ravani's father looked at him.

"I don't know," he said in his quiet voice. "Are you, son?"

Ravani imagined tossing out a boast, saying, "'Course I am, and I'm gonna give Donnie a run for his money!" with a wink and a reckless grin. Every child in Slaughterville lived for the Red River Raft Race every year and lay awake at night dreaming about the glory of being crowned champion in front of the whole town. Every child except Ravani. He hadn't raced in it last year, or the year before, and he wasn't going to be racing in it this year, either. Because the Red River Raft Race was not a solo event: to race, you needed a boat, and a friend.

Ravani Foster didn't have either.

"I . . . ," Ravani said, eyes darting from his father to Mr. Carter. His words caught in his throat. "I don't . . ."

Mr. Carter's brow furrowed. He cocked an eyebrow at Ravani's father.

"Well? Is he or ain't he? What kinda boy wouldn't wanna race? Ain't he gonna try and beat the reigning champion?" He slapped Donnie on the shoulder hard enough to nearly knock him down.

Ravani opened his mouth to answer. Saw his father frown and look down to the floor. Ravani just shook his head.

"Well," Mr. Carter said, smirking. "Probably for the best. Wouldn't want to see him get hurt." He turned and started talking to the rest of the crew, his arm around Donnie's shoulder.

Ravani walked up to his father and held out the lunch tin.

"Thanks, son." The words were murmured, quiet. "What happened to your shirt?"

Ravani couldn't meet his father's eyes, so he looked at the big man's scraped knuckles, his blood-splattered coveralls, the burly muscles of his arms, the solid square sturdiness of his size thirteen boots. He was so much *more* in every way than Ravani, it seemed.

"I fell," he said. True words. More or less. Maybe less.

His father sighed and nodded.

Ravani kept his eyes down. Being a disappointment to his father was not a new feeling.

"Go on home," his father murmured, and Ravani glanced up to see his father looking at Donnie, still grinning around at his father's crew. Now was Ravani's chance to leave alone, and his father knew it. He knew who was the cow, and who was the butcher.

"Yes, sir," Ravani mumbled. And then he made his escape.

Once outside, he looked at the empty road. Then he looked at the woods. If he walked home through the woods, he'd have to walk right through the Croward yard. He could peer, perhaps, through windows. Find, perhaps, hiding children.

He was halfway to the tree line when he saw the cow. The same one, still standing at the fence, watching him with begging eyes.

Ravani stopped. And then, for reasons that he wouldn't have been able to explain, Ravani chose to walk over to the doomed and lonesome animal. Stories, after all, are about choices.

The cow watched his approach. Its ears perked up.

Ravani stopped in front of the condemned creature. He put his hand on the barbed wire and looked into its eyes. There was a sparkle there. A warmth.

The cow was a deep chestnut brown all over, but with a white blaze on its forehead that was in the unmistakable shape of a cloverleaf. A cloverleaf that, if Ravani squinted right, seemed to have four leaves. Ravani knew what he would've named the cow, if it had been his.

"*Hello, Lucky,*" he said quietly.

The cow's breath was warm on Ravani's hand.

The cow was trapped, in a sad place where monsters lurked, with seemingly no hope of salvation.

"*You and me are a lot alike, Lucky,*" Ravani whispered. "*Maybe we could be friends.*" Lucky poked her head through the fence. She rested her velvet chin on Ravani's hand. She blinked her long eyelashes.

When two lonely souls find each other, sometimes there is a reaching out.

Ravani swallowed, feeling all the things that a soul feels when it makes a friend it knows it is going to have to lose.

But then Ravani saw: Lucky wasn't just standing by the fence. She was standing by a *gate*.

The gate was closed with a latch. But there was no lock. Cows, after all, couldn't open gates.

Ravani looked around quickly. There was no one in sight.

His hand reached for the latch, and then froze. It was an incredibly stupid thing to do. He would be in serious trouble. His father could lose his job.

But then he looked, again, into Lucky's eyes.

A choice was made. A mistake, perhaps, but a choice to be sure.

Ravani undid the latch. He swung the gate open, cringing at the creak of the hinges. Lucky looked at the path to freedom, then back to Ravani.

"*Go on.*"

Sometimes a soul, when it sees the chance to have what it's always wanted, doesn't have the courage to seize it.

That cow, though, *did* have the courage. Or maybe she was just bored. It's hard to tell with cows.

She walked out through the gate, past Ravani, and over toward the shade of the trees by the creek, its hooves a quiet thunder in the muddy turf.

"*Good luck,*" Ravani whispered, then closed the gate and hurried into the shadowy safety of the forest. He glanced back once and saw the cow, grazing in the long grass.

It wouldn't make a difference in the long run, he knew. The cow wouldn't wander far, and they'd probably find her in a few minutes. But it was, Ravani figured, better than nothing.

At least this way the cow could enjoy a little bit of freedom before being turned inside out.

Chapter Three

In Which a Friend Is Eaten, and a Gift Is Given

Ravani had one brief stop to make on his way to investigate his mysterious new neighbors. After double-checking that Donnie wasn't following him, he slipped down the faintest of paths. He wound between mossy cedars, pushed through the broad leaves of a vine maple, then he was there: his secret sanctuary.

A fern-floored clearing between the ancient trunks. Rays of sunlight shooting in sideways. And, up between the branches all around, his own addition: birdhouses. Not two, or three, or four. A dozen, more even. Different styles, different colors, different sizes. Some high, some low, facing in all directions. His own little town, his own little village for the birds. Haven Hollow, he called it.

The clearing thrummed with life, with birds coming and going, chirps and songs, the flutters of wings, the cries of babies snug in their shelters. Ravani smiled, like he always did when he visited. No one else knew about Haven Hollow . . . not his father, not his mother, certainly not Donnie.

"*Hello, sparrow,*" Ravani whispered, eyes up as he stood in the center of the clearing. "*And you, flicker. And you, goldfinch.*" The birds were the only friends Ravani needed. Or at least that's what he always told himself. But, like almost all people, Ravani was even better at lying to himself than he was at lying to others.

After a minute or two of standing there—the birds, unafraid of him, swooping so near him at times that he almost felt their feathers—he said goodbye to Haven Hollow and walked away on quiet feet.

When he came to Carcass Creek, he slipped off his shoes and waded into the water and turned upstream toward his house.

He was nearly home when he heard the whispers.

The whispers came from around a bend in the creek just ahead, where the old Croward house sat. The creek marked the back edge of its overgrown backyard.

Ravani stopped, one foot dangling in the air above the water.

He couldn't hear the words clearly, but he could hear the tension in the voices.

"*Watch out!*" he thought he heard, and perhaps "*Be quiet!*"

He stepped along a log, careful and quiet.

Then, clear as dewdrops on a spiderweb, he heard words that prickled his arms with gooseflesh.

"*If I catch him, I'm gonna kill him!*"

Ravani froze, mouth dry. He took a step backward.

"*If you did, you know I'd hate you forever.*"

"*Aw, geez. Just joking, sister. If you really wanna frog for your birthday, I'll get you a frog.*"

Ravani's shoulders slumped in relief.

"*Then stop talking and start catching. We gotta get back before he notices we're gone.*" A girl's voice, he thought. A silver-haired girl? he wondered.

"*I'm trying. They're too fast.*" A boy's voice, he was pretty sure.

There was the churning splash of someone charging through knee-deep water, then a hissed curse.

Ravani smiled. Catching frogs was tricky for most folks. Especially folks who charged through the water like a rhinoceros.

He took a step forward, then another, trying to peer around the corner to see the whispering frog-catchers.

Bad things can happen, though, when you're looking one way and walking another. Especially when you're teetering on a log. Ravani's toe caught on a knot. He wobbled, flapping his arms like a windblown wren, battling for balance.

He lost the battle.

There was a *whoosh*, a brief shriek, and then a splash.

The cool water snatched his breath away, and he came up gasping on all fours in the knee-deep creek. Then he froze, listening.

The sound of footsteps, running away. At first through shallow water, and then thumping on dry ground.

Ravani jumped to his feet and struggled, dripping, after them. He came wading around the corner just in time to see a blink of sunlight flashing on what might have been golden hair, fleeing toward the Croward house.

"Wait!" Ravani called out. He wasn't sure why. He was more used to hiding than chasing. And yet.

He ran faster after the retreating footsteps, up into the Croward back lawn. Just in time to see, he thought, the back door swinging shut.

He stood there, gasping, being eaten alive by curiosity.

Ravani was a quiet soul who kept to himself. But his usually quiet soul was shouting now, hollering a question that he simply had to know the answer to: Who in the world were these strange children?

When Ravani's father got home from work that night, Ravani was sitting in the shadows of the front porch, reading a book and watching the house across the street.

"Hello, son," his father said.

"Hello."

"Did you . . . did you have a good day, then?"

Ravani knew what he was asking. Did he make it home all right without a new bruise or bloody nose from Donnie?

"Yes, sir," Ravani answered.

His father nodded.

"I, uh . . . I . . ." His father trailed off, as he often did. He seemed to have a harder time catching words than some folks did catching frogs. His burly shoulders rose and fell in a sigh. "All right," he finally said, and then walked inside.

Ravani heard his mother greet his father, heard their hellos and quick kiss. A few words murmured back and forth that Ravani couldn't make out. But he knew they were talking about him, could tell by the sad and worried tone in their voices.

And then he heard his mother say, "Me too. He'll find his place, though. He'll find a friend."

And then he heard his father answer, "How is a boy like that ever gonna make a friend?"

Ravani's face flushed hot.

His father wasn't being cruel. He was being truthful. But the truth, sometimes, can be the cruelest thing of all.

Those cruelly true words rang in Ravani's heart all through

dinner. He stared at the steak on his plate, oozing pink juices into his mashed potatoes. His father had brought it home from work. He thought of Lucky.

"Did . . . did any cows escape at work today?" Ravani asked his father.

His father frowned, chewing on his sirloin. "Nope."

Ravani's stomach twisted.

"*Sorry, friend,*" he whispered to his steak. He'd wished the cow well, but it had ended up medium rare. Lucky, it turned out, hadn't been after all. He pushed his plate away. "I'm not hungry," he said.

How is a boy like that ever gonna make a friend?

He thought about those words as he washed the dishes, while his mother played the piano and his father dozed beside her and the sunlight faded and the shadows stretched from their daytime hiding places. Through the kitchen window, he saw the fireflies begin to blink between the trees outside. And as their floating lights flickered into life, so did an idea in his soul.

He thought of midnight children, and silver-haired girls, and tears wiped from cheeks, and uncaught birthday presents. He thought of being woken up by loneliness.

And he thought of how in the house across the street, behind those darkened windows, was a girl who seemed just as quiet and just as alone and just as sad as he was.

It's all right to be afraid. It's all right to be lonely. It's all right to be sad. This is, after all, a world with darkness and fists and killing floors and cruel truths.

But if there is ever going to be a hope for something else, there has to be a reaching out.

Ravani nodded.

A choice, once again, had been made.

Catching frogs was tricky for most folks. But not for him.

A few moments later, he was walking out his front door into the dim gloaming. He held a glass jar under each arm. He kept on, eyes straight ahead. Down to the creek.

He took off his shoes and his socks and he waded into the water and then across, to the slow backwater against the far bank where the creek was deeper and slow and choked with leaning cattails and lily pads. It was where the frogs lived, he knew.

Their singing stopped as he drew near, but he didn't need their song to find them.

It didn't take long. One quiet minute, a quick grab with his hand, and then he was sloshing back to the shore, a meaty frog wriggling between his fingers. Into one of the jars it went, along with an inch of creek water.

The next part was trickier, but it was also something he was uncommonly good at. A few jumps and dives, some clapping of hands, one stumble over a devious tree root, and then he had them: seven fireflies, glowing in the other jar.

He walked up to the back porch of the Croward house, a little muddy and a lot scared but completely determined. His soul, after all, was thirsty.

He set the jars down on the warped wooden floorboards of the porch, then pulled something out of each of his pockets: a single white candle from one, a box of matches from the other.

A strike, a spark, a sputter, a flame. Light, reaching out through the darkness.

He held the candle over the jar with the frog inside, letting the hot wax drip down onto the lid between the air holes. Then he pressed the bottom of the candle into the wax puddle until it stuck and stood.

He stepped down, off the porch. Looked at his gifts.

The frog sat blinking in its jar beneath the candle, looking longingly through the glass at the dancing lights of its neighbors.

The candle was a nice touch. It was a birthday present, after all.

How is a boy like that ever gonna make a friend?

Ravani smiled. *Like this, maybe,* his smile said.

He leaned forward and knocked on the door. One, two, three knocks.

Then he turned and walked home through the darkness, fairly sure that the children (if they even really existed) would not open the door as long as he stood there.

≈

Later that night he opened his bedroom window to let in the breeze before going to bed. From the birdhouses around his window came the small flutters and peeps of feathered families settling in for the night.

The sky was black now, and cloudy, so that even the light of the moon was hidden.

The house across the street was the same as it had been all day: soundless, dark, and empty. There was, however, one small difference.

One of the second-story windows, directly across from his own, was open. The white curtain drifted like a ghost.

Glowing faintly on the windowsill was a jar full of swirling fireflies.

Small differences can actually make quite a big difference, sometimes.

Ravani smiled.

"*You're welcome,*" he whispered.

CHAPTER FOUR

In Which Claws Are Sharpened, and the Hunt Begins

Sometimes—a lot of times, perhaps—there are things happening in a soul's story that it can't see and that it doesn't know about. Other stories, connected to that soul's story like the gears of a clock, turning and turning, quietly, and far away. And as the clock hands slowly turn, those other stories can become very, very important. They can make the clock's bell ring. Or they can make the clock stop.

Miles and miles away from Ravani and Slaughterville, a man was sitting in a dark room. He almost never turned on a light. He liked his eyes to be used to the dark, for when he was hunting. And he nearly always hunted at night.

The man was very pale. He had very short, very white hair. His eyes were very blue behind his very round glasses. The man was very.

The man was filing his fingernails. In smooth, deliberate movements. Everything the man did was very smooth and very deliberate.

Critch went the nail file. *Critch. Critch. Critch.* The man liked his claws to be sharp. Very sharp.

The man did not think of himself, really, as a man. He thought of himself only as a hunter.

The Hunter switched the file from his right hand to his left.

Critch went the nail file again. *Critch. Critch. Cri—*

Brrrrng!

The telephone interrupted the Hunter's sharpening. He didn't jump. The Hunter was always very calm.

He set down the nail file. And he rose from his chair.

Brrrrng!

He walked to where the telephone hung on the wall.

Brrrrng!

He pulled the black earpiece off its cradle. He put his mouth with its very straight and very white teeth very close to the mouth piece.

"Hello," he said, in a very soft and very smooth voice.

"I have a case for you," a woman's voice said from the earpiece. Her voice was deep, and her voice was angry.

"Of," the Hunter said, "course."

Because, after all, that was the only reason his phone ever rang.

"They escaped last night. I'd hoped they would turn back up today."

"How," the Hunter asked, "many?"

"Seven," she said. And she said it like it meant something, and it did.

The Hunter blinked. A slow smile stretched his pale lips.

"It's," he whispered, "*them*."

"Yes."

The Hunter had hunted those seven before. He had caught them, once. And he had missed them, several times.

They were the only prey the Hunter had ever missed.

The Hunter always only chased one kind of prey: people. But that one kind of prey came in many flavors. Children, sometimes . . . runaways, kidnap victims. Grown-ups, too: fugitives, criminals. Escaped prisoners. Scared people who owed bad people money.

The Hunter never hurt his prey, not on purpose. But he often handed them over to people who would. The Hunter did not care why the prey that he chased was wanted, or what happened to them afterward. He only cared about the hunt.

"I'll pay," the woman said. "Of course."

"Mmmm," the Hunter murmured. He was not thinking about the money. He would take the money, of course, but he did not care about the money. The Hunter loved the hunt.

"I'll," he said, "find," he said, "them."

He said it like it was very true.

CHAPTER FIVE

In Which a Ghost Is Met, and a Lie Is Spoken

The window across the street was empty in the morning.

But Ravani knew what he'd seen.

They were over there. *She* was over there. Who were they? Where had they come from? Why were they hiding?

It's not just that they were something mysterious. It was more that they were something *different*. And something different was something Ravani wanted very much. Because if something was different, there was always the hope that it would be something *better*.

Downstairs, his mother was at the kitchen table, sipping coffee. She was wearing her painting smock, hair pulled back in a sloppy ponytail.

"Painting day?" Ravani asked her.

"Indeed." She smiled at him. "I'm just waiting for inspiration. And a subject."

Ravani's mind sparked. He thought about the house across the street.

"How about cattails?" he asked.

Moments later he was out the door, wiping toast crumbs off his lips. He had a folding knife in his pocket. He walked slow through the Croward yard, whistling conspicuously. Craned his neck to squint into the windows as he passed. There was no answering whistle, no face looking back at him from a window.

On the other side of the creek, in the deeper backwater where he'd caught the frog the night before, the cattails stretched up out of the water, tall and slender. Off with his shoes, up with his pant legs, out with the blade, and into the water he went.

He shivered when the water rose above his knees, but soon he was among the thrushes, seeking out the fattest ones and cutting them from their stems. One, two, three. Four, five. Six. One more. And there it was, a step away and the biggest yet, fatter around than a sausage. A frog sat on a lily pad next to it, blinking doubtfully at Ravani.

"It's all right," Ravani said to the frog. "I'm not after you today."

He stepped forward and was reaching toward the cattail when a voice spoke out behind him.

"Careful with that knife."

Ravani jumped, dropping the knife into the water around his knees with a *plop*.

He spun around. And there she was.

The girl with the silver hair. He'd been right, too, that first night: her hair was golden in the sunlight, though it was still pulled back with a black ribbon like it had been in the moonlight. She was barefoot, wearing holey-kneed old jeans rolled up to her knees and a dingy white T-shirt just like before.

Ravani opened his mouth, but no words came out.

The girl looked at him with solemn eyes.

"Thank you. For the frog, I mean. And the fireflies." She had a strange, flat way of talking. Her voice didn't go up or down all that much. It wasn't a voice that reached out and hugged you; it held you at arm's length, and maybe even frowned a little.

Ravani knew a "you're welcome" was in order, but still his voice was stuck, somewhere between his heart and his throat. He'd half believed that the children in the moonlight hadn't been real, that they'd been nothing more than a dream, but now here she stood in front of him.

So Ravani, wordless, just nodded.

The girl raised one of her eyebrows. Then she walked toward him. A slow splashing stroll right into the water and across the creek.

"Don't you talk?" she asked. Before he could answer, she went on. "It's okay if you don't. Most people don't say anything worth hearing, anyway." Her face was serious, thoughtful, and her voice was low with a scratch at the bottom of it. It sounded like how a campfire smells. Her eyes were greenish-blue, but so pale that they were nearly gray.

The corners of her mouth tucked down and her eyes narrowed. "But I heard you talking to that frog. So you *can* talk. What, you just don't talk to people, then?" She leaned forward, looking deep into his eyes, and her next words she spoke in a whisper. *"You can talk to us, though, if you want. 'Cause we're not real people. We're ghosts."*

The hair on Ravani's arms stood up, and not because of the cold water swirling around his bare legs.

The girl with the golden hair was crazy. Ravani could see the sunlight on her cheeks, and the breeze flicking at her hair, and the way the water rippled around her legs. She was as real as he was.

Ravani cleared his throat.

"I can talk," he said.

"Oh." The girl took a step back. She looked almost disappointed. "That'll make this easier, I guess. What's your name?"

Ravani licked his lips. He'd been teased all his life, by Donnie and many others, at lots of different times for lots of different reasons. One of the most common, though, was his name.

"My name's Ravani," he said with a sigh, waiting for the laugh and the scoff that would come next. "But people call me Rav."

The girl didn't snort or roll her eyes, though.

"Ravani. I haven't heard that one before" was all she said, but she didn't say it mean. She just said it true. "*Ravani.* Hmm. I like it." Ravani's heart skipped a little when she said that. He nearly smiled. *He* actually liked his name, too. "Where'd you get a name like that?"

"Um. My mother gave it to me." Which was true.

"Why?"

Ravani's mind raced.

"Well. It's a family name. I'm named after my grandpa."

The girl tilted her head to the side. Her lips pressed together.

"Liar," she said. Somehow, she managed to say the word not mean at all. She said it plain, like it was just a fact. Which, in this case, it was. "Tell me the truth."

There was no way in the wide, woeful world that Ravani Foster wanted to tell that strange, solemn girl the truth of his name. And yet. There was simply something about her stillness, and her eyes, and the way her voice was scratchy and soft at the same time, like old corduroy.

"It's . . . it's a kind of dessert in Greece, I guess," he said. "And she's always wanted to go to Greece. When I was born, she said—" He stopped, realizing he'd gone too far. What was he thinking? It was too late, though.

The girl blinked.

"What did she say?"

Ravani gulped. He dropped his eyes to the water.

"She said, well, she said I was the . . . sweetest thing she ever saw. So she named me after that dessert."

He flinched, waiting for the laugh, or the taunt.

Again, though, it didn't come.

Instead, the girl reached forward and grabbed his hand. She lifted it up toward her face. Ravani gaped at her like a caught fish.

And then that girl licked the back of his hand.

"Bullspit," she said flatly. "You're not sweet at all. You're salty. Your mother should've named you Pickle."

Ravani grinned and started breathing again.

"Or . . . French Fry," he said, and for the first time the girl smiled. Or, nearly did, perhaps. It was small, and it didn't last long—it flickered like a goldfinch through the trees—but it was there. She let go of his hand.

"I saw you all," he said, "that night, with the truck, and—"

But the girl interrupted him.

"Are those for us, too?" she said, looking at the cattails in his hand.

"No. They're for my mother. She's gonna paint 'em."

The girl nodded.

"They'd make a nice picture, I think."

Just then, a sound rang out from the direction of the house

behind her. It was a sound Ravani had heard before. Like the hoot of an owl.

The girl frowned.

"I have to go," she said softly, looking deep and serious into his eyes.

"Wait," Ravani said, as she took a step back. But then a voice barked at them. It was hidden by the trees between, but it coursed with authority. Her father's voice, Ravani was sure.

"Virginia! Get in here, now!"

Ravani's heart raced, but the girl just rolled her eyes.

"Is that your name?" Ravani asked. "Virginia?"

"Sure," she said, then she bent down and slid her hand into the water. When she stood back up, she handed Ravani his dropped knife, dripping with creek water.

"Thanks," he said.

"Virginia!" the voice shouted again.

"You better stay here for a minute, where he can't see you," she said, still looking gravely into Ravani's eyes. "I'm not supposed to talk to you yet."

Ravani's brow furrowed.

"Who?" he said. "Why can't you—"

But Virginia held a finger up to her lips, just like she had that first night. She shook her head slowly from side to side. "Not yet," she whispered. Then she turned and walked away, back across the stream. When she got to the other side and the sound of her splashing was over, Ravani suddenly remembered something.

"Hey!" he hissed in a hoarse whisper, as loud as he dared. "Happy birthday!"

She looked back at him, over her shoulder. For a moment, it looked like she was going to smile. Instead, though, she frowned.

"I'm not looking for a friend," she said.

Ravani swallowed. His skin stung cold.

"Me neither," he lied.

Her eyebrows went up, and her mouth opened just a bit. She stood there for a breath, looking at him.

"Goodbye, Ravani," she said, and then turned and walked away, leaving him with a damp hand and, somehow, more questions than he'd started with.

Chapter Six

In Which There Is a Spectator, a Sparrow, and Spit

Ravani's mind was still thick with questions the next morning. He'd had blurry dreams about ghosts and girls with scratchy voices and monsters that hooted like owls. All he wanted to do was get answers, but it was Friday, which meant that what he *had* to do was deliver newspapers.

The year before, his mother and father had said that if he wanted to house and feed dozens of birds outside his window, it was up to him to pay for it. The very next week the boy who had been doing the route had been struck by a delivery truck and broken both his legs, an accident that had earned him a headline in the newspaper but cost him the job of delivering it. Ravani, having both a bicycle and two unbroken legs, had gotten the job and had been pedaling the paper around town three days a week ever since.

"What's the news?" Ravani called out toward Hortense Wallenbach, owner, manager, journalist, and editor of the *Slaughterville Spectator*. She sat in her office, leaning back in her chair with her boots up on her desk, drinking coffee. It's what he always asked when he walked in, and she answered like she always did.

"Read it and find out."

Ravani knelt by the stack of fresh papers and started rolling them in rubber bands and stuffing them into his bike bag, checking the headline on the front page while he did: *Skinister Meats to Produce New Line of Lean Ground Chuck.*

"Huh. That's not much of a story, Ms. Wallenbach."

"You're telling me. I don't make the stories, kid. I just write 'em and print 'em."

"It'd be a better story if Mr. Skinister was doing something *really* different, like . . . making buffalo wings or salmon burgers. Don't you think?" He looked up at her expectantly, knowing she couldn't help but take the bait.

Hortense's eyes brightened.

"Sure. And it'd be a *much* better story if old man Skinister fell madly in love with a trapeze artist in the traveling circus, but she was already married to a short-tempered and famously jealous lion tamer . . . and then the lion tamer turned up mysteriously missing, and the next day someone found his wedding ring in a Skinister Meats burger patty, but when the sheriff turned up at Skinister's door to arrest him he was already gone, having run away with his adoring acrobat to Brazil. *That* would be a better story." She took a sip of her coffee and shrugged, drowsily blinking away the spark in her eyes. "But . . . that ain't the story. I'm stuck with the facts, kid. And the fact is, this just ain't the kind of town where exciting things happen."

Ravani thought about a group of children showing up in the middle of the night and almost argued with her, but kept that to himself.

Ms. Wallenbach yawned.

"Enough silly storytelling. Get those papers out the door.

There's a whole town just dying to find out about that lean chuck."

Ravani followed the same route he always did, weaving on his bicycle through the mostly-sleeping-but-just-beginning-to-wake-up town, tossing and dropping papers as he went.

After delivering the papers to the houses in the dozing neighborhoods, he turned back toward downtown. The sun was fully risen by then, the larks and jays awake and singing, and he was no longer alone on the streets of Slaughterville.

He moved on to Fred Frotham at the café, who was outside topping off Sheriff Quigley's coffee where she sat at a patio table.

"Morning, Ravani," Fred said with his usual bored warmth.

"You have one for me today, Mr. Frotham?" Ravani asked, stopping with one foot down and handing him a paper. "Maybe that lovesick sailor?"

Fred smiled with half his mouth. He was youngish, maybe twenty-five, with skin the same rich dark brown as the flight feathers of a peregrine falcon. He'd taken over the café from his grandmother, who'd run it since before it had electric lights. The menu hadn't changed.

Fred set the paper down on the sheriff's table and cleared his throat. He squinted one eye shut and hunched over.

"*Yar, boy!*" he growled, his voice an octave lower and dripping with a salty mariner accent. It was like he became a whole other person. "*Why d'ya bring up love, 'fore a miserable soul like me? Aye, my love lies far away across the sea, and a bonny lass she is! But cursed I am to sail these seas, far from her warm embrace. Away with you, sinister siren!*"

Ravani laughed.

"Amazing!" Sheriff Quigley exclaimed.

"Not bad, eh?" Fred grinned, straightening up. "I was lead in the Slaughterville High play every year, and—"

"What? No, I was talking about this!" The sheriff stabbed her finger at the newspaper spread across the table. "A new line of lean chuck? I never thought I'd see the day!"

Fred's grin faded. He looked at Ravani and sighed.

"Thanks for the paper, Rav," he said. "Usual bacon and sausage platter for you, Sheriff?"

"Of course."

Rav had one paper left in his bag, and he pedaled his bike toward Bread & Butter Bakery, his last stop. Lee Chin was behind the counter, blinking sleepily at a tattered paperback book.

"Mornin', Rav," he said when Ravani's entrance jangled the bell above the door. "Got some hot-from-the-oven news for me?"

The day's loaves were wrapped in brown paper and waiting in baskets for hungry customers: white sandwich loaves, brown sourdough rounds, and skinny baguettes with crispy-crunchy crusts. They were the same choices the bakery had on Friday and were the same choices the bakery would have the next day.

Ravani handed over the newspaper.

"Say hello to your mother for me," Mr. Chin said, and turned back to his book.

After a quick stop back at the newspaper office to return the now-empty newspaper bag, Ravani headed toward home.

He was weaving down the sidewalk on Main Street, thinking about a design for a new birdhouse—a bird *hotel*, actually, with six different rooms, each with its own round door hole—when he glanced down an alleyway.

And saw Donnie Carter. He was crouched behind a garbage can, thirty or forty feet down the alley. Kneeling next to him was Stevie Mueller. Stevie was Donnie's greasiest and most reliable sidekick. Their bikes were leaning against the wall beside them.

It only took Ravani a moment to see the string in Donnie's hand, which led to a stick, which was holding up a box, underneath which was half a hot dog. Then he noticed the stray cat, thin and mangy, approaching the trap.

Ravani didn't know what Donnie planned to do with the cat once he caught it, but he was sure it likely involved a firecracker, or the river.

The cat was already halfway under the box. One more second, and it'd be over.

Choices.

Ravani made one.

He stooped down, quick. Picked up a crushed soda can off the street. Brought his arm back.

Down the alley, Donnie looked up and saw him. Their eyes locked.

Donnie narrowed his eyes and shook his head. Ravani gulped. Then he threw.

His plan had been to throw the can so that it hit the box, knocking it down from the stick and scaring the cat to safety.

But what Ravani's mind *planned* and his body actually *did* were often very different and only dimly related things.

The can careened through the air, off target from the moment it left his hand. It bounced off one alley wall, ricocheted off a fire escape ladder, and then, regrettably, *thunked* into something just as hard: the side of Donnie Carter's skull.

Ravani's heart stopped, briefly.

The cat *yrowr*ed and scampered off.

Donnie rose to his feet. He was breathing through his nose, which Ravani knew from experience was never a good sign.

"*You . . . are . . . dead!*" Donnie snarled.

Ravani kicked his bike into action and took flight. Legs churning and muscles burning, he flew down the street. He heard Donnie and Stevie emerge from the alley behind him. He pedaled harder, heart hammering and lungs billowing.

Once, Ravani had watched a sparrow being hunted by a kestrel. The kestrel was making vicious, whip-fast dives at the flitting, fleeing sparrow. The sparrow was flying for all it was worth, but it was over an open field, far from any trees. The sparrow, and the kestrel, and Ravani had all known that it was going to end in blood and feathers. And it had.

Now, deep down inside, Ravani knew as well. It was hopeless. He knew how fast his predators were, and how fast—or rather, how *slow*—he was. But hope is a funny thing. A soul doesn't have to have it to feel it. And the less a soul has of it, the more it wants to believe that it does.

So Ravani pedaled like he had a prayer. But he knew better.

He raced past the slaughterhouse, the *hiss-moooTHUDs!* punctuating the churning of his legs.

A frantic look over his shoulder showed him that Donnie was only twenty feet back and gaining. There was still at least a hundred and fifty yards until the homeward turn onto Offal Road. He wasn't going to make it.

His only chance was to find cover. He knew the winding paths and hidden places of the forest better than Donnie and Stevie. There he had a chance.

As he crossed the bridge, he saw Donnie's bicycle tire creeping up beside him at the edge of his vision. It was now or never.

The moment he was past the end of the bridge's railing, he cut hard to the side, shooting off the road and into the branches and bushes of the forest's edge. He leaped from his bike and ran. Already he could hear Donnie thundering through the foliage behind him and Stevie calling after.

He sprinted over a log, veered onto the wisp of a game trail, shouldered sideways through a crowded stand of trees.

Then he saw it, through the trees: the sun-splashed openness of the Croward back lawn. He was going to make it. Once there, he'd be able to dash around to within sight of his own house, or even knock on Virginia's door and—

Alas.

In this world there are kestrels and there are sparrows, and there is hope and there is truth, and there are roots and there are feet.

Ravani's hopeful foot snagged on the hard truth of the gnarled root of a fir tree, and then he was flying—fast as a sparrow— and then he was landing, his face plowing through dirt and pine needles, his mouth filling with dirt, and then he felt the kestrel's talons sink into his back.

Donnie, sweaty and panting, turned him over so that he was kneeling with one knee on Ravani's chest. His brow was furrowed in fury, his face red, his eyes narrowed.

"Gotcha, Ravioli!" he spat between breaths.

Stevie trotted up behind Donnie, out of breath but already grinning like a troll.

"That wasn't very nice," Donnie huffed. "He ruined our game, didn't he, Stevie?"

"Yeah!" Stevie chimed in. "Ruined our game!"

Ravani wiggled helplessly and Donnie shifted, grinding the weight of his knee down on Ravani.

"Don't you think he owes me an apology?" Donnie sneered.

"Yeah he does!"

Donnie leaned in so close that Ravani could smell his black jellybean breath.

"Say you're sorry," he hissed through clenched teeth. "Say you're sorry and maybe I'll let you go."

Tears sprang hot to Ravani's eyes. Tears because Donnie's knee hurt, tears because he had dirt in his mouth, tears because he was tired of the cruelty and the loneliness, and tears most of all because he knew it was no use. That no matter what he did, no matter what he did or didn't say, that he would always be the sparrow caught in the kestrel's claws. He was the cow, lured by the open gate, then served with mashed potatoes. And he always would be.

Ravani, blinking blurry through his hot tears, mumbled.

"What? I couldn't hear you, Ravioli."

"I'm sorry," Ravani said, louder. The words tasted like rancid pickles in his mouth.

Donnie's putrid mouth spread wide.

"There. That wasn't so hard, was it?"

Donnie straightened up, still perched on Ravani but no longer eye to eye with him. For a second it seemed to Ravani like that might be it. But then Donnie's eyes narrowed, and his smile darkened.

"Oh no," he said, voice dripping with mock concern. "You got some dirt in your mouth, buddy. Lemme help you rinse it out." He slumped forward, a palm on the ground on either side of Ravani's head, his foul face right above Ravani's. "Open wide."

Ravani's blood chilled colder than the water in Carcass Creek. He clamped his lips shut.

"I said, *open wide.*"

"Yeah, open wide!" Stevie jeered.

Ravani shook his head desperately. He shoved at Donnie with his arms, but Donnie just grabbed him by the wrists. He pinned one to the ground with his own meaty fist and pinned the other under his knee. With his free hand, he pinched Ravani's cheeks and squeezed, hard, slowly forcing his mouth open.

"*Hoikkk!*" Donnie hacked, bringing up a mouthful of wet spit. Then he opened his mouth. *Pppt.*

Ravani managed to jerk his head to the side at the last moment. The spit landed on his cheek, warm and sloppy. He wanted to gag.

Donnie's nostrils flared.

"Now you're making me mad," he seethed. "Open your mouth, or it gets worse." Donnie's grip tightened. He stabbed his knee down harder, sending flames of pain up Ravani's wrist and cutting his breaths short.

HOIKK!

Ravani screwed his eyes shut, resigned to a sour mouthful of Donnie Carter spit.

Instead, he heard a small thud. Felt Donnie's body give a little jerk. Heard him gulp, swallowing the loogie he had in the chamber. Ravani opened his eyes.

"Why'd you throw that?" Donnie asked, whipping his head toward Stevie.

"Throw what?"

"That rock!"

"I didn't throw—"

Stevie's words were interrupted by a small *ding*, and this time all three of them saw the stone drop to the ground after it bounced off Donnie's belt buckle. It hadn't come from Stevie. It came from the thick underbrush in the other direction. From the direction of the Croward house.

"Hey!" Donnie snarled. "Who—"

Another rock whistled out of the shadowy tangle of limbs and leaves, nicking Donnie's ear. He ducked and swore.

"Who's there?" he shouted, hands loosening on Rav as he straightened up to peer into the fallen logs, hanging vines, shifting shadows, and crumbling stumps of the forest. There were a hundred places to hide and duck and not be seen.

"Hey, uh, Donnie, maybe we should, um," Stevie stammered, taking a step back.

"Shut up, Stevie. *Hey!* Who's out there? You're gonna be sorry, I promise!"

Ravani knew who it was, who it *must* be.

Ravani blinked away his tears. And he said something.

"What'd you say?" Donnie spat, turning back to him.

Ravani cleared his throat.

"It's ghosts," he said.

Donnie's eyes squinted in scorn.

"What'd he say?" Stevie squeaked.

"What are you talking about?" Donnie said through heavy breaths. "There's—"

But right then three more rocks flew, each from a different direction. One hit Stevie in the stomach, one bounced off Donnie's shoe, and the other bounced on the ground between them.

"It's ghosts," Ravani said again, louder.

"I'm getting outta here, Donnie," Stevie said, his voice high.

Donnie opened his mouth to bark something but then a rock arced through the air and bounced off the back of his head. It wasn't big enough to do any real damage, but it was certainly big enough to sting.

"Ouch!"

Donnie rubbed the back of his head and licked his lips, eyes darting around. Most of his face was defiant and angry, but his eyes blinked and darted and widened and narrowed.

Donnie Carter was scared.

"This ain't over, Ravioli," Donnie said, standing up. "You owe me a cat!" But he followed after Stevie, shoulders hunched and hands clenched.

A rock flew after him. It flicked his other ear. Donnie walked faster.

After a moment, Ravani sat up.

He didn't look toward where the rocks had come from. Toward where, he was mostly sure, the ghosts were watching him. He had dirt in his mouth and spit on his face and tears in his eyes, and he couldn't look. His cheeks burned with shame. They'd seen him, like this. *She'd* seen him. She knew what he was, now. The little cottony thread of hope that he'd had since he'd seen her that first night blinked out like a blown candle.

How is a boy like that ever gonna make a friend?

He felt like perhaps he should say *Thank you* or *I'm sorry* (though he wasn't quite sure why) or *Goodbye.*

Instead he said nothing. He stood up and walked home through the forest, his eyes on the ground.

CHAPTER SEVEN

In Which Something Is Taught,
and Someone Is Warned

Later that afternoon Ravani returned for his bicycle.

He was trudging back toward his garage when a voice stopped him.

"Hey, Ravani." He looked over and there she was, standing in the shadows of a tree in the side yard of the Croward house. Like she was hiding. "Come here."

Ravani frowned. His soul still shook with shame. But he set his bike down and walked over.

She wore the same clothes and the same solemn expression from the day before.

"I need your help," she said. Ravani couldn't imagine anything that he could possibly help someone with. Bird identification, perhaps. But that seemed like an unlikely favor.

"With . . . what?"

"You gave me a frog," Virginia said in her serious way. "Give a girl a fish, and she'll eat for a day. Teach her to fish and she'll eat her whole life. I don't want to just eat for a day. I want you to teach me how to catch frogs myself."

Ravani's stomach dropped. "You . . . you *ate* that frog I gave you?"

Virginia blinked at him. "No. Sweet juniper. It's a metaphor. So will you help me?"

Virginia had, probably, saved him from Donnie that morning. He owed her one.

"I guess."

She grabbed him by the arm and yanked him out of the sunlight and into the overgrown strip of unruly woods between her house and Skinister Street.

As they pushed through shrubs, she talked over her shoulder. "It's harder than I thought. Catching frogs, I mean. We've been trying all afternoon."

When they broke free from the woods and into the clearing of the creek bank, Ravani saw who the "we" was.

Another boy was already in the water. He had the legs of his blue jeans rolled up but Ravani wasn't sure why, since every inch of him was sopping wet. He was older than Ravani by a bit, maybe thirteen or fourteen. Skinny, with bony arms sticking out of his white tank top undershirt, and blond hair buzzed short. A younger girl sat on the bank watching him, five or six years old, once again holding the stuffed giraffe she'd been clutching the night they'd arrived. In the daylight Ravani could see that it was shabby and worn, with frayed seams and one missing glass eye.

"Thank God," the boy in the creek called out, grinning at them. "The cavalry has arrived! My heart was gonna break if I had to watch Virginia fail miserably one more time!"

"That's my brother," Virginia said. "I'd call him obnoxious but that would be meeting him more than halfway."

The boy splashed over their way, wiping water off his brow

with a muddy arm, smearing his forehead brown. He held a hand out to Ravani.

"Howdy. My name is Mr. Amazing . . . but you can just call me Amazing."

"Nuh-uh!" the younger girl cried. "Your name is—"

"Colt," the boy cut in quickly. "My name's Colt. And that there is my little sister, Ugly."

"No!" the girl protested, jumping to her feet. "My *real* name is—"

"Annabel," Virginia finished, shooting Colt a dirty look.

"Hello," the girl said, slipping from scowl to smile in a heartbeat.

"Hi," Ravani said to her, blinking around at them. He saw Colt's soggy hand still hanging there waiting and he shook it. "My name's Ravani. Rav."

"Nice to meetcha, Rav," Colt said with a nod. "I think you're just the fella we need."

Ravani fought the warm blush that crept up his cheeks. It was a new feeling, hearing kind words from someone who wasn't his mother.

Colt put his fists on his hips and squinted at him. "So we've been jumping and diving like two otters with their tails tied together, but all we're getting is wet. What's the trick, Rav?"

"Um . . . well, there isn't a *trick*, really. First thing is you gotta know where they are."

"I can help with that!" Annabel chirped. She pulled something from around her neck and held them out to him: a pair of binoculars. They were cheap, scuffed plastic; just a toy, really.

Ravani was just about to decline the offer when Colt caught

his eye. The older boy's eyes were serious. He shook his head, just once, and small, but Ravani got the message.

"Oh," he said, taking them. "These are . . . perfect." He held them up to his eyes and squinted through them. "Ah. Yep. Now I see 'em. Over there in the lily pads and weeds." He handed the binoculars back to Annabel with a smile. "Thanks. Those are swell."

She beamed back at him, eyes sparkling. Colt gave him a little nod of thanks.

"Catching 'em isn't about speed. It's about stillness." Ravani saw the doubt on Colt's face. "If you run up to a frog, it's just gonna jump in and swim away every time. You gotta go in slow, have your hand ready, and when you're close enough, you grab it quick."

Colt sniffed. "Show us how it's done, pal."

So Ravani did. Colt and Virginia followed him out into the water, and the hunt began.

He caught one first and made it look easy.

Within a few minutes, Colt was standing triumphant, a mile-wide smile across his face and his hand held up in dripping victory, clutching a meaty handful of frog. Annabel cheered from the shore.

Virginia, however, kept coming up with nothing but a wet hand. With each failure her body tightened, her face grew redder. Ravani could tell she was close to giving up. But he remembered the stones, flying from shadows. He owed her one.

"You can do it," he said quietly into her eyes, when her frustrated face looked back his way.

She blew a breath out through flared nostrils and nodded

grimly and turned around and then, sure enough, she did it. Moved in slow, kept the water still . . . then her hand flashed and splashed, and when she stood up and turned around she was holding a frog.

"Way to go, sis!" Colt crowed, and Annabel clapped and hooted.

Virginia's and Ravani's eyes locked. He smiled, and she nearly did, too. Sometimes a soul can speak without talking, though. And her eyes were saying *Thank you*.

I owed you one, Ravani said with a shrug. And then she did smile, even if it was only for a second.

Afterward, they all flopped down on the grassy slope of the creek bank.

"You sure got the magic, Rav," Colt said, and Ravani was glad Colt wasn't looking at him close enough to see his blush.

"Yeah," Annabel said. "You're a good teacher."

Their words washed over him like sugar.

Colt sniffed at the palm of his hand.

"Ugh. My hand smells like frog now."

"Then it smells better than the rest of you," Virginia said.

They lay for a minute, feeling the warm sunshine and smelling the pine trees.

Then Annabel broke the spell. "Who were those boys who were picking on you this morning?"

All of Ravani's good feeling leaped and skittered away.

"Shut up, sister," Virginia said, quiet and quick.

"Don't you tell her to shut up," Colt snapped.

The words hung for a second in the air between them, waiting. Ravani's eyes burned.

"They were just . . . just kids from school." It was true, what he said. More or less.

"Why do you owe them a cat?" Annabel said.

"Oh. Long story," Ravani said, although it wasn't.

"They always like that?" Colt asked.

Ravani shrugged and looked away to hide the wetness of his eyes. For a little while, he'd been something different from what he was used to. He'd known it couldn't last, that good feeling. A soul can't fly forever.

"Well, they're not going to treat you like that around us," Virginia said.

"We don't like bullies," Annabel added.

Ravani gulped and blinked. Feelings swirled inside him. Mostly good feelings, but also a fair bit of confusion, and at least a dash of disbelief. Maybe even a sprinkle of suspicion. Who were these midnight children? How could they promise something like that? *Why* would they promise something like that?

"Okay?" he mumbled, more as a question than an answer.

"And next time they come around, we ain't throwing rocks," Colt said. "We're throwing *frogs*."

They all laughed. Snorting, loud laughter . . . the kind that's a relief after hard feelings.

And then they lay there in the sunlight dappling down through green leaves and pine needles, and they talked. Not any sort of important talk. Just lying by a creek on a summer afternoon talk. Talk about ice cream, and radio shows, and movies, and birds, and school, and bets over who could throw something the farthest. There was some joking, and some giggling.

To most children, in most places, it would have felt like the most normal of normal things.

But to Ravani, in Slaughterville, it felt like visiting another world. It felt like what he'd always imagined having a friend would feel like.

So, all the while, Ravani bit back his curiosity. He wanted to ask these strange children a dozen questions, a hundred . . . but he didn't want to break the spell. He chose, for the moment, friends over answers.

Annabel blew out a sigh. "I think I like it here," she said, wistful. "It's a good place."

"We'll see," Virginia said, quiet, then *tsk*ed her tongue. "Don't get your hopes up, little sister."

Ravani frowned up at the clouds. "What do you mean?"

"We move a lot," Virginia said, after a little pause. She said it bored, with a yawn. It was funny, though. Ravani didn't quite believe in her boredom, but he couldn't say why. "On account of our dad's work."

"Oh. What does he do?"

"He's a truck driver," Colt said. "On the road all the time."

Ravani nodded. So the cigar-smoking man who he'd seen drop them off *had* been their father. Then he frowned.

"If he's on the road, then why do *you* have to move?"

"It's complicated," Virginia said.

"What do you mean?" Ravani asked, his pulse quickening. He had a string of questions lined up—Why did you come in the middle of the night? Why do you hide all day? Where is your mother?—but he didn't get the chance to ask them.

"They mean you should mind your own business," a hard voice said from behind them. They all jumped and sat up.

And there he was. The oldest boy, the one with the angry body in the moonlight. He stood there, stern-faced, black-haired, tight-jawed.

"Time to come inside."

"Tristan!" Annabel exclaimed, scrambling to her feet. "Guess what? We were trying to catch frogs, and Virginia was just terrible at it, so she went and got Rav, and—"

"Come on. Mom wants you to clean up for dinner," the boy said, cutting off Annabel's excited voice. His voice was a little gentler when he spoke to Annabel. But only a little.

Annabel gave Ravani a fleeting smile and whispered "*Goodbye*" before walking away up toward the house. Colt followed behind, mumbling a quick, "Farewell, Frog Master," as he left.

The older boy, Tristan, stood there waiting with crossed arms. "*Now*, sister."

Virginia blew out a bored sigh. Ravani could almost hear her eyes roll. She got to her feet, taking her time. Ravani was still sitting in the grass, stomach knotted with worry. They were in trouble, all of them, somehow, and he didn't know why.

Virginia bent down and held out her hand to help him up and he took it and stood and when his ear was by her mouth she whispered, "*Tonight. Midnight. The old graveyard.*"

Ravani blinked at her. But he saw the look in her eyes, waiting for an answer. So he nodded, once, small and fast, so only she could see.

"Thank you for your help," she said louder, her voice sulky. "You're a peach."

Tristan was glaring at them, impatient and brooding. Virginia dropped Ravani's hand and strolled away, up past Tristan, unhurried.

She marched up the porch steps and inside, letting the screen door slam shut behind her.

That left Ravani, standing alone . . . facing Tristan, standing alone. It felt like a lot of alone, but like even more together.

Ravani looked at his hands. Then his feet. At the grass between them.

"Um," he said.

He started to walk home, but the older boy's voice stopped him.

"You live across the street," he said, and he didn't say it like a question. But Ravani nodded anyway, eyes down.

Tristan breathed in, deep, and let it out through his nose. Scratched at his jaw, and looked down toward the creek. Then he said the most surprising thing of all. "Thank you. For helping them."

Ravani stood speechless. Tristan's *Thank you* didn't feel like it was waiting for a *you're welcome*.

Tristan fixed his stony eyes on Ravani. "Go on. Get outta here." His voice was winter cold again.

Ravani, grateful to be let go, turned and started off. But once again his steps were stopped by words from Tristan.

"I don't want you over here anymore, you understand?"

Ravani looked back at him.

"You leave her alone. Leave all of us alone." And with that, Tristan turned and walked across the lawn and up the steps and inside.

His words, though, lingered in Ravani's heart. Like carcasses dangling from meat hooks.

You leave her alone.

They were sharp, those words. Menacing. Cold to the touch.

But they weren't the only words echoing inside Ravani. There were a few others, flitting from branch to branch in his heart. And their song was low and soft and scratchy at the bottom. Like the smell of a campfire.

They were *tonight.*

And *midnight.*

And *the old graveyard.*

Chapter Eight

In Which a Soul Leaps,
and a Trap Is Sprung

Ravani shivered, his foot hanging off the porch step.

It was nearly midnight.

He hadn't quite made the choice yet: whether he was going to sneak out, to walk through the woods alone in darkness, to meet a strange girl in the old graveyard. Almost all of him didn't want to. It was a lot to risk for the hurried whisper of a girl he'd barely met.

And yet.

The first night they'd come, his loneliness had been so strong, it had woken him up.

He was tired to his soul of being lonely. And he'd thought, for too long: *Someday. Someday I'll be happy. Someday I'll have a friend.*

Well. Maybe it wasn't meant to be someday, after all. Maybe it was some *night.*

When two souls find each other in the darkness, sometimes there is a reaching out. And sometimes, there is a leap.

Ravani leaped.

Over the three stairs of the back porch, knowing that they creaked and that the window to his parents' room was right overhead. He flew through the cool night air and landed on the moon-washed grass, then tiptoed across the lawn to the forest's edge.

He knew the old graveyard, and he knew all the ways there. He didn't know how *she* knew about it, though ... It wasn't easy to find. She must have gone exploring on her own. It was an old place, almost entirely forgotten, lost in the woods and overgrown.

Ravani crept through the forest, stepping over logs and ducking under branches. The world was a middle-of-the-night sort of quiet, but it wasn't any sort of still: crickets chirped, insects buzzed, and small living things skittered and scurried all around him.

Finally, up ahead, he saw it: the clearing where the graves lay waiting. He hopped over one more log and then stopped at the graveyard's edge. He'd never seen it at night.

The grave markers rose up out of the long grass, shining like crooked teeth in the moonlight. Some were crosses, some were rounded tombstones, some were statues, some were wooden, some were stone; all were crumbling, leaning, decaying. It was eerie, in the silver light and inky blackness.

The hairs on Ravani's arms rose up, tingling.

He stayed in the shadows along the graveyard's border, scanning for Virginia.

A sound stopped him, his foot dangling an inch above the ground.

It wasn't a footstep, or a branch breaking.

It was a *crack*, a soft *pop*. It didn't come from the graveyard, but from off to the side, in the thickness of the forest. Ravani stood, frozen. Then he heard it again. And with it, the murmur of a voice.

It must be Virginia, he thought. Making her way toward him.

Lost, perhaps. Looking for the graveyard. He walked toward her, listening close. The sounds got louder.

Then, he smelled it. And saw it. Smoke, and the yellow flicker of flames. A campfire, snapping and crackling.

He took a few quick steps closer. Why had Virginia built a fire?

But then: a bulky shadow that definitely did not belong to Virginia lurched into the firelight. Ravani would've recognized the brutish shape of the shadow anywhere.

Donnie Carter.

Ravani's blood shot hot with cold electricity.

He tried to take a step back, but a hand clamped hard over his mouth and a voice hissed into his ear, *"Don't. Move. A. Muscle."*

CHAPTER NINE

In Which a Monster Is Fled,
and a Test Is Passed

Ravani Foster didn't move just *a* muscle when that hand grabbed him and that voice whispered into his ear. He moved every one of them.

He bucked like a pony and squealed, or did the best he could to squeal with a hand over his mouth.

The grip on his face tightened, and he felt hot breath in his ear again.

"*Hold still, or they'll hear us.*" And, this time, Ravani recognized the voice. He stopped struggling and took a breath. Virginia.

But it was too late.

Ravani, eyes gaping, saw the shadow at the fire spin in their direction. Another silhouette stumbled into the circle of light: Stevie Mueller, carrying an armload of wood.

"What was that?" Donnie asked, squinting into the darkness.

Ravani and Virginia stood stock-still, breath held. Donnie couldn't see them yet, standing in a forest thick with shadows and trees.

But: it was only a matter of time. Ravani's heart thundered in his chest, and he could feel Virginia's pounding, too, pressed against his back.

"*Run*," Ravani said into the hand across his mouth, quiet as he could but as loud as he dared, so that Virginia would hear. "*Now*."

They ran.

At first, they tried to flee quietly, sprinting on soft feet . . . but then Virginia thumped her foot on a log, and Ravani snapped off a branch with his shoulder, and from behind them came a Donnie-throated holler: "*Someone's spying on us! Come on!*" Then, through their panting breaths and thumping footsteps, the unmistakable sounds of pursuit at their backs.

Ravani followed the flitting shine of Virginia's hair through the forest, weaving and leaping and running. He knew the woods, though, and she didn't, and she was leading them back toward Offal Road. If they burst out into the open moonlight with Donnie only thirty feet behind them, they'd be caught. So when she tripped and stumbled and skidded to her hands and knees, Ravani helped her up and whispered breathlessly, "*Follow me*." He found the thread of a deer trail, invisible to anyone who wasn't looking for it, that curved around back into the forest.

He ran as fast as he could in the darkness.

It sounded like they were pulling away from Donnie. Hope fluttered in his heart, but then he heard Virginia cry out. He looked back and saw her, stuck, ponytail snagged in a branch. She jerked her head, breaking free, and Ravani was about to spin and keep running when he saw it.

The dark shadow of a hollow space, under the log he had just jumped over. Big enough to hide a person, perhaps.

Virginia vaulted over the log and started to sprint his way, but he ran back and stopped her.

"*There*," he whispered, pointing at the nook and shoving her toward it.

Virginia didn't hesitate. She dropped to her belly and slithered under the log, pulling herself in and disappearing into blackness.

"*Come on*," she hissed out at him. "*There's room.*" Her hand, ghostly white in the moonlight, stretched out of the shadows toward him. Ravani paused, unsure. But then, twenty feet away at most, he heard Donnie crashing through the woods and a growled "*They went this way.*"

He dove to the forest floor and took her hand and she pulled him in. He wiggled and rolled back, tight up against her.

They lay there, pressed together in the blackness, catching their breath and trying to still their hearts.

There was a rock jamming into Ravani's side and something scratchy poking into his cheek but he didn't so much as twitch.

Virginia shifted so her mouth was against his ear.

"*Hey. You came.*"

The words were almost soundless, but they were also casual. Like Ravani and Virginia were just hanging out, talking, and not squished together in a hole in the forest, hiding from a villain.

Ravani nodded, hoping that was the end of her attempt at conversation.

Above them, footsteps pounded and branches snapped. Close. *Very* close.

"*I didn't think you would,*" Virginia said. Ravani grimaced. Their only hope was to lie there silently and pray that Donnie and Stevie didn't look down, or hear them.

So he shrugged, and let that be his answer.

The log over their heads shifted. A little shower of fine dust rained down on them.

"Where'd they go?" Donnie asked, breathing hard. He was standing on the log right above them.

"I dunno," Stevie answered, his whisper shaky and nervous. "You sure it ain't a bear?"

Donnie snorted.

"Bears make way more noise than that." The log trembled and he jumped down to the ground. Ravani flinched back and Virginia's arms tightened around him. Donnie's shoes were right in front of his face, less than a foot away. "It's some weirdo spying on us."

Ravani felt a tickling on his cheek and realized with horror what it was: a spider, crawling across his skin. He swallowed and screwed his eyes shut, willing himself to hold still, clenching his jaw tight to hold in his whimper.

"You got your flashlight?" Donnie asked, taking a step forward and crouching low. Ravani's blood froze . . . With a flashlight's beam, Donnie would find their hiding spot in no time.

"No. It's back by the fire."

"Darn. Come on, then." Donnie started walking forward, head swiveling. "They was headed this way."

"Why don't we just go back, Donnie? We could—"

"What, you scared, Stevie?"

"No," Stevie said quickly, but even people hiding under a log could tell he was lying.

"Then don't be such a *girl*." Virginia's fingers tightened viciously, digging into Ravani's arm. "I ain't afraid. Come on. Spread out over there and we'll both head that way. We'll find 'em."

Stevie snapped through the brush way off to the right, deeper into the woods. A second later Donnie's shoes followed.

Virginia and Ravani waited until Donnie disappeared through a dense thicket of trees and out of sight. Ravani took his first deep breath in what felt like an hour. His body melted into the ground, going soft with relief.

"*What. A. Jerk.*" Virginia's whisper was a cold kind of angry.

Donnie was far enough away that Ravani thought it was okay to finally whisper back.

"*Yeah. He's—*"

"Go on, get moving," Virginia interrupted, hardly whispering at all. She gave him a little push with both hands on his back. "You're sweating way too much for us to be this close."

"*Wait! We should stay hidden. Wait for them to—*"

"No," Virginia said, calm and unarguable. "I've got a better idea."

She dug a knuckle into his back so he had no choice but to wiggle out into the open, ears straining for any sign of Donnie's return. She scooted out and knelt beside him, listening as well. Way off in the distance they heard Donnie's and Stevie's voices calling back and forth, still moving away from them.

They looked into each other's eyes. To his surprise, Ravani felt a smile creep onto his face.

"*That was close,*" he whispered.

The corners of Virginia's mouth smiled back.

"Yeah." Her eyes narrowed. "You have a spider on your face."

Ravani flinched and squeaked and batted at his head like it was on fire.

"Cheese and rice, Rav. I said a spider, not a rattlesnake. Come on," Virginia said, grabbing Ravani by the shirt and yanking him after her, back in the direction they'd fled. She ran swift and silent as a nighthawk, darting and dodging. Ravani wasn't sure where she was taking them until he saw the cheerful light of the campfire ahead through the trees. He stopped at the light's edge.

"*What are we* here *for?*" he hiss-whispered. Virginia walked up to the fire and turned to look at him with her serious eyes.

"Justice," she said matter-of-factly.

Ravani took a reluctant step into Donnie's camp. There were two sleeping bags spread out, a backpack on the ground between them, some food wrappers scattered around, and a flashlight propped up against a log.

"What do you mean? They didn't even do anything to us."

Virginia's eyebrows lowered darkly.

"*Don't be such a girl?*" she said. "What was that supposed to mean? Keep an ear out." Virginia unzipped the backpack and started rifling through it. She pulled out a sloshing canteen. "'Girl' is not an insult, Ravani Foster. Anyone who says it is needs to learn a lesson."

She reached over and grabbed the flashlight, then straightened up and fixed Ravani with one of her solemn stares.

"I'm a girl. And I'm every bit as brave as he is." She said it simply, like it was true . . . because it *was* true, and Ravani knew it. "And, as a matter of fact, when he said he wasn't afraid, he was lying."

"How do you know that?"

Virginia pursed her lips.

"I just know. And I'm every bit as tough as he is. And I'm every bit as smart as he is." Ravani nodded. He was sure that for every smart bit that Donnie had, Virginia had at least two. There was a fire in her eyes twice as hot as the embers glowing behind her, but her voice was still solemn and flat. "I don't like people who try to make me feel smaller than I really am. You should know that, Ravani."

"Okay."

"The only bad thing about being a girl is having to deal with boys like him."

Ravani swallowed. He looked away from her shining eyes.

"I have to deal with boys like him, too," he said.

There was a moment of near quiet. No sound but the popping of the coals, and the rustle of the needles and leaves.

"Yeah," Virginia said at last, and her voice was softer. "I know you do." He looked back to her. The fire was gone from her eyes, but not the truth.

Ravani looked out at the woods beyond the firelight. There was a monster in the woods, and they were standing in its den. The night forest was quiet, but it wouldn't be for long.

"Tell me, Ravani. Why do you think I asked you to meet me out here tonight?"

Ravani turned back to her. She moved closer, so close that he almost jumped back. Their toes were nearly touching. Her eyes were alight with flames from the fire.

"I . . . I don't know."

"I was testing you."

"Testing me?"

"Yes."

"Testing me for what?"

Virginia blinked. Her face, which always seemed so serious, went even more somber. Sad, almost.

"I have secrets, Rav. Big secrets." The fire spat and crackled. Somewhere, out among the trees, an owl called. "I wanted to see if you were the kind of person a secret would be safe with."

Ravani waited, breathless. And waited. Finally, he gulped. "Uh. So. Did I, um, pass?"

She gave him a long, grave look. "Flying colors."

"How?" he asked. He thought of the last twenty minutes of his life. How he'd squealed, and run, and hid, and been nothing but scared the whole time.

She cocked her head to the side, just a bit.

"We were being chased by Donnie through the woods at night." She leaned in even closer, so close that he could feel the warmth of her breath and see speckles in the gray irises of her eyes. "But when you found that hiding spot, what did you do?" Ravani tried to swallow but couldn't, lost as he was in her eyes and the scratchy spell of her voice. "You gave it to *me*. That's something, Ravani Foster. *You're* something, I think."

There was a breathless sort of moment.

Sometimes, when two souls find each other in the darkness, the darkness goes away.

There were songs inside Ravani, right then in the firelight. Songs he'd never heard before.

Virginia stepped back. She tossed the flashlight a few feet away into the underbrush.

"They'll find it in the morning," she said. Then she unscrewed the lid to the canteen and upended it over the fire. The fire sputtered and hissed and steamed and, splash by splash, went dark. Ravani blinked, trying to reorient his eyes to the darkness.

Virginia dropped the empty canteen and looked down at the sleeping bags. She frowned and wiggled her hips a little bit.

"I wish I had to pee," she said.

"Why?" Ravani asked, though he had a pretty good idea.

"Doesn't matter," she shrugged. "Let's go."

When they got to the gravelly end of Offal Road, they stopped, catching their breath in front of their houses.

After being terrified spitless for half an hour, Ravani suddenly didn't want the night to end.

"Your secret," he asked, feeling bold. "Is it a good secret? Or a bad secret?"

Virginia's smile faded into a thoughtful sort of frown.

"It's a terrible secret." She blinked once, twice. Her throat bobbed with a swallow. She raised one shoulder in a shrug, just barely, and let it drop. "And it's a wonderful secret."

"Both?"

She nodded, just a dip of her chin.

"Both."

"So . . . what is it?"

Virginia opened her mouth. Ravani waited, soul on tiptoes, like the moment just before you sneeze. He could see it, see the secret burning behind her eyes, wanting to come out into the world.

But then her mouth closed. She blinked, fast.

"The first secret is that I have secrets," she said. "The rest you'll have to wait for. Good night, Rav."

And then she walked away, without looking back, toward her own silent house.

Chapter Ten

In Which a Bag Is Filled,
but a Stomach Remains Empty

The Hunter, as always, prepared for the hunt very carefully. He did not rush.

A large gray backpack stood open on his narrow, tautly made bed.

Into it went the dark tools of his grim trade, in the reverse order that they were likely to be needed, so that what he might need would always be at hand.

First: ten black cloth gags, which the Hunter rarely used, but which were very useful when they were needed. His prey only numbered seven, but the Hunter always brought extra. One never knew how a hunt would play out.

Then, one by one, ten pairs of handcuffs went in. He coiled each pair carefully so that they didn't get tangled. Tangled handcuffs can lead to mistakes. The Hunter was not in the business of making mistakes.

Then several throwing nets and bolos, which were in fact *designed* to tangle, but around fleeing legs rather than one another.

A soft-sided leather case that held pliers and screwdrivers and a small crowbar. All terribly useful.

Two sturdy metal flashlights, both with fresh batteries. One had a red bulb, one a bright white one. Each could be useful.

Finally: a lock-picking set, scrupulously oiled and organized.

Everything had its place. Each bird to a nest.

The Hunter pulled the zipper slowly closed.

He did not pack any food.

Because the Hunter always hunted best when he was hungry.

And the Hunter was very hungry.

Chapter Eleven

In Which a Friend Is Not Made

Early the next morning, Ravani stepped out onto the dark porch, still half asleep. He nearly wet his pants when a voice spoke from the porch swing, only a step away from him.

"Good morning."

Ravani jumped so high his feet actually left the ground.

"Sorry I scared you," Virginia said calmly once he'd landed. "That was quite a jump. You almost hit your head on the ceiling."

"What . . . what . . . what are you doing here?" Ravani sputtered.

"I'm coming with you on your paper route," Virginia said, standing up. "To see something of this town besides the creek and the graveyard."

"How did you . . ."

"I saw you leave yesterday morning. It *is* a paper route, right?"

"Well, yeah." Ravani thought of Tristan, of his warning and his watchfulness. "Are you . . . allowed to?"

Virginia stood up. "Allowed? I was *told* to."

Ravani rubbed at his eyes, trying to clear his sleep-fogged brain. "Told to? What does that mean?"

Virginia dropped her voice into a steely imitation of Tristan's voice. "It means you should mind your own business." She smiled with half her mouth. "Let's go before I fall back asleep."

Hortense Wallenbach sat up straighter when Ravani walked into the *Slaughterville Spectator* office with Virginia behind him.

"Who do we have here?" she asked.

"Ms. Wallenbach, this is Virginia. She's, my, uh . . ." Ravani trailed off, looking to Virginia. The words *I ain't looking for a friend* echoed in his heart.

"I'm Ravani's new neighbor," Virginia finished for him.

"Well, there's a scoop! I didn't hear that someone interesting moved into town!"

"Oh, I'm not interesting," Virginia said in her deadpan voice. "Not even a little bit. Me and my family, we're boring as mashed potatoes."

"Homemade garlic mashed potatoes, with turkey gravy?" Hortense asked, raising a hopeful eyebrow.

Virginia shook her head. "Powdered potatoes. No gravy."

Hortense's face dropped. "You sure? This town could use something fresh."

"I'm sure, ma'am. We're nowhere near as interesting as"— Virginia grabbed a newspaper off the waiting stack and read the headline out loud—"*'Skinister Quality Meats Considers New Spicy Meatball'*?"

Virginia blinked at the headline, then looked up at Hortense. The editor sighed and shrugged.

"I don't make the stories," she said glumly. "I just write 'em down and print 'em out."

"Well, it *could* be interesting," Ravani said, trying to cheer her up. "What if it's, like, *really* spicy. Like, *dangerously* spicy."

Virginia furrowed her brow, but Hortense Wallenbach picked it up.

"Yes! One by one the townspeople start dying horrible, unexplainable deaths, and then a local amateur detective—a new girl in town, perhaps, or a plucky newspaper editor—uncovers the sinister truth: Skinister seasoned the meatballs with cursed chile pepper looted from a lost jungle tomb, and the curse will only be lifted if Skinister is thrown into a volcano!"

Ravani guffawed. Hortense grinned. Even Virginia's brow unfurrowed.

"*That's* the story you should write," she said.

But Hortense was already settling back into her chair. She yawned and rolled her eyes. "Yeah, right. Who'd wanna read that nonsense?"

"Lots of folks, I bet. I know I would." Virginia turned her serious eyes on Ravani. "Wouldn't you?"

"Oh. Sure, I guess."

"Yeah, well, duly noted," Hortense said with a snort. "Lemme know when you're old enough to buy a paper." But as Ravani bundled the papers into his delivery bag, he noticed Hortense chewing on her cheek, staring thoughtfully at the ceiling.

Virginia and Ravani walked his route in sleepy silence, taking turns sticking newspapers into mailboxes and throwing them onto porches—or more or less *near* porches, in Ravani's case.

"So, which of these are your friends' houses?" Virginia asked, chucking a paper and landing it squarely onto a porch's welcome mat.

Ravani almost stumbled. "Oh. Well." Ravani took a few more steps, mind racing and heart dropping.

The truth was, of course, that Ravani's friends didn't live in any of the houses that subscribed to the *Slaughterville Spectator*, because Ravani's friends didn't live in any houses at all, because Ravani's friends didn't exist. But that was the sort of truth that hurt even more to say with your mouth than it did to hold in your heart.

"There," Ravani said at last, pointing at the dreary brown house they just happened to be passing at that moment. "I've got a friend that lives there."

Virginia's face turned toward him, a little wrinkle between her eyes. "Liar."

It was the second time she'd called Ravani that name, and once again it was strange how she managed to say it like she wasn't calling him a name.

"I'm . . . um, not lying," Ravani said, not even convincing himself.

"That's a lie, too," Virginia said. "Why are you lying?"

Again, her voice painted with curiosity, not accusation.

I'm not lying, is what Ravani meant to say next. But the words didn't come.

"I don't know," he said. But he did know, of course.

The wrinkle between her eyes got deeper. She stopped walking, so he did, too.

"Liar," she said again, but so soft that it was nearly a whisper. They stood there, facing each other in the street. She held him in her wide eyes, waiting. She was waiting for the truth, and he knew it.

And, to his surprise, he said it. There was just something about her.

"I don't have any friends," he said.

Her eyebrows went up.

She didn't call him a liar this time. He was, after all, telling the truth. She just nodded, lips pursed.

"Neither do I," she said.

A little fluff of hope rustled its feathers in his heart.

"Maybe we could be friends," Ravani said, and his soul held its breath.

"No." Gentle. Not like a slap, like a handshake.

"Why not?"

"I just can't," she said. "It's got nothing to do with you. But we can't be friends. So let's be . . ." She bit her lip and looked down, thinking. Then her eyes flashed up. "Comrades." She nodded, once. "Yes. Comrades."

"Comrades? What does that even mean?"

Virginia breathed in through her nose and blew it out. "It means that I'm on your side. And you're on mine." She stuck her hand out toward him. "Deal, comrade?"

Ravani looked at her hand. He'd never had a comrade before. He didn't know if it was as good as having a friend. But he was pretty sure that having a comrade was better than not having one. And he was also absolutely sure that if he was going to have a comrade, he was glad it was Virginia. He took her hand and shook it.

"Deal."

She handed him a rolled-up paper. "Your turn."

He took the paper, squinted one aiming eye, and hurled it at the nearest front porch. The paper bounced off the gutter and landed in a rosebush.

"Not bad," Virginia said. "Your closest one yet, comrade."

They finished the last of the houses and took the turn into downtown.

At the café, Fred was clearing an empty, greasy plate from the sheriff's usual table.

"Oh," Fred said when Ravani walked up with Virginia, clearly surprised. "Who's your friend, Rav?"

"I'm Ravani's neighbor," Virginia said, holding out her hand gravely. "Virginia."

"Fred. Pleased to meet you." He did a dramatic bow. "Welcome to my establishment."

Ravani handed him a newspaper.

"New in town?" Fred asked.

"I like your restaurant," Virginia said as an answer, looking around at the patio tables under their weather-worn umbrellas. "It isn't trying too hard."

"Thanks?" Fred said with a shrug. "I guess you could thank my grandmother. She's the one who started this place."

"You know," Ravani said, "Fred used to own a restaurant in Paris." He shot Fred a hopeful look.

"Really?" Virginia asked.

"Yep." He raised his eyebrows at Fred, who just sighed. "Until . . . tragedy struck?"

Virginia looked at Fred. He narrowed his eyes at Ravani, but they were sparkling, and he grinned ruefully. He set the newspaper down on the table behind him, and when he turned around he was transformed.

"*Oui! Mon dieu*, what *tragédie*!" His eyes were wide in soulful sorrow, the back of one hand held to his forehead, his voice suddenly melodic and raspy and dripping with a French accent and melancholy. Ravani could almost hear accordions in the background. Virginia snickered.

"It was a—how you say—*zeppelin*? Oui, a blimp! Full of ze gas of the hydro*gen!* Its sinister shadow fell across my *petit café,* and I looked up into ze sky and I cried out, '*Sacre bleu!*'" Fred's gaze was heavenward, his face twisted in anguish.

"It crashed on your restaurant?" Ravani asked through a wide smile.

Fred's eyes dropped to Ravani's, and his voice lowered to a haunted whisper. "No. Worse zan zat, *mon ami.* It—oh, and how it destroys ze heart in my chest to say it"—he paused dramatically, hand over his heart—"it emptied its *toilette*. Ze sewage, it rained from the sky upon my *bistro.*" Ravani laughed through his nose. Virginia laughed out loud, too, which was a first. "*Poopoo* in my porridge. *Le crap* on my croissants. It was a *désastre total.* I knew I could never—how you say—*wipe* zat memory clean. So I said *ciao* to my *café* and left it behind, but I made a sacred vow to one day open again, but *zis* time . . . with umbrellas!" He finished with a dramatic flourish, holding both arms out toward the closest umbrella.

Ravani applauded. Fred took a bow.

"Unbelievable!" the sheriff's voice exclaimed from behind Fred.

"*Merci!*" Fred beamed, turning around.

But the sheriff was looking down at the newspaper on the café table. "A *spicy* meatball? I never would have predicted *that* one!"

"Oh. Yeah," Fred said, turning back to Ravani with a roll of his eyes. "*Oui,* it's a shocker, all right."

"He's great, isn't—" Ravani started to say to Virginia, but then realized that she was no longer standing next to him.

"Your friend went that way," Fred said, pointing down the street and pulling a rag out of his apron to wipe the table.

"Oh, thanks. See ya."

"*Ciao*, Rav."

He hurried down the sidewalk. There was no sign of Virginia . . . It was like she'd just disappeared. But then a familiar voice called his name from the alleyway and he saw her, standing there in the shadows.

"Virginia! Why'd you leave?"

Virginia blinked at him. "I didn't want to get a sunburn."

Ravani looked up at the sky. It was *kind* of sunny, he supposed.

"Is . . . everything okay?"

"Of course. Why wouldn't everything be okay?" she asked. She stuck her head out of the alley and looked back toward the café. Fred was heading inside with an armload of dirty dishes. The sheriff was walking away from them, back toward her office. "I should get home. Let's finish this route up."

They only had one more stop: the bakery.

Mr. Chin, as always, had elbows on the counter, hands propping up his head.

"New in town, huh?" he asked Virginia after Ravani's introduction. "Well, then, pick something out for your family. My treat as a welcoming gift." He spread his hands to show the same selection of loaves and rolls he'd had the day before.

"Thank you," Virginia said, eyes scanning the case. "Do you have any cupcakes?"

Lee shook his head. "Nope. Just the loaves."

"How come?"

Lee blinked, confused. "Well. I mean." He scratched at his

cheek, leaving a floury white fingerprint on his brown skin. "I've always only done the loaves. Same as my dad." He shrugged. "It's what we do."

"Huh," Virginia said, one corner of her mouth frowning. "I had a cupcake in a bakery once. In Mineral Springs. It was cinnamon carrot cake. With ginger-maple frosting." She sighed. "It was incredible," she said flatly.

Lee's eyebrows rose. "I love maple," he said wistfully.

"Who doesn't love maple?" Virginia looked back down at the loaves. "I'll take the white sandwich loaf, please. Thank you very much."

A few minutes later they were walking home, Ravani pushing his bike and Virginia holding her loaf, wrapped in a brown paper bag.

"It's a nice town," she said. She sounded almost sad, but it was hard for Ravani to tell with Virginia. She always sounded kind of sad.

"I guess." Ravani shrugged.

"I think it's the kind of place I'd like to live."

"You *do* live here."

"Yeah," Virginia said vaguely.

Just then, though, another voice interrupted their conversation.

"Well, lookee here. Fresh Ravioli."

No, Ravani moaned in his soul. *No, no, no. Not with her here.*

It was, of course, inevitable. It was how Ravani's life went. Of course Donnie would show up. He always did.

Chapter Twelve

In Which There Are Both Trolls and Gold

Donnie and Stevie emerged from under the bridge like trolls.

They were wet and muddy and sneering.

Their eyes took in Virginia, and Donnie's sneer turned to a scowl.

"Who are *you*?" he asked.

Virginia looked him up and down. The thin line of her mouth curved into a frown.

"No offense," she said calmly, "but you don't seem like the kind of person I enjoy spending time with."

Most of Ravani's body broke out into a sweat.

"What did you say?" Donnie asked, blinking.

"Nothing," Ravani squeaked quickly. "This is Virginia. She, um, just moved in next to me."

Donnie squinted at Virginia, sizing her up. "Yeah? Well, ain't that sweet." He smeared some version of a smile onto his face. "Welcome to Slaughterville. But you oughta be careful who you choose to be friends with."

"I am," Virginia said. She sounded almost bored, which was almost exactly the opposite of how Ravani felt.

"Well, then you should be *more* careful. 'Cause Ravioli here *ain't* the kind of kid *anyone* wants to be friends with."

Ravani's face burned red.

"Says who?" Virginia asked.

Donnie snorted.

"Says *everyone*. He's a freak. A loser. Look at him."

Virginia turned her head and looked at Rav, face thoughtful. Her brow furrowed when she saw the tears waiting in his eyes.

"*I* like him," she said softly, and even though she said it to Donnie, she said it into Rav's eyes, and she said it like it was true. "I like him a lot."

Ravani's soul tingled.

Ravani had seen a bird, once, trapped in his garage. Fluttering in desperate circles, battering its fragile wings against the rafters, the walls. The garage door was closed, and Ravani wasn't strong enough to open it. So he crawled up and opened the small cobweb-choked window. But the wren didn't understand; too blinded by fear to see the sunlight, it still crashed around the garage, shedding feathers like tears. It thought it was trapped, because it had *been* trapped. Ravani had almost cried, watching the anguish of the wren. But then it had landed for a moment on a wheelbarrow, its tiny chest heaving. The sparkling black jewel of its eye had fixed on the bright square of blue sky. *Ah*. A triumphant flutter of wings, and the wren was free in the great green world.

With Virginia's words, Ravani felt the same feeling. Virginia had opened a window.

It doesn't have to be a big moment, when a soul realizes that maybe life doesn't have to be what it has been so far. It can be small. A glance across a garage. Simple words, simply said. It was just a start, when Ravani heard Virginia say those words. A seed, not an oak tree. But the magical thing about seeds is that they grow. Just ask an oak tree.

"You *like* him? Ravioli?! *Nobody* likes Ravioli! He's a weakling. He *cries*, and—"

"So?" Virginia cut in, again without any fight in her voice, turning her head back to Donnie. "Don't you ever cry?"

"No," Donnie shot back through a churlish chortle.

Virginia tilted her head to the side. "Liar," she said. Soft and easy, like it was nothing.

Ravani died a thousand little deaths on the inside when she said it, the open window forgotten.

"What did you call me?"

"I called you a liar. Because you just lied. It isn't that complicated."

Donnie sputtered. His face turned red. Then white. Then white with red blotches. Ravani didn't think that was a good sign.

He was right.

Donnie's hands curled into fists. He stepped forward, right into Virginia's face, his muscles tensed and ready.

Ravani didn't exactly plan on opening his mouth. He certainly didn't plan on saying anything. But, really, he hadn't *planned* on giving a stranger a jar of frogs for her birthday, and he hadn't *planned* on sneaking into a graveyard at midnight. There was just something about Virginia that seemed to change his plans.

"Leave her alone," Ravani said, and then nearly vomited.

Virginia looked to him. Donnie's head turned slowly toward Ravani, too. Eyes blinking furiously, nostrils flaring, jaw muscles working. The word *rhinoceros* came to mind.

"What did you just say?" he growled. Even Stevie looked a little scared. Virginia, however, did not.

"We know you heard him," she said, rolling her eyes. "You're very dramatic, you know."

The world jostled, just a bit, off its axis. Ravani nearly lost his balance . . . although that could've been because he wasn't breathing, and his heart had stopped.

Donnie's demonic gaze shifted, thankfully, away from Ravani and back to Virginia.

"*You're lucky,*" Donnie finally managed to say through gritted teeth, "*that I don't hit girls.*"

"*You're* lucky that you don't hit girls," Virginia said calmly. "Because this one hits back."

Donnie's mouth opened and closed. His face twitched.

"You know what you are?" he asked finally, glaring her up and down.

"Yes," Virginia answered simply.

But Donnie's question had been rhetorical.

"Dressing like a boy. Talking like that. You're a dirty little *creep.*" His narrowed eyes slid back to Ravani. "And you're a dirty little freak." He smirked and shook his head. "Look at the two of you. A couple of weirdo losers. The *Creep* and the *Freak.*" Donnie let the words slide out of his mouth like greased eels. He cocked his head back with a gloating sneer.

"The . . . Creep and the Freak?" Virginia repeated doubtfully. She looked at Ravani. A smile grew slowly on her face. It was the biggest smile he'd seen from her yet. It was, to be honest, pretty creepy. "That's got a real ring to it," she said, nodding. "The Creep and the Freak. I *like* it." She held out a hand to Ravani who, too stunned and terrified to think, shook it. "The Creep and the Freak. We should have T-shirts made."

Donnie's face went from gloat to glare. His eyes glittered with angry confusion. "You're trash," he spat, apparently determined to keep shooting until something landed.

And, finally, it seemed that something had.

Virginia's smile faded.

"No," she said, low but strong and sure. "I am not trash. I am *gold*."

She put an arm around Ravani.

And she said, "And he's gold, too."

Ravani's heart started beating again. And it was beating in a whole new way.

Virginia *tsk*ed her tongue.

"Well, this has been a real delight," she said blandly. "But I need to get home. Come on, Rav."

And then, like it was nothing, they walked away. Just walked down the road, leaving Donnie and Stevie gaping.

"I'm starving," Virginia said after a while, sniffing at the wrapped loaf in her arms.

Ravani, however, was still reeling from the near-death experience they'd just survived.

"That was . . . that was . . . ," he started, but didn't know how to finish. *Amazing? Crazy? Terrifying?* "Weren't you scared?"

"What, of that jerk?" She shrugged. "He ain't nothing new."

"Uh, you don't know Donnie."

"Sure I do," she said. "I've known plenty of Donnies." She reached into the bag and ripped off a chunk of the loaf, then tore it in two and handed half to Ravani. She popped the other half into her mouth. "The thing about this world is that there's all kinds of people in it, and there's nothing you can do about that," she said through a crusty mouthful. "The only thing to do is decide what kind *you* are, and then be it. Don't worry about anyone else. Especially the Donnies."

Ravani snorted. "Well, that's easy to *say*. It'd be great just to do that, just to . . . just to . . ." Ravani, once again, wasn't sure what words should come next. *It'd be great just to . . . be who I want to be . . . to be okay . . . to not be alone . . . to not be scared . . . to be happy.* Each answer welled up from deep inside him, but each one was yanked back down by his soul before he could say it.

"Maybe someday." He sighed. *Someday.* It's a word that's dressed up like hope, but is really sadness all the way down. It feels like a wish, but is almost always a surrender.

Virginia wiped at her lips with a sleeve. "*Pfft.* Someday. There'll always be people who want to make you feel small, Rav. But they shouldn't do it with your permission."

Ravani bit off a piece of the bread, thinking.

"Were you really gonna hit him back?" he asked through a doughy mouthful.

Virginia chewed, then swallowed. "No. My arms are almost as skinny as yours, Rav. But I have very sharp knees. I was gonna knee him where it counts."

Ravani laughed out loud, almost spitting his bread out.

Virginia snuck him a quick smile. "I have three brothers. I know what works."

They turned the corner onto Offal Road and were soon standing on the street between their houses.

"I'm liking you more and more all the time, comrade."

Again, just like the night before, Ravani had no idea what he'd done to earn Virginia's kind words. Sometimes a soul just doesn't think it deserves kindness. Every time a soul believes that, though—any soul at all—it's wrong.

"Why?" Ravani asked, honestly.

Virginia squinted through the midday sunshine at him. "You really don't know, do you?" she said, almost to herself, then shook her head. "You gave me a frog for my birthday. You met me in the moonlight," she said. "And you stood up for me to Donnie just now." She pursed her lips. "Well, kind of. It wasn't all that impressive, really. But it wasn't nothing. I wasn't lying back there, Rav. I think you're gold." Like everything Virginia said, she said it flat and matter-of-fact, just as though she were calling him a *mammal*, just as though she was merely stating an unremarkable fact and not, in fact, making his heart soar like a sunrise lark.

Ravani tried to swallow. "So . . . when are you gonna tell me your secret?"

Virginia arched an eyebrow.

"Never, probably," she said, then shrugged. "Or soon, maybe. I haven't decided yet."

She picked a piece of bread from between her teeth and flicked it to the ground, then took a backward step toward her house. "Well. See you around, Freak."

CHAPTER THIRTEEN

In Which Grapes Are Thrown,
and Tears Are Shed

"Who was that girl you were talking to?" His mother's question took Ravani by surprise as he climbed the porch steps.

"Girl?" he asked, startled. He had walked all over town with Virginia, but somehow she still sort of felt like a secret. "Oh. Um, that was Virginia. Her family just moved in across the street."

"Really?" His mother was, quite reasonably, confused. Usually a move involved a moving truck, a marching in of boxes and furniture, a commotion. "And you've met them?"

Ravani nodded.

His mother put her hands on her hips, which was rarely a good sign. "When were you going to tell me?"

Ravani swallowed. "Right now?" he tried.

"Really. Well, I feel rude. Wash your face and change out of those dirty clothes and then run over and invite them for lunch. I want to welcome them to the neighborhood."

Ravani blinked. There was something about Virginia and her family that was so *strange*, even beyond their mysterious midnight arrival. They just didn't seem like the inviting-them-over-for-lunch types.

"What neighborhood? It's two houses on a dead-end road."

"Then I want to welcome them to the dead-end road, darling."

Ravani chewed his lip, looking back across the street.

"Go," his mother said. "Now."

≈

A few moments later he was freshly changed and rapping his knuckles on Virginia's front door.

From the other side, he heard some hushed footsteps and back-and-forth whispers.

He was just about ready to retreat back home and tell his mother that he'd tried, when the door opened a crack.

A sideways face appeared from behind the door. Brown eyes, peeking out from under brown bangs, with a smattering of freckles underneath. Ravani could only see it from the nose up.

"Who is it?" the eyes asked.

"Um . . . it's . . . me?" Ravani stammered.

"Knock it off! You know who it is!" said a fierce whisper, and the eyebrows in the doorway furrowed. The door opened a bit more, so that Ravani could see a mouth missing a couple of teeth. The face was older than Annabel's but younger than Virginia's. Seven or eight years old, maybe.

"You're the frog kid, right?" the face asked.

"Uh, yeah. I'm Rav. I live across the street?"

"We know."

Another head popped out from behind the door. Almost

identical to the first, but a girl. She had the same eyes, the same freckles, the same straight brown hair. Twins.

The two pairs of eyes stared at him.

"Uh. Well. Is . . . Virginia home?"

"Yeah," the girl said. "She's taking a bath. You her boyfriend or something?"

"No!" Ravani said quickly. His face burned hot. "No," he added, then clarified, "No."

He stood there, sweating and blushing and rocking on his feet like he had to go to the bathroom. He had completely forgotten why he was there.

He was rescued by the familiar face of Colt, walking down a flight of stairs. He wasn't wearing anything other than a towel tied around his waist, and he was chewing loudly on an apple.

"Frog Master!" he said through a mouthful. "How's it going?"

"F . . . fine?" Ravani stuttered. In Ravani's house, no one ever walked around mostly naked.

Colt saw him eyeing the towel. "It's bath day. And I like to air-dry." He held the half-eaten apple toward Ravani. "Wanna bite?"

"Oh. Er. No, thanks. I'm, um, supposed to see if you want to eat."

Colt stopped mid-chew and squinted at him.

Ravani blew out a breath and tried again. "I mean, my mother wants to invite you all over for lunch today. If you want. To come."

Colt poked a bit of apple out of his teeth with his tongue.

"All of us?"

Ravani nodded.

"Your parents, too."

Colt shrugged and swallowed his bite and muttered under his breath, "You must have a big table."

"What's for lunch?" the younger boy asked from behind the door.

"Egg salad sandwiches."

"I'll come," the boy said without a beat.

"Hold on," Colt cut in, stretching his mouth to take a big bite off the core. "I'll ask Mom." He turned and walked away up the stairs.

The four silent eyes continued to stare at Ravani from behind the door. A finger crept out and picked one of the noses, then disappeared back behind the door. Hopefully not toward a mouth.

"So," the girl said. "You're the frog killer."

Ravani shook his head. "I don't kill them. I just catch them. Then let them go."

"That's weird."

Ravani breathed a sigh of relief when Colt came jogging back down the stairs, the towel replaced by his usual uniform of blue jeans and a white tank top, followed by a wet-haired Virginia.

"Howdy, comrade," she said.

"All right, we're coming," Colt said. "Just the kids, though. Mom's got a doozy of a headache. And Beth's staying, too. That's our eldest sister," he added to Ravani.

Ravani thought about Tristan. Those angry eyes, the cold voice. An image of the older boy, chewing an egg salad sandwich while glaring at Ravani across the kitchen table, made him shudder.

"What about your . . . older brother?" he asked.

He tried to make his voice sound casual but apparently failed, because Colt scrunched his nose and said, "Don't worry. He's out hunting for gainful employment." He winked at Ravani, then clapped his hands at the younger children still mostly hidden behind the door.

"We are invited guests," he said. "So everyone needs to put on shoes."

Matching groans sounded out from behind the door.

"*And* socks?"

"Yep. Underwear, too. *Clean* underwear. Hop to it!"

There was another groan of protest, and then the twins emerged from behind the door and trudged up the stairs. The boy, Ravani noticed, was definitely not wearing clean underwear. He could tell, because the boy wasn't wearing any underwear at all, which he could tell because he wasn't wearing any clothes whatsoever.

Colt saw Ravani's surprised look and shrugged.

"It's bath day," he said again.

A few minutes later, they were all stomping up the front steps of Ravani's house. Virginia was still wearing her faded denim overalls, but they were now strapped over a green button-down shirt instead of the usual white T-shirt.

"Listen up," Colt said when they were on the porch. He looked into each of their eyes, waiting for them each to look back. Then he pointed at each one as he said their names. "Annabel Deering. Winnie Deering. Benjamin Deering. Virginia Deering. Remember what Mom said. You will all be on your most sterling behavior. Pleases and thank-yous and excuse-mes. No weird or embarrassing behavior. Absolutely no cursing. Understand?"

Virginia snorted.

"Yes, sister?" Colt asked.

"You, dear brother, are the crown prince of weird and embarrassing behavior."

"Well, then that makes me royalty."

"Your shirt's on backwards, Your Majesty," Virginia answered. Colt looked down quick. His hand flew up to finger the tag sticking out at the front of his collar. "And inside out."

"*Damn it,*" he said, and pulled his arms into the armholes and wiggled and writhed but only had the shirt halfway turned around when the front door opened behind Virginia. Ravani's mother stood there, wiping her hands on a towel.

"Oh, hello! I *thought* I heard voices out here."

"Hello, Mrs. Foster," Virginia said. She held out her hand formally, and Ravani's mother shook it. "My name is Virginia Deering. Thank you for inviting us to lunch. My mother sends her apologies." Virginia pulled a small white envelope from her pocket and handed it to Ravani's mother.

"Thank you, dear," she said, opening the envelope and scanning the card inside. "Oh, I'm so sorry to hear that she's not feeling well! We'll be sure to send some food home with you, then."

She looked up and scanned the crowd on the porch. Colt had stopped wrestling with himself and was standing there, shirt halfway turned around, his arms still pinned inside. He slapped on a winning smile.

"Good afternoon," he said.

Ravani's mother laughed.

"Good afternoon. Well, it looks like we're short on sandwiches. And chairs." She smiled. "So we'll do blankets."

While Ravani's mother made a few more sandwiches, Ravani and the others spread a couple of blankets in the backyard.

"So," Mrs. Foster said once she'd joined them on the blanket, "let's do names. Virginia I know, but I'll need introductions from the rest of you." She looked to Benjamin and Winnie, but Virginia jumped in.

"This is Winnie and Benjamin," she said.

"Twins?" Ravani's mother asked, stretching to shake their hands.

"Yes." Winnie smiled. Then her smile dropped. "I mean, yes *please.*"

"I had a bath today," Benjamin announced. "*And* I'm wearing clean underwear. Thank you."

Virginia's face stayed calm, but Ravani noticed her nostrils flare.

"Well," Ravani's mother said through a smile, "then you and I already have two things in common, Benjamin. And such good manners!"

Benjamin smiled and stuck his tongue out at Virginia. Her eyes smoldered, but she forced a smile at Mrs. Foster and moved on.

"This is Annabel," she said. "Annabel Deering."

"Wonderful to meet you, Miss Annabel."

"And this is my older brother," Virginia cut in. "He—"

"Saved the best for last!" Colt exclaimed, jumping to his feet and dropping into a dramatic bow. "My name is Colt Deering." He held out his hand and took Mrs. Foster's, then kissed it with a loud *smack.* "It is truly a pleasure to make your acquaintance, Mrs. Foster."

"My, what a gentleman!" She laughed.

"Isn't he, though?" Virginia said through gritted teeth.

"Five beautiful children! That's quite a houseful."

"Seven, actually," Colt said.

"Our oldest brother and sister couldn't make it," Virginia explained.

"Seven! How lovely, to have such a big family. I always wanted a big family."

"Then why didn't you have one?" Benjamin asked.

"*Benjamin!*" Virginia hissed at him.

"Sorry," he said quickly. "Then why didn't you have one, please?"

Her smile tightened at its corners.

"A fair question. One doesn't always get what one wants, though," she said softly, her smile fading. "I always thought, someday . . ." But her voice dwindled to silence. Ravani swallowed and leaned in, so that his shoulder touched hers. He knew the truth, of course, and the pain of it. She blinked, and the warmth came back to her smile. "But we are very lucky and grateful to have *one* miracle." She rubbed Ravani's back, and his face burned hot. "It would be greedy to want more than that. Now, let's eat, shall we?"

Eating lunch with most of the Deering family turned out to be fairly messy and more than a bit noisy. It was very different from the quiet, only-child lunches that Ravani was used to. It was sort of like lunch in the Slaughterville Elementary School cafeteria, Ravani thought, except less lonely and less dangerous. And much more fun.

At one point, when Colt threw a grape and it hit Winnie right between the eyes, Ravani laughed so hard that lemonade came out his nose, which only made him laugh even harder.

And then, like a sudden flock of starlings that fills the sky with wings and life and then swoops just as suddenly away, they were gone. Colt herded the horde back across the street, while Virginia lingered to help finish washing the dishes.

"Thank you for having us over, Mrs. Foster," Virginia said as Ravani and his mother walked her to the front door. "That was the best egg salad I've ever had."

"Well, thank you, dear. It's my own recipe. I'll need to have your mother over soon. I'd love to meet the woman who raised five such charming and well-behaved children."

"She would love that. I'll let her know." Virginia stopped in the hallway. She was looking at a painting hung on the wall. It was a picture of a young boy, holding out a pudgy hand. A black-and-white chickadee was perched on the boy's finger. "This looks like you, Ravani. But smaller."

"Well, um," Ravani mumbled, "it *is* me."

Virginia blinked, then looked to Mrs. Foster. "You painted this," she said in her serious voice.

"Oh, yes, forever ago," Ravani's mother said, waving her hand dismissively. "I don't know why I have it up. It's silly—"

"No," Virginia murmured, looking back to the painting. "It's not silly at all. It's wonderful."

Virginia said it like it was true. And Ravani, looking closer at the painting that had hung for years in his own hallway, realized that it *was* true. The chickadee looked alive, as though it could fly right off the canvas. And his own face in the painting was half in golden light and half in shadow; he was about to smile or laugh, his cheek dimpled, one eye squinted, mouth open. You could nearly hear the giggle, it seemed, and almost feel the sunshine. It *was* wonderful.

Sometimes a soul needs to see something through another soul's eyes to really see the thing at all.

"Oh, well, goodness. Thank you, dear." His mother sounded shy, which was not something Ravani was used to. "Painting was a little dream of mine, a long time ago."

"What happened?" Virginia asked, her voice plain and her eyes back on Mrs. Foster.

"I don't know," she answered, and it sounded true. "I guess the funny thing about dreams is that sometimes you wake up." She sighed, eyes lost in the painting. Her voice sounded far away. "I always thought that someday I'd live in some special place." Ravani frowned; he'd never known that his mother had ever dreamed of leaving Slaughterville. "That I'd be a chef, or a painter, or a pianist, and—"

"You play the piano?" Virginia interrupted.

"Mm-hmm."

"I've always wanted to play the piano."

"Really? Well, I'd be happy to teach you, if you'd like."

Virginia blinked. She raised her eyebrows. "You have a piano?" Her voice was still soft, still flat, but was suddenly much more intense. Breathless, almost.

"Yes, right here in the parlor. Would you really like to learn? I used to offer lessons . . ."

Virginia's eyes dropped.

"I . . . I can't pay, I don't think. I mean, I'll ask my mother, but—"

"No charge for neighbors," Mrs. Foster cut in. "So . . . shall we make beautiful music together, Virginia?"

Then something very strange happened. Virginia didn't smile. Or blush. Or roll her eyes.

Instead, her eyes filled with tears. Quietly. Eyes are always quiet, technically, but at some moments they are even more quiet than usual.

Virginia blinked wetly up at Ravani's mother. "I would love that."

She didn't just say it like it was true, which it was. She said it like it was the sort of truth that a soul says, and not just a mouth.

"Splendid. Tomorrow morning, then. Say, eight o'clock. I'll be looking forward to it."

A moment later, Ravani and Virginia stood alone on his front porch.

"Your mother is wonderful," Virginia said.

Ravani, like many children, had rarely thought about whether his mother was wonderful or not. It's easy, if they're always there, and they're always kind. It's harder if they're not.

"Um. Yeah, she's all right, I guess," Ravani said.

"She's sad, though."

"What? No she's not."

"Yes, she is. I can tell." Virginia narrowed her eyes and cocked her head to the side, and when she asked her next question her voice was gentle. "How come you're an only child, Rav, if your mother wanted a big family?"

Ravani chewed on his lip. He blinked, fast. "Um," he said, then looked away and cleared his throat, trying to swallow the sharp pain that was there. "My, um, mother. She wanted more children. She . . . tried. But . . ."

Through his blurry eyes, Ravani saw Virginia nod.

"Sometimes, the baby just didn't last. Miscarriages. Sometimes, the baby made it, but . . . when they came, they were already gone." Ravani remembered it all: hope, and excitement, and tiny bought clothes. And he remembered: midnight rushes to the hospital, and sad-faced doctors. He remembered: very small funerals, with very small coffins. Tears spilled onto his cheeks, though he tried to hold them back.

"I'm sorry," he mumbled, wiping his face and looking down. "It's silly, I guess. To be sad over losing a baby that never even was, really."

Virginia took one step closer to him. "It's not silly. It's not one little bit silly. They were souls. And you loved them. And then you lost them. That's sad, Rav. Of course it is."

Then Virginia did something very unexpected. But beautiful things are often unexpected. She wrapped Ravani in a hug. Soft. But then stronger, and stronger. Like the sun rising. It was warm and it was tight.

Ravani wasn't sure what to do, at first. But a soul, when it's surprised by something unexpected and beautiful, almost always knows what to do, really. So, after a shaky breath, he wrapped his arms around her, too. And he squeezed her back.

Virginia was a good comrade.

Sometimes, when a soul is very sad, it doesn't really want to not be sad; it just wants to not be sad alone.

Finally, she pulled back. She kept her hands on his shoulders, though, and looked gravely into his eyes.

"You've been awful lonely," she said. "So have I. So tell the truth, Ravani. Will you ever betray me? Can I trust you?"

Ravani took a breath. "Yes."

Virginia blinked. "Yes you'll betray me, or yes I can trust you?"

"Oh. The second one."

"Then say it. Say it loud, so I can hear."

Ravani gulped. And he looked straight into that girl's gray eyes. That girl who had thrown rocks at the monsters, and run with him through moonlight, and opened a window so he could see the sunlight, and said out loud that he was gold. All that, in a few days.

"You can trust me, Virginia. I'll never betray you."

Virginia listened close, head tilted to one side. Then she nodded. "Good." She let go of him and walked away down the stairs, then looked back over her shoulder at him. "Come over tonight. After dinner. Then I'll share it with you."

"Share what?"

"The secret."

Chapter Fourteen

In Which There Is Hiding,
and Finding

"Where can we hide?" Virginia's voice murmured in his ear. "Someplace he can't find us."

"I don't know. This is *your* house."

"Barely," she muttered, and pulled Ravani by the hand toward the backyard.

Darkness hadn't come completely yet, but it was well on its way. The first sprinkle of stars glowed dimly, and the moon was just rising over the pine trees.

Around them, Virginia's brothers and sisters were darting and dashing, looking for their own hiding spots. Winnie and Benjamin sprinted away hand in hand before diving down into the bushes at the yard's edge. Ravani could still hear, from the front porch, the sound of Colt counting down. Soon, he'd come looking.

"How about down by the creek?" Virginia asked.

"No. Up there." He pointed. There was a trellis climbing up the back wall of the house, next to the chimney. The vines were overgrown and wild but the wood looked strong, and it rose right up beside the shadow-cloaked roof of the back porch.

Virginia went first, clambering quickly up the frame. The trellis shook but it held, and when she stepped off it onto the porch roof, Ravani followed. Soon he was pulling himself onto the rough shingles.

They wiggled over against the wall, under a dark window, one of them lying on either side of the porch roof's peak, so that they were face-to-face in the shadows of the eave, invisible.

Beneath them, the grass was silver with moonlight. Ravani smiled when he saw Annabel, crouched in the middle of the yard behind a birdbath much too small to conceal her.

"This is perfect," Virginia whispered. They were close enough that Ravani could smell the butterscotch on her breath.

"Yeah. He'll never look up here."

"No. I mean this is the perfect time to tell you. The secret."

To Ravani, the middle of a game of hide-and-seek seemed like a very odd time to start sharing terrible secrets.

"It is?"

"We're being chased. And we're hiding. It's the perfect time. You'll see."

She gave him a long look. Eyes wide. Mouth tight.

"Tristan won't be happy if he finds out I told you." Ravani thought about Virginia's older brother, his clenched jaw and smoldering eyes.

"Then . . . why are you telling me?"

Virginia frowned.

"The first time we met, we both said that we weren't looking for friends. You were lying." She took in a big breath, let it out. "Well, guess what? So was I. I haven't had a friend in *forever*, almost. We move too much. But I see other kids with friends. How they look out for each other. How they trust each other. How they share secrets. That's what friends do, right?"

Ravani, who had watched all the same things, nodded.

"It looks wonderful. To not be alone like that. Shouldn't I have that, too?"

Ravani, who had felt all the same things, nodded.

"I have lots of brothers and sisters," Virginia said, her voice scratchy and low. "And I love them more than anything. But I don't have any friends. And a person can get tired of things always being the way that they've always been, Rav."

This was a truth that she didn't have to tell to Ravani.

"I'm never alone, Rav. But I'm always lonely." She took another breath. "I don't feel lonely when I'm with you, though."

Ravani's skin tingled at those words. It was like hearing another soul say all the things that his own soul had been dying to say. And perhaps that's all our souls are ever really looking for: another soul they don't feel lonely with.

"I know I can't have a friend. Not a real one. It's not safe. But why can't I have something close? Something just like it?"

"A comrade?" Ravani asked in a hoarse whisper.

Virginia half smiled, with half her mouth, for half a second.

"A comrade. I wanna have a comrade to trust. To share secrets with. And I pick you, Ravani Foster."

I pick you.

"Ravani's soul soared on the wings of those words."

"Okay. You ready for the secret, then? Because once you're in on the secret, there's no going back. For either one of us. You should know that."

"I'm ready."

In the world below them, there was the pounding of bare feet on grass. Gasping breaths of someone running, someone seeking. But on the roof, there was only the gravity of Virginia's eyes, and the weight of her whispered words.

"Us kids?" she said. "All of us Deerings? We don't have a mother. And we don't have a father."

"Wh . . . what do you mean?"

"I mean just what I said. There aren't no grown-ups with us."

"What, are they . . . on a trip, or something, or—"

"We don't have them at all. No father off at work. No mother home with a headache. It's just us, by ourselves. Always. We don't have any parents, Ravani."

"You mean . . . you're all alone? You're orphans?"

Virginia's eyebrows clouded down. "No. We're not alone. We have each other. And we're not orphans. We're a family."

Ravani's mind tried to make sense of what she was saying. It failed. Below them, a triumphant call of "I got you!" echoed through the night.

"So . . . your brothers and sisters and you, you . . ." His question stumbled, too many places for it to go.

"We're not really brothers and sisters, not blood-wise. Except for Winnie and Benjamin."

"But you all have the same name."

Virginia whisper-snorted.

"What, Deering? That's just what Tristan picked this time. We have a different name in every town. There's only one real thing we call ourselves." Virginia hesitated, just for a moment. Then she motioned with her chin and Ravani wiggled up closer so his chin was next to hers, their cheeks nearly touching. Her breath was warm on his ear.

"*We call ourselves . . . the Ragabonds.*"

Goosebumps rose up on Ravani's arms. Virginia said that word like it was powerful, like it was the most secret of secrets.

But then, with a click and a flash, the spell was broken.

The window beside them glared bright with electric light.

Virginia and Ravani jumped.

Tristan was standing in the window, his jaw tight.

"Come inside," he said, his voice quiet.

"Tristan . . . I . . . ," Virginia stammered.

"Come inside," he said again. "Now."

Ravani started to slide back toward the trellis, his stomach in his throat and his heart hammering.

"I'm sorry," he said. "I'll see you later, Virginia, I—"

"No," Tristan said, his voice stopping Ravani like a chain on a dog's neck. "Inside. Now. Both of you."

CHAPTER FIFTEEN

In Which a Truth Is Told,
and the Promise Is Made

The only light in the room came from candles. The curtains were drawn, locking the outside world away, and making the inside world feel very small and very warm.

Ravani stood in the middle of the room, sweating and nauseated. There were six other people inside, but Ravani felt completely alone.

Virginia stood beside him. She was staring at the floor with big eyes and a worried mouth, her hands clasped tight in front of her.

Tristan stood before them, leaning against the fireplace mantel, arms crossed and face stern.

The other children—the other *Ragabonds*, Ravani supposed—were in a loose circle around them. All of them except for Beth, who they could hear walking around the house, latching windows and locking doors. She closed each latch and lock three times, and the *click-click-click*s echoed through the waiting stillness of the house. When the last lock was in place, she joined them in the living room. She took a spot next to Tristan. Her face wasn't as cold or angry as his was, but it was every bit as serious.

When Tristan spoke, Ravani was surprised that his voice was soft, not seething.

"He is not one of us," he said, tilting his chin at Ravani. "He is an outsider." He worked his jaw from side to side, eyes circling the room. "Virginia spoke him in."

One of the children gasped. Another muttered something. Colt blew out a breath and shook his head.

"Does this mean we have to move again?" Winnie asked. "We just got here."

"Aw, I *like* it here," Benjamin said, and his voice cracked a little. "We gotta leave already?"

"I don't know yet," Tristan said. "That depends."

"On what?" Colt asked.

Tristan's eyes cut to Ravani. "On him."

Ravani squirmed. Tried to swallow, but it was no use. His throat was dry as salt.

Tristan stepped toward him. Lowered his head to look right into Ravani's eyes, his own sparkling blackly.

"You're in on the secret now. A big secret. Bigger than anything you've ever had to carry before." His voice wasn't angry. It mostly just sounded tired. "It's *our* secret. But now you've got it. We're at your mercy, kid. You can help us . . . or you can ruin everything."

"How much does he know?" Beth asked.

"Just about everything. He knows we're by ourselves. He knows our names aren't real. And he knows our *real* name." He paused, chewed his lip. "He knows we're the Ragabonds."

Another ripple murmured through the crowd. Not a happy ripple, either.

"Darn it, Virginia," Colt spat out.

"I'm sorry," she said, quick and quiet. "I just—"

"Leave her alone," Tristan interrupted. His voice was still low, but still somehow hard. "It happened. She trusted him. Now we just have to see if he deserves it."

Ravani could feel all their eyes on him. They were scared. Ravani knew what that felt like.

He looked at Virginia. She was looking back, eyes pleading quietly. She pressed her lips together and gave him a small nod.

"I . . . I won't tell," he said. But he knew it was too soft, his voice too timid, so he said it again, louder, and he said it right into Tristan's unblinking eyes. "I won't tell."

Virginia slipped her hand into his. And she squeezed.

But Tristan shook his head.

"That's easy to say. Here, now, with us all around. It gets a lot harder when you walk out that door. You've gotta be with us for keeps. So that it's not just you keeping *our* secret. It's gotta be your secret, too."

"Okay," Ravani said. But he must've said it too quick, too easy. Tristan's jaw tightened.

"This is not a game, Ravani. This is our family at stake. We're not looking for you to just *agree*. We need you to *understand*." He clasped his hands behind his back. "So ask. Ask us anything. We'll tell you the truth. So you'll know. So you'll be a part of it. Ask."

Ravani bit his tongue. There was so much to ask. His voice dried up inside him.

But then Virginia squeezed his hand again. *I'm here.* He nodded.

"How long have you been living like this?"

"We all became Ragabonds at different times," Tristan said. "I've been one for ten years. Annabel joined just last year. But there were other Ragabonds before us. Long before. There've been Ragabonds for over a hundred years."

"How do you know that?"

"It's in the *Always and Forever*. We'll get to that later. Next question."

"Okay. If there were other Ragabonds before you, where are they? Where are the grown-up ones?"

"They leave," Beth said. "It's one of our rules. When a Ragabond turns eighteen, they gotta leave and find their own way."

"And you never see 'em again?"

Tristan shrugged. "Sometimes they visit. Help out. There's Ragabonds living all over. They're teachers, carpenters, truck drivers."

"Charlotte's a doctor," Annabel chipped in.

"That's right." Tristan nodded. "She was Shepherd when I joined. That means she was the oldest. Like I am now. Left about nine years ago. But she checks in from time to time."

Ravani's trembling was fading, replaced by wonder. The questions were flying fast into Ravani's mind.

"How do you pay for food and your house and stuff?"

"Old Ragabonds, mostly. They send money, when they can. Some can only send a little, some more. But they all send something. And we all do what we can. Get jobs if we're old enough. Babysitting and lawn mowing and stuff for the younger ones. But with so many mouths to feed, we never have much."

Ravani nodded to himself, thinking of Virginia and Colt always wearing the same threadbare clothes.

"Where did you all come from, though? Did you all run away from home? Where are your parents?"

"We each have our own story before the Ragabonds. Some of our parents died—" Tristan's voice broke off for a moment. Ravani saw a few heads around him drop. "Some of them abandoned us, on orphanage or firehouse or police station doorsteps. Some of us have no idea how or why we ended up alone. But all that matters is that we're not alone anymore. Our grown-ups, for whatever reason, couldn't take care of us. So now we take care of ourselves. And we take care of each other."

"But—this isn't . . . *allowed*, is it? To just live like this, with no grown-ups?"

Tristan's face darkened.

"No. It's not. And that's why we have to hide. Always. Because there are people who are looking for us. Wolves. That's what we call them. Wolves with badges, Wolves with handcuffs, Wolves with custody papers and court orders. And other Wolves, too, who aren't looking for us, Wolves who smile, Wolves who *care*, but when they find out about us, they want to turn us in. Send us back to the orphanages."

"What's—" Ravani stopped his question. He knew it might sound cold, coming from him: a boy with a mother, and a father, and a warm bed. But Tristan had said to ask anything. So he did. "What's so bad about that? Why not just live in an orphanage? Are they that bad?" Tristan, to his relief, didn't seem offended by the question.

"Not all of them. They were horrible when the Ragabonds first started, or could be. They're better now, most of them. But . . . but they're still not a *home*. They're not a *family*. We chose to become Ragabonds because we wanted to be a part of something. Something better. We love each other." His voice shook for a moment. Beth reached out and put a hand on his shoulder. He nodded at her, and sniffed, and then kept going. "We're a family. We're Ragabonds."

Tristan cleared his throat. His voice got steady and resolute again.

"So we always gotta be ready. We can't wait until someone catches on, or catches up. If the Wolves show up, it's already too late. When a Wolf comes knocking, we gotta make sure they're knocking at the door of an empty house."

Ravani looked around at the pale faces of the Ragabonds. Some were holding hands. None were smiling. They looked a little sad. And a little scared. But also: a lot determined. There were teary cheeks, but there were also stubborn mouths, and fierce eyes, and set jaws.

He understood Tristan, then. How he'd acted since that very first night. The hard glares. The caution. The rules, and the cold words, and the warnings. He wasn't being cruel. He was taking care. And, as he stood there in the flickering candlelight, Ravani didn't feel scared of him. He felt sorry for him.

Ravani couldn't even keep his one little soul safe, sometimes. Tristan was trying to protect seven.

"Any more questions?"

Ravani thought. He thought about Virginia, sneaking out to play in graveyards. And Colt, laughing, muddy in the creek. Annabel giggling in the grass. He thought about hide-and-seek in the moonlight with a truckful of children. He thought about living in a house with six other souls, each one looking out for you. And he thought of his own lonely life.

"One more," he said. "Is it . . . fun?"

Tristan's eyebrows went up. It was, clearly, not a question he'd been expecting.

"It's . . . hard," he said.

"It's scary," Annabel added.

"It's exhausting," Beth said.

"But . . ." Tristan stopped short. Then, to Ravani's surprise, he grinned. Well, *kind of* grinned. It was a distinctly Tristan sort of a smile. Half of his mouth went up, showing his teeth, and a dimple popped onto his cheek. ". . . yeah. It *is* kind of fun, sometimes."

Beth pursed her lips and nodded.

"Aw, heck. It's *way* fun," Colt said. "I mean, when we're not running for our lives."

"I read a book once," Winnie jumped in, "and the girl in the book had a slumber party with all her best friends. Being a Ragabond is kind of like that, all the time. Except there's also police chasing you."

"Yeah," Benjamin agreed. "And there's not enough food. But, also, no bedtime."

"There's no mother to tuck you in," Virginia said in her soft voice, and the room quieted. "But you never wake up alone."

Ravani looked into Virginia's eyes. He squeezed *her* hand. He remembered what she'd told him, that night in the woods.

"So it's terrible," he said. "And it's wonderful. Both."

She smiled, mostly with her eyes. "Exactly."

"So," Tristan said, stepping forward again. "Can we trust you? To keep the secret? Are you with us?"

Ravani nodded. "Yes. You can trust me."

"Promise, then. Say it out loud. Do you promise, on everything, always and forever?"

Ravani looked again at Virginia. Into her waiting eyes. They were reaching out to him, those eyes. He nodded. And she nodded back.

Sometimes, when two souls leap, they catch each other.

"Yes," he said, turning back to Tristan. "I promise. I'll keep your secret. Always and forever."

He said it like it was true. Because he was sure that it was.

Tristan looked to Virginia.

"It's true," she said, with a little nod.

Tristan licked his lips.

"All right." He looked to Beth, and then to Colt. "Get the book."

CHAPTER SIXTEEN

In Which There Are Wolves, and Angels

When Beth walked back in, she was cradling a book in her arms. She carried it like it was holy, like it was sacred. The room grew even more hushed.

Tristan slid a small table in between him and Ravani and set two of the candles on it. Beth laid the book down between the glowing flames.

The book was ancient. Ravani could tell just by looking at it. The cover was scarred, time-smoothed leather that had begun as deep red, perhaps, but had faded to the color of dried blood. It was as big as one of his mother's cookbooks, but thicker, with hundreds of yellowed pages. Their edges were uneven and ragged, like they'd been put in the book at different times, by different people. Bright little bits of ribbon stuck out from the pages here and there, some of them with small paper tags tied at their ends.

It looked as though it was handled every day, but with extraordinary care and gentleness.

Beth traced a light circle on the book with her finger. She looked up into Ravani's eyes. "This is the *Always and Forever*."

Ravani's skin went tingly at the way she spoke those words, and at the shine in all the Ragabonds' eyes when they looked at the book.

"What is it?" he asked breathlessly.

"This is our book," Tristan answered. "Our history. Our secrets. Our stories. Ragabonds like us have been keeping this record since the beginning. For more than a century. It's got the names of all the Ragabonds over the years, the addresses of where they live now, the addresses of the homes we've lived in. The names of people to beware, the names of people we can trust." He paused, and then looked up at Ravani. "And now you will be in it, too."

Ravani's racing heart slowed. The moment felt thick around him, like syrup. Important, in a very deep and quiet way.

The other Ragabonds crowded around, feet shuffling almost soundlessly on the wood floor, until they were all shoulder-to-shoulder around Ravani and the book.

"I'm not alone," Tristan said. Then, one by one around the circle, they each spoke.

"I'm not useless."

"I'm not unwanted."

"I'm not scared."

"I'm not lonely."

"I'm not abandoned."

"I'm not trash." The last voice was Virginia's.

Seven souls, each alone but all together, saying what they weren't.

Tristan looked around at them and nodded.

"I'm a Ragabond," he said. Then, one by one around the circle, they each said it.

"I'm a Ragabond."

"I'm a Ragabond."

"I'm a Ragabond."

"I'm a Ragabond."

"I'm a Ragabond."

"I'm a Ragabond."

Ravani could hear smiles in some of their voices.

"Always," Tristan said.

"And forever," they all finished, in unison.

Tristan nodded then poked through the ribbons marking the book's pages until he found an ivory-white one. He opened the book to the page that it marked.

The page was yellow, the paper rough and almost wavy. In faded purple ink at the top, written in spidery cursive letters, was the word *Angels*.

"These are all the people who have helped us," Beth said. "Through all the years, and all the Ragabonds."

There were three columns of entries below it, each in different handwriting. A name, then a place, then a date.

The first, so faded that Ravani could barely make it out, read, "*Rebecca Hempstead—Fort Mill, South Carolina, 1818.*"

Then, "*John and Grace Bradley—Doylestown, Pennsylvania, 1821.*"

"*The Ching family—Cedar Rapids, Ohio, 1860.*"

The names went to the bottom of the page, and then continued at the top of the next.

The last entry, halfway down the page in the third column, read, "*Guadalupe Garza—The Dalles, Oregon.*" It was dated eight years previous.

Ravani blinked. It had been eight years. Eight years since the Ragabonds had trusted somebody with their truth.

He realized, then, the magnitude of what Virginia had risked for him. Tears warmed his eyes.

Beth held a pen out toward him.

"Signing your name in this book is a promise," she said. "A solemn vow to never betray our trust, to never tell our secret. Always, and forever. Look at all the names of those who've come before you. We remember them, and we honor them, and we thank them. Even though most of them are long dead by now, as are the Ragabonds they helped. They kept our secret." She pressed her lips together. "Are you ready to join them, Ravani?"

Ravani's mouth was as dry as summer ash. But it didn't matter. "Yes. Yes, I am."

He let go of Virginia's hand so he could take the pen. He bent down to the *Always and Forever* and pressed the tip of the pen to the paper. That close, he could smell it . . . smell its age, its long history, its ancient ink. Like the smell of a library, but alive.

His hand shook at first, but he gripped the pen harder and brought the strength of his soul to bear.

The pen steadied, so that his promise could be clear.

Ravani Foster—Slaughterville.

He looked at his name, written in that book. Would some other child, in some other place, in some other year far from now, see his name there and wonder who he was?

He set the pen down and let out his held breath. His legs were quivery.

A shaky smile grew on his face.

"Now we seal the promise," Tristan said. "Say what you're not, Ravani Foster."

For a breath, perhaps two, Ravani's mind went blank. He wasn't so many things, after all. But he knew he needed to choose the right one.

Then he thought of the shadows that Tristan said were always chasing the Ragabonds, always on their trail. And he thought of Donnie and Stevie, their cruel eyes and their snarling mouths. He thought of his own blood and bruises. He knew what he wasn't.

He raised his chin. "I'm not a Wolf." He said it, and it was true.

Tristan blinked, then nodded.

"Now say what you are."

Words flew through Ravani's mind: *I am worthless. I am strange. I am lonely. I am pathetic.* But, he realized, they weren't really his words. They had been given to him. His soul had held them, for a long time. And his soul was tired of them.

He needed new words.

Gold had been given to him, too, but that didn't seem right. *Hero*, either.

He looked at Virginia.

I'm on your side, and you're on mine, her eyes said, silently.

"I'm a comrade," he said.

Tristan blinked.

"Um," he mumbled, leaning in. "You were supposed to say *angel*. But that'll work."

He held out his hand, and Ravani took it. Tristan's grip was strong. Ravani tried to match it. Tristan nodded at him. His eyes were still intense, but his gaze was different from before: more like a handshake, instead of a shove away.

Beth smiled at him.

"You're in, Ravani Foster," she said. "Welcome."

Six voices echoed hers, welcoming him in.

He felt hands on his shoulders. Patting. Squeezing. Touching.

He smiled, looking down at the book, and his own name in it.

His soul had felt, for so long and so deeply, that it was *apart* from other souls. But in that flame-lit moment in that locked room in that empty house with those quiet children, he felt like he was *a part* . . . a part of something, a part of someone.

There is a powerful difference between feeling apart and feeling a part. There is a world in that space.

Then Ravani saw them again, the threads of different colors trailing out from the pages, each with a slip of paper tied to the end. One of them was lying faceup, and in the dim light he could just make out a name written upon it: *Joseph.*

He reached out and followed the black thread with his fingers to the page that it marked.

"What's this?" he asked.

Tristan's hand shot out fast and clamped hold of Ravani's. Hard. Ravani flinched.

"No," Tristan said. His voice was back to cold iron.

"Those pages are private," Beth said quickly. "But you didn't know," she added, looking at Tristan with pointed eyes. He blinked, and his grip softened, and he released Ravani's hand.

"Those are *our* pages, each of ours," Beth went on. "Every Ragabond has their own pages. Marked with their name. Tied with a knot. For their eyes only. We can open them whenever we want, but no one else ever can. We keep our own stories there. Our real names. Where we came from, our fears, our dreams. Our memories, good"—her voice caught, just a bit—"and bad. When we join the Ragabonds, we gain a lot—so much—but we lose so much, too. Our names. Our homes, whatever they were. But we can hold it, there, in those pages."

Ravani looked at all the fragile little threads. He wondered which one was Virginia's.

"When a Ragabond grows up and leaves, they take their pages with them. We don't have much. But we have those pages. They're ours. That's part of the magic."

Ravani's head tilted up. *The magic.*

"What does that mean? What is the magic?"

All around him, eyes flashed back and forth. He waited, breathless.

It was Tristan who finally spoke.

"The magic is what's kept us safe since the beginning. We don't understand it. We can't see it. We don't control it. But we know it's here. It's around us, all the time, and it follows us wherever we go. It gives us powers, each one of us. To keep us together, to keep the Wolves away."

Around Ravani, the faces of seven children were serious. Eyes big.

But Ravani's heart dropped, just a little.

He'd expected more. He'd wanted wands. Sparkling light. Something he could see. Something he could believe. Something, maybe, that would keep *him* safe, too. From his own Wolves.

He wanted truth. Not a story.

"That's it?" he said, soft. "It's just . . . something you believe in?"

Tristan's eyebrows gathered like storm clouds. "No. It's something we *know*. It's real. And it's powerful. It keeps us safe." He tapped the book with a firm finger three times. "Three houses ago, everything seemed fine. There were no warnings. We'd been as careful as ever. But, one night, the magic woke me up. It whispered to me, in the dark: *Run, Shepherd*. So we did. In the middle of the night. We slipped out the back door. And just before I got in the truck in the alley, I saw another truck pulling up to the front door. To grab us. It was the magic that saved us, Ravani."

"What about last time, though, Tristan?" Annabel asked. "We got caught." Her voice was small, but it wasn't doubting. It was seeking. *Tell me we're going to be okay.*

Tristan's mouth tightened. His gaze dropped. "Yes. That's true. The magic didn't fail, though." His voice lost its edge. It was soft as torn fabric. "I did."

His eyes rose to Ravani's, but now they were troubled.

"Our last house," he said, his voice now scratchy and low, almost a whisper, "the Wolves got us. All of us weren't as careful as we need to be." In the corner of his eye, Ravani saw Colt's head drop. "I wasn't watching and listening close enough, I guess. I wasn't there when it happened. I came home, and everyone was . . . *gone.* The book was still there, in its hiding place, but the house was empty." Tristan swallowed. His eyes were still on Ravani, but it didn't feel like he was really looking at him. They were far away. "It took me three days to find them. At an orphanage. Madame Murdosa's. I'd been there before, before I was a Ragabond. They were split up, and locked up. I watched them from the woods behind the fence. Waiting for my chance. It took me a week to break them out. But that night, when I came for them . . ." His eyes came back. They sparkled, in wonder. "A window was left unlocked. Madame Murdosa *never* left windows unlocked. And, as I was sneaking down the hall—when I was right out in the open, caught in the moonlight—Madame Murdosa came out of her office. But just when she was about to see me, when I was *sure* I was caught, her phone rang. She turned around. And I snuck by her. And I got them out." Tristan blinked. "And we came here. *Magic*, Ravani Foster. It's real. And we have it."

Ravani could feel it all around him.

Not the magic. But the need for it. In all of them. It was belief, but it was a kind of belief that was very close to hunger.

Sometimes, when souls feel like they're lost in the dark, they'll clutch onto anything that looks like light.

"Okay," he said. It didn't matter if he believed in their stories.

Tristan closed the *Always and Forever*.

"It's time for you to go," he said. But he didn't say it the cold way he had the first time they'd met. He said it the same way Ravani's mother would tell him it was time to go to bed.

Virginia reached out and gave his hand one more squeeze.

"Goodbye, Rav," Annabel said, and she gave him a quick hug. "*I'm glad you're in*," she whispered. Her face was shining, like they were sharing a fun secret. A few more voices said goodbye. Hands patted his shoulders. "Welcome aboard, Frog Master," Colt said with a wink, punching him on the shoulder.

When he stepped out into the darkness of the front porch, a piney breeze and the summer smell of cut grass filled his lungs. Moonlight, silvery compared to the yellow light of the candles, painted the night. It felt like he was stepping out into a whole new world.

And Ravani, for the first time in, well, about as long as he could remember, didn't feel something. And the something that he didn't feel was *lonely*. The silent wish that his soul had made on that moonlit night when the Ragabonds had appeared had come true. Not for *always*, perhaps . . . and not for *forever*, perhaps . . . but at least for a while.

He smiled. And he smiled like it was true.

Chapter Seventeen

In Which There Is No Ice Cream

The sun had long since set when the Hunter parked his truck very straight between the lines in the parking lot. The sign on the grim building beside it read MADAME MURDOSAS HOME FOR WASTRELS FOUNDLINGS & ORPHANS. Madame Murdosa believed that commas and apostrophes were a waste of paint.

It was a white truck, and it was very clean. It had white-walled tires, and very shiny chrome bumpers, and two doors that opened into the back, which had no windows.

The words *Delicious Ice Cream!* were painted on both sides of the back of the truck in very red letters above a picture of a dripping pink ice cream cone.

If any of the wastrels, foundlings, or orphans inside Madame Murdosa's had looked out a window and seen the ice cream truck arrive, they might have gotten excited. They shouldn't have.

The white truck had never once held delicious ice cream. The white truck had only ever held one thing: captured prey.

The Hunter walked up to the front door, but he didn't knock. He did not check in at the office, or seek out Madame Murdosa. She was not his prey, after all, so he didn't care about finding her.

Instead, he pulled a flashlight from his pocket. Then the Hunter began to walk around the building. Very slowly. And looking very closely. At the ground, and at the drain pipes, and at the fire escape, and at each window. He did not smile, and he did not frown.

When he was halfway around the building, Madame Murdosa caught up with him. She had seen him looking at her office window and had hastily thrown on a coat and shoes.

"Hello!" she called, walking as quickly as she could in her high-heeled shoes. The Hunter didn't answer. He was looking very closely at a window that looked in on a long hallway.

"I don't understand it," she trilled. Her voice was high and wavery, which was how it always sounded when she was nervous, which is how she always felt around the Hunter. "They just *disappeared.*"

"No," the Hunter said, "they," he whispered, "didn't."

His eyes were very sharp and very shiny and they were looking at the windowsill very intensely. More specifically, they were looking at the shadow of a hint of an echo of a dirty footprint *on* the windowsill.

People don't often stand on windowsills.

"Go," he said, looking toward the woods nearby, "inside."

Silently following instructions immediately and without question was something that Madame Murdosa always expected from the children in her custody but almost never did herself. But, silently and immediately and without question, Madame Murdosa went inside.

The Hunter walked across the lawn toward the woods that the trod-upon window looked out on. As he walked, he swept the beam of his flashlight in slow arcs across the grass. If a wastrel, foundling, or orphan inside had looked out and seen him, they might have thought: *oh, what a gentle and quiet man, out for a pleasant stroll*. They would have been wrong. Very.

There was a lot to look at in the woods, but the Hunter wasn't looking for a lot. He was looking for a little.

Twenty yards into the trees, the Hunter found a road. An old road, dirt, overgrown with grass. It was the kind of road that hadn't been used in a long time. Or, rather, it was the kind of road that *shouldn't* have been used in a long time. Just like people *shouldn't* stand on windowsills.

But the Hunter, bending down, saw that, here and there, the weeds in the road ruts were bent. Flattened. And, in a patch of dirt, he found a tread mark. The kind of mark that a heavy truck tire might make.

Walking along the road, looking very closely and moving very slowly, the Hunter stopped again. And he bent down. Pinned in his flashlight beam was a small, crumpled piece of paper. It was in the mud, beneath the broad leaves of a dandelion plant. Most people would never have seen it. The Hunter was not most people. Very carefully, he picked it up.

Written on the piece of paper was a phone number.

The Hunter did not smile. If someone had been bold enough to take the Hunter's pulse at that moment, they would have found that his heart wasn't beating any faster than it had been a moment before. But, really, the Hunter *was* excited.

He was very excited.

PART TWO

Chapter Eighteen

In Which Blood Is Smelled, and Something Is Not Noticed

The next morning's paper route was a blur. No matter who Ravani was talking to, or which porch he was badly missing with a newspaper, one word echoed like the persistent *caw* of a crow in his mind: *Ragabonds. Ragabonds. Ragabonds.*

Hortense Wallenbach told him one of her fantastic stories, he was fairly sure; it involved the sheriff joining a ballet company to catch a jewel thief, perhaps. Fred Frotham had performed a flamboyant character on his café's patio, Ravani dimly remembered; a burly Russian bear trainer, he thought he recalled. It all faded, though, beneath the story playing behind Ravani's eyes: a story of a family of children, banding together and fleeing the Wolves. It was a true story, as hard as it was to believe, and he was now a part of it, which was even harder to believe.

As he walked back up the porch steps of his house, though, he heard the melodic plinking of piano keys from inside. He stopped outside the door and listened: a murmur of two voices, both familiar, and the chiming of the piano. Strong, confident notes when his mother played; then Virginia's echo, timid and clumsy, but daring all the same.

Ravani stepped inside just as the lesson finished. Virginia

was clutching a battered folder to her chest, out of which Ravani could see yellowed pages of music poking.

"Welcome back," his mother said, smiling. "You found me a fine piano student. This girl has music in her soul. She's a fast learner, too."

"I can't even play a song yet, Mrs. Foster," Virginia said, but she was fighting a proud smile.

Mrs. Foster *tsk*ed her tongue and rubbed Virginia's shoulder. "You have to learn your words before you can tell a story. But I can see that *you* have a story to tell, sweetheart."

Virginia's face spread in a smile that on anyone else could have been called *lukewarm*, but on her counted as *beaming*.

"And *you*," Mrs. Foster continued, looking to Ravani, "have a lunch to deliver."

"Again?" he protested with a groan.

"I tried a new curried potato salad recipe this morning, and it had to chill. This one has *lemongrass*." She said it like Ravani would care. He did not. "The sack is in the fridge."

"I'll come with you," Virginia said. "I'd like to see the meat factory."

"You would?" Ravani and his mother asked in unison.

Virginia shrugged. "I've never been in a meat factory before."

So it was, then, that Ravani found himself walking up to the office of the Skinister Slaughterhouse with both Virginia and Colt Deering at his side. When they'd stopped by the Ragabonds' house to pretend to ask for permission from Virginia's "mom," Colt had excitedly joined them when he'd heard what their destination was. His excitement dimmed, though, when he saw the cows waiting miserably in the lot outside.

"Oh," he said uneasily. "I . . . guess I thought the cows showed up already dead."

"No." Ravani sighed. "They're alive. But not for long."

Hiss-moooTHUD, the building coughed. *Hiss-moooTHUD*.

Like always, Mr. Skinister was frowning behind his desk. His eyebrows rose when he saw Ravani.

"Young Mr. Foster. And with some companions, I see."

"Good morning, Mr. Skinister. These are my new neighbors. Virginia and Colt."

There was a shaking of hands and an exchange of hellos, and then Mr. Skinister eyed the sack in Ravani's hands.

"What's for lunch today, then?"

"Potato salad," Ravani answered. Mr. Skinister looked almost disappointed.

"Curried potato salad," Virginia said. "With lemongrass. Chilled."

"Mmmm. Is there . . . ?"

"Yes, sir." Ravani handed over the small jar his mother had made for Mr. Skinister, who took it with eager eyes and licked lips.

Hiss-moooTHUD. Hiss-moooTHUD.

"What's that sound?" Colt asked.

Mr. Skinister's eyes dimmed. "It . . . *was* a cow. At least the 'moo' part was."

Colt's forehead wrinkled doubtfully. His curious enthusiasm seemed to fade a bit with each *moo,* and more than a bit with each *THUD.*

"Cows are nice to look at," Mr. Skinister said. "So are hamburgers, I suppose. It's all the steps in between that are a bit unpleasant."

Virginia frowned. She and Colt both looked a bit paler than they had before.

"You don't have to go to the killing floor," Ravani said to them.

"The . . . killing floor?" Virginia asked, looking more than a little unsettled.

Mr. Skinister winced.

"I hate that term. It's grisly. And inaccurate."

"Oh," Virginia said hopefully. "Why isn't it accurate?"

Mr. Skinister frowned and answered in a soft voice.

"Because it isn't the floor that kills them." He sighed. "It's us."

Mr. Skinister's words hung in the air for a moment, before being swept out by a *hiss-moooTHUD*.

"All right," Colt said abruptly, putting an arm around Virginia. "Have fun in there, Frog Master. I think we'll wait right here."

Mr. Skinister nodded somberly.

"An industrial slaughterhouse killing floor may not be the best place for a nice young girl," he said. Then he frowned, and mumbled mostly to himself, "It may not the best place for *anybody*, really. Certainly not for the cows." He sighed glumly, then brought his attention back to them. "Getting you all splattered with blood wouldn't be the best way to welcome you to town."

It wasn't, unfortunately, lunch break on the killing floor yet.

The details of Ravani's walk to the lunch benches were like toilet paper: best left unshared. He did, at one point, have to make eye contact with his father across the slaughterhouse floor to let him know his lunch had arrived. Ravani willed his eyes to block out everything except the burly shape of his father. He waved, but his father didn't wave back. His hands were, quite unfortunately, quite full at the time, which Ravani also tried to block out.

His father nodded and offered an attempt at a smile. At that moment, there was an especially loud and nearby *Hiss-moooTHUD!* A blast of air blew back Ravani's hair, and a sickeningly warm mist spritzed his face.

Throat tight and stomach curdling, Ravani left the chilled curried potato salad with lemongrass on a bench, then made his scurried escape. He did his best to keep his eyes averted and his breakfast down. He burst back into Mr. Skinister's office.

"The secret to a good alfredo sauce," Mr. Skinister was saying, his lunch on the desk in front of him, "is using—"

The secret to a good alfredo sauce was cut off by Ravani's abrupt arrival. He stood with his back pressed to the door, gasping and gagging.

"Hello, Rav," Virginia monotoned. "Did you have a nice visit to the killing floor?"

"Can we go?" Ravani asked, still fighting the rising bile from his belly.

"This is top-notch sauce," Colt said to Mr. Skinister, ignoring Ravani. He was licking his finger and smacking his lips thoughtfully. "Real premium stuff, Mr. Skinister. You oughta bottle this and sell it."

"Sell sauce?" Mr. Skinister repeated, befuddled. "There isn't even any meat in it."

Colt shrugged.

"There ain't no meat in soda pop, and folks seem to buy up that." He grinned, and his eyes sparkled. "You know why pea soup is better than roast beef?"

Mr. Skinister frowned. "No."

"Because anybody can roast beef."

It took a second for Mr. Skinister to get the joke. But then his eyebrows rose and he sat back in his chair and barked out a guffaw of a laugh.

"I'm telling you, sir, you got a winner here," Colt said, licking his lips again and pointing at the alfredo.

"Huh," Mr. Skinister said, scratching at his cheek.

Hiss-mooooTHUD.

Back outside, they stopped for a moment while Ravani sucked in great breaths of fresh air. Virginia looked into his still-frantic eyes and pursed her lips.

"You okay, Rav? You look like you got punched in the guts."

"Please don't say *guts.*"

Colt squinted at him.

"I don't know if now is the right time to ask this question, Frog Master . . . but, theoretically speaking, if you had blood splattered on your forehead, would you want someone to tell you, or just wipe it off?"

Ravani's nausea perked right back up.

"Wipe it off, I guess," he answered shakily.

Colt pulled a bandanna out of his back pocket and daubed it along Ravani's forehead. He was sticking it back in his pocket when the flyers on the bulletin board by the slaughterhouse door caught Virginia's eye.

"Red River Raft Race," she read. "What's that?"

Ravani frowned and started walking.

"Just a dumb thing that happens every year."

"Huh. You ever won?"

"I've never even raced."

She looked at him.

"Why not?"

He shrugged.

"I don't want to. I hate the stupid raft race."

"Why wouldn't you wanna do a boat race?" Colt asked, chucking a rock at a tree they were passing. "Sounds fun to me."

"Well . . . I mean . . . I don't . . . well, Donnie always wins, anyway," Ravani sputtered. He blew out an exasperated breath. "And besides, you need a team of two to race, and I never . . ." He trailed off, looking away.

"Oh," Virginia said quietly. Ravani's face burned.

"I don't want to do it," he insisted.

"No offense, buddy, but it kinda sounds like you do," Colt said.

Ravani opened his mouth. He had his next lie ready. But as his soul cast around for the right words to lie, instead they stumbled onto a truth. A truth he hadn't known until that moment.

He *did* hate the raft race. But not because he didn't want to do it. He hated it because he *did* want to do it.

He remembered sitting on his father's shoulders as a kid, watching the older children splash and laugh and holler their way down the river, the rest of the town cheering and laughing along. "Okay, when I was little, I always thought, like, when I was older, I'd . . . I don't know . . . that I'd have . . . that . . ."

There were too many truths, and too many wishes, and too many fears, and too many lies, for Ravani to know which of them to say. And, finally, he landed on a truth that surprised him even as he said it.

His shoulders slumped.

"I guess maybe I *have* always wanted to do the race. Someday."

"*Someday*," Virginia echoed. "You mean, someday when you're old enough? You're twelve, right?" He opened his mouth, but nothing came out. "You mean, someday when you've got all the time in the world to make a boat? You mean, someday when you've got a creek across the street to practice in? You mean, someday when you've got a comrade to do the race with?" She raised an eyebrow at him. "Welcome to someday, Rav. You're already here."

Ravani's mouth opened and closed. He looked from Virginia to Colt.

"If there's something you've always wanted to do, and you get the chance, you probably oughta do it," Colt said wisely. "Take me, for example. I have always wanted to say the words, *Lay it on me, old man.* And if the chance ever presents itself, you can be darn sure I ain't gonna let it pass me by."

"'Lay it on me, old man'?" Virginia said with bored incredulity. Ravani snickered.

"Yep. Heard someone say it on a radio show once. It sounded spectacularly nifty, the way the kid said it. Been waiting for my chance ever since."

"What an inspiring story," Virginia said. "I cannot believe that I willingly call you my brother."

"Likewise, sis," Colt said, reaching around Ravani to slug her lightly on the shoulder. Then he nudged Ravani. "So?"

Ravani walked for a few steps between them.

He took a steadying breath. And then he took a leap.

"Virginia Deering, do you want to do a boat race with me?"

"Took you long enough," she said. "Of course I do."

Ravani grinned. They'd just reached the bridge. Colt stepped to the side and leaned on the railing and looked over the edge. Virginia and Ravani joined him, peering down at the flowing waters of the creek below.

Then a thought occurred to Ravani that flattened his smile.

"But . . . will Tristan let you?"

"Oh, he'll let her. It's all part of the plan, Frog Master," Colt said.

"Plan?"

"Sure," Virginia said. She looked up and down Skinister Street, making sure no one was there. "People *are* looking for us. Police and stuff, probably. But we can't have folks get suspicious. We only hide out for a week or so. Then we start letting ourselves be seen. Become part of the scenery."

"Imagine if school started and all seven of us just showed up out of nowhere," Colt added. "There'd be a lot of questions, right? So we gotta be out and about—walk along on newspaper routes, talk to slaughterhouse owners, splash around in a boat race, for example—so that folks get used to us. *Hiding in plain sight . . .* that's what it's called in the *Always and Forever*."

Ravani stared at the water. It was a lot for a group of kids to have to think about.

"Don't you ever get . . . *tired* of all that?"

Colt *pttt*ed a great glob of spit down into the current. When he spoke, his voice was uncharacteristically soft.

"Sure we do. At least, I know *I* do. Tired of hiding. Tired of running. But running and hiding is better than getting caught and locked up. Madame Murdosa said if we ran away again, she would send me to some horrible boys' reform school she knows. Some prison on an island, basically." He shook his head. "I belong with my family."

Ravani nodded. Sometimes a soul just does the best it can to survive. He knew that firsthand.

"Well, your secret is safe with me."

Colt threw an arm around his shoulder. "I know it is, buddy." He gave him a squeeze, then raised his arm in a stretch. "Let's skedaddle. You two got some work to do. And my afternoon nap ain't gonna take itself."

Standing there, Ravani noticed the summer smell of mud and leaves rising up from the creek bed. And he noticed the pair of goldfinches flitting from tree to tree upstream. And he noticed how Colt's words and Colt's arm around his shoulder had him feel a sort of good he'd never really felt before.

There were things he didn't notice, though, there on that bridge. And sometimes the things a soul doesn't notice are even more important than the things it does.

Stories are about choices, yes.

But they're also about mistakes.

Even if a soul doesn't know it made them.

CHAPTER NINETEEN

In Which There Is Both an Undertaking and an Undertaker

"We can't use a real boat," Ravani told Virginia. "We have to build our own, or paddle in something else that's *not* a boat." He grunted, struggling to lift open his garage door. "Last year a team rowed the whole way in an old pig trough."

"Are you serious?"

Ravani shrugged, still yanking on the door handle.

"Well, they didn't win. *Urrgh!*" Ravani's hand slipped free and he fell back onto his rear.

Virginia bent down and grabbed the handle, then jerked the door up with a rattling clatter. She looked down at Ravani. "I should probably do most of the paddling."

They poked through the dusty piles and stacks of junk, shouting whenever one of them found something promising. There wasn't a lot of shouting. Except when Ravani came across a particularly large spider.

When they'd gone through the whole garage, they stood shoulder to shoulder and considered the pile of possible raft-building supplies they'd rounded up: a few old two-by-fours, a couple of buckets, an old patched-up tire, and a rusty piece of tin roofing.

"I don't think we have enough for much of a boat," Ravani said.

"Hate to break it to you, Rav," Virginia answered. "I don't think we have enough for a *paddle*."

"Well, shoot. You got anything good at your house?"

"Nope," Virginia sighed, shaking her head. "There was just some furniture when we moved in. No garage. I don't think—" She stopped. Her eyebrows flashed up and her eyes got a sparkle of inspiration. "Rav. Have you ever been in the Croward basement?"

≈

The stairs creaked under their feet as they descended into darkness. A musty cellar smell hit Ravani's nose. The air grew a little cooler with each downward step, and he was pretty sure he heard a rodent-sized rustling in the blackness below. Virginia was one step in front of him. They were both holding long white candles, flames trembling behind their cupped hands. She stopped on the last wooden step before the packed dirt floor of the basement. "So, Rav. What did Mr. Croward do? As a job, I mean?"

"Um, well, he's been retired forever. But before that, he ran the funeral home, I think."

Virginia nodded. "That makes sense."

"Why?"

She stepped down onto the dirt floor, then moved to the side and swept out her hand at the dark room around her. "Behold," she announced, "our winning boat."

Dimly, at the edge of the candlelight, Ravani could see bulky shadows lurking, but he couldn't quite tell what they were. He stretched his candle arm out toward the shrouded shapes. Boxes, perhaps?

Squinting his eyes and holding his breath, he moved closer.

Then Ravani blinked. And he gulped. And he nearly dropped his candle. His head swiveled toward Virginia, who was standing with a small but proud smile on her face.

"You . . . you . . . want us to build our boat out of a *coffin*?"

"Of course. They're perfect," Virginia said, like it was the most obvious thing in the world.

"Please tell me," Ravani said slowly, "what's *perfect* about using a *coffin* as a *boat*."

"They're the right size," Virginia said simply. "The right shape. They're made of wood, with room for us both to sit. They basically *are* boats, Rav. Just . . . meant for a different kind of passenger."

"A *dead* passenger."

"Obviously. Why would you bury a live person?"

Ravani frowned. "That's not what I—"

"Here, take a look," Virginia said. She strode over to the far wall and with a grunt and a screech of rusty hinges she threw open a giant cellar door that led out to their side yard, flooding the basement with daylight. Ravani shielded his eyes.

"Why didn't we just come in that way?"

"The candles were more dramatic. Now, look at these beauties."

At least twenty coffins were stacked in crooked piles around the room, and leaning up against the walls. There's a limit to how cheerful a roomful of coffins can be, perhaps, but the sunlight and birdsong drifting in from the cellar doors certainly made it all seem a bit less sinister.

"Geez. I wonder why old Mr. Croward kept all these down here?"

"Maybe he was a murderer," Virginia said, "and he was planning ahead."

"Um. Probably not." Ravani looked closer at the coffins. They were simple and plain, not much more than boxes of bare wood. "I think they're just really old. I went to my great-uncle's funeral last summer, and his coffin was all shiny and polished, with brass handles and fancy carved corners and stuff. Maybe he couldn't sell these boring old-fashioned ones but he didn't want to just throw them away."

"Either way, it sure worked out for us," Virginia said. "We got a whole fleet to choose from."

Ravani lifted the lid of the closest coffin just an inch and peeked cautiously inside.

"Don't worry, they're all empty," Virginia assured him. "We checked. They were a big hit when we found them down here. Colt dragged one upstairs to use as a bed." Ravani gave her a queasy look, but she shook her head. "Tristan made him bring it back."

Ravani opened the lid all the way. It was, indeed, empty. All that the casket held was some dust, a couple of silky spider egg nests, and a black padded felt lining. It looked solid and watertight. And, Ravani had to admit, downright comfortable.

He flashed her a smile.

"You're right. These are *perfect.*"

"I know. They're canoes, practically." Her eyes drifted up. "Oh, and you have a spider on your forehead again."

Ravani squealed and flapped, dancing in a circle and slapping it away.

Virginia frowned.

"For someone who so often has spiders on their forehead, you sure overreact. If you keep doing that, I'm going to stop telling you."

Ravani and Virginia browsed through the coffins.

"This one's too heavy," Virginia said, shaking a thick-sided one.

"Yeah. And this one's too basic," Ravani replied, examining one that was barely more than a few planks nailed together. "We need one that's sealed real good. And I like the ones with the lining inside. They look comfier."

And then Ravani saw it. Apart from the others, sticking out from under the stairs they had just walked down.

"Virginia," he said. "That's it."

She followed him over to the coffin. He bent down and opened it up.

It was lined with plush red velvet. Its black-painted sides looked sturdy but not too heavy. What had caught his eye from across the basement was its shape. It wasn't a rectangle like the others. It was wider at the shoulders, and then narrowed sleekly down at the head and the feet. There were a couple of simple brass handles on the sides.

"Hot darn," Virginia whispered over his shoulder.

"It's, like, *streamlined*," Ravani said, grinning back at her. "It's *made* for the water!"

"I'm pretty sure it's made for the dirt," she replied. "But it will make one heckuva boat."

They hefted the casket up by its handles and lugged it over to the brightest patch of basement dirt, in the full sunlight of the cellar door. Virginia pulled a screwdriver out of her back pocket and got to work unscrewing the tarnished hinges so they could yank the lid off.

"The foot end can be the front," she said.

"You mean the bow?"

"No. I mean the front. I'm not a sailor, Rav." Virginia popped the first hinge off and moved on to the second. "We could bend that metal roofing we found and nail it on the front—you know, make it pointy instead of flat. Like a canoe."

"And we could paint it! I've got some leftover birdhouse paint, I think."

The second hinge fell to the dirt and Virginia stood up, wiping sweat from her forehead. Together, they lifted the lid off and set it to the side. The fancy cabin of their boat shone in the sun, red as a gutted steer. Ravani couldn't keep the wide smile off his face.

"Let's go get the paint," he said, and started off, but Virginia grabbed his shirt and yanked him back.

"You're putting the cart before the horse," she said. "Or, before the hearse, I guess." She stooped down and gripped the handle on one side and then looked at Ravani. "We have to make sure she floats."

Awkwardly, they lifted it and made their way up the cellar stairs, out into the sunlight, and through the trees and shrubs and down to the creek, stumbling and straining the whole way.

"This is . . . way heavier . . . than it looked," Ravani wheezed.

"Imagine it with a dead guy inside."

"I'm trying not to."

They peeled off their shoes and carried their vessel out toward the deeper, slow part of the creek. The water was only knee-deep, but that's all they needed.

They traded here-we-go looks, then lowered the casket into the creek.

The coffin sank a few inches, but then settled and bobbed, the waterline halfway up the side.

"It floats!" Ravani gasped out.

"Get in," Virginia replied, and Ravani's smile disappeared.

Ravani looked down at the waiting red velvet, suddenly feeling sick to his stomach. The *idea* of climbing into a coffin had been quite a bit less eerie than the reality of it.

"I've . . . never been in a coffin before."

"I'd assumed that, comrade." Virginia blew out a breath. "Fine. I'll go first. Hold it steady."

Ravani gripped the handles. Virginia lifted a dripping foot from the creek and set it carefully in the coffin. She grabbed hold of both sides, hopped her other foot up and in, then lowered her body down so that she was sitting scrunched up in the middle of the casket.

It wobbled a bit, and it was riding lower in the water, but it held.

Virginia stretched her feet out, then wiggled down so that she was lying flat on her back.

"She floating steady?"

"Yeah. It's looking good."

She shifted, settling in. "You were right, Rav. This is comfy." She folded her arms across her chest and closed one eye, peeking up at Rav with the other, her face solemn as always. "Do I look dead?"

Ravani looked down at his comrade in the coffin. The

peeking eye was sparkling, and the hint of a smile was playing at one corner of her mouth. Her hair was dazzling gold against the bloodred of the casket lining.

"No," Ravani said. "You don't look dead, Virginia."

"Oh. Well, plenty of time for that later, I guess." She sat up gingerly and held on to the coffin's sides, then scooted forward a bit. "Now get in behind me. Don't tip us."

Ravani splashed around to the back of the coffin, holding it level as he went. He got one foot in, then stood there halfway into the casket, trying to get up the nerve to make the leap. The coffin started to float away. Ravani hopped on his anchored foot to keep his balance.

"Come on, Rav!" Virginia urged him.

Far closer to doing the splits than he was comfortable with, Ravani had no choice; he screeched and sprang off his creek-bound foot, twisting as he tumbled clumsily into the coffin, so that he ended up backward on his rear, facing away from Virginia.

The casket spun and tilted dangerously, water sloshing off its sides, but then it steadied and settled and then they were sitting there, backs pressed together, drifting in the water.

"Very graceful," Virginia said. "You'd never know it was your first time boarding a floating coffin."

"Thank you," Ravani gasped.

She relaxed back into him, and he did the same. They sat there together, holding each other up. Ravani could feel her breathing, through his back. Then he felt her back shaking, just a little. And he heard little breaths puffing out through her nose.

"Are you . . . laughing?" He'd never seen Virginia Deering laugh. He'd hardly seen her smile.

"That was quite a sound you made jumping in the boat," she said through snickers. "Like a chicken getting plucked."

Ravani's face burned red for a second, but then he started laughing, too.

Virginia dropped her head back, so it was lying on Ravani's shoulder. He dropped his, too, so it was resting on her shoulder. The boat spun in a slow circle, floating in that muddy frog-heaven backwater. They looked up at the sunlight winking through the dancing leaves.

Virginia took a thoughtful breath. "You ever have the feeling that you are exactly where you belong?"

Ravani stared at the sky, considering. He considered bullies, and beatings. And slaughterhouses, and silence. And loneliness, and lies.

"No," he answered. "Not really."

"Fair enough. Me neither. At least not, ever since—" Her voice broke and cut off. There was a story there, Ravani could tell. A sad story, he was pretty sure. A story that wasn't his to know just yet. She cleared her throat. "Ever since. But sitting here? I feel like this is exactly where I belong, for now."

"You think a coffin is your destiny?"

"I think a coffin is everybody's destiny, Rav. But a coffin *boat*? That's a special kind of destiny."

Ravani snorted.

Virginia blew out a sigh. "You've seriously never felt like you were where you belonged? Not once?" She *tsk*ed her tongue. "Not gonna lie, Rav. That's kinda depressing."

He thought about her question. When he'd answered before, he'd thought he'd been telling the truth. Maybe, though, he hadn't been.

"Well," he said, then stopped.

"Well what?"

He pursed his lips. It's hard for a soul to reach out, sometimes, when all it's ever had is its hand being slapped.

"There's one place," he said.

"Where?"

He gulped. But then he made the choice. "I'll show you."

≈

A few minutes later, he pulled Virginia by her hand through a tangle of vine maple. Walked her out into the center of a little clearing. She blinked, eyes wide, looking around at the myriad birdhouses of Haven Hollow. The birds fluttered and flittered and sang all around her.

"You made this?" she asked, her flat voice hushed.

"Yeah," he said, his face burning. "It's stupid, I guess. Just a bunch of—"

"Shut up," she said, and he did. She spun in a slow circle, taking it in, then looked at Ravani and shook her head. "No doubt about it."

"What?" he asked.

"You," she said, almost smiling. "I picked the right comrade. You're gold, Rav."

Ravani smiled back, standing there with his golden-haired comrade, surrounded by songs and sunlight, feeling like he was, perhaps, exactly where he belonged.

CHAPTER TWENTY

In Which a Secret Is Revealed, and a Truth Hidden

The next day, Ravani was walking his bike home from his paper route, feeling a kind of happy that settled all the way down into his bones. It was a deeper sort of happy than he was used to. A *friendship* sort of happy. A *belonging* sort of happy. A *hopeful* sort of happy. An *at last* sort of happy.

Alas, though, *Nothing lasts forever* is something that people say, and they say it because it's true.

"Hey." Spoken with a rough smirk, that one word was all that it took to drain that happiness right out of Ravani's bones.

Obviously it was Donnie.

He was sitting on the railing of the bridge over Carcass Creek. Ravani had just been too lost in his happiness to notice.

Ravani kept his eyes down on his handlebars as he passed Donnie. He allowed himself a hopeful, shaky breath. Was Donnie going to just let him pass?

"How's it going, Ravioli?" Donnie asked.

"Fine," Ravani mumbled. He kept moving. He didn't like the tone in Donnie's voice.

"Why don't you stop and talk a second?" Donnie said.

"I gotta get home," Ravani said, shuffling faster. "Sorry."

"What's the rush? You got a date with that creepy friend of yours?"

Ravani did, in fact, have a date with that creepy friend of his; they were going to paint a coffin, which sounded exactly like something a creepy friend would do.

"No, I just..." Ravani trailed off and moved his feet even faster; he was almost running. He was five feet past Donnie and tantalizingly close to getting past him unscathed.

It looked like he was going to make it. He was nearly to the other end of the bridge; Donnie was still leaning lazily against the railing.

When Donnie stopped him, he didn't stop him with a grab or a kick. He stopped him with a question.

"You good at keeping secrets, Ravioli?"

It seemed like an innocent question, but Ravani knew that Donnie Carter was rarely innocent of anything.

He stopped walking. His stomach clenched. He looked back at Donnie.

"I guess," he said.

"Hmm. I ain't. And I gotta big one. Why don't you come back here and talk about it."

Ravani grimaced, and chewed on his lips, and turned his bike around and walked back across the bridge. He didn't know what Donnie was up to.

Donnie's eyes glinted sharply.

"Funny thing," he said. "Yesterday I was down under this bridge, working on my boat, when I overheard a very interesting conversation."

Ravani's blood ran colder than Carcass Creek in February. He remembered leaning against that rail himself yesterday, talking with Colt and Virginia.

"You know what that conversation was about, Ravioli?"

Ravani shook his head.

Donnie frowned.

"Huh. That's weird. 'Cause I woulda swore you were a part of it. Sure of it, in fact." Donnie took a step toward Ravani. "It was something about that creepy friend of yours and her family. Ring any bells?"

Ravani shrugged. He was frantically trying to act calm and cool and, he was sure, failing miserably.

"No? Lemme help you out. It was something about them hiding. And lying. And being wanted by the police."

"You're not gonna tell, are you?" Ravani squeaked quick.

Of course he was, Ravani knew.

"Of course I am," Donnie said.

"You can't. Please, Donnie. You can't tell."

Donnie's eyes narrowed. "I can do whatever I want. I don't like that creep."

Ravani felt it all slipping away. Not just that morning's happiness: the next day's, and the next day's, and the days after that. He pictured the Ragabonds led away in handcuffs. The house across the street empty. Virginia gone. Their coffin unsailed. Himself, alone again. Always and forever.

"Please don't. Please don't, Donnie. Please don't."

Donnie took a lazy, snuffling breath and leaned back against the railing again. He looked like he'd won. "Why shouldn't I? They're dangerous criminals."

"They're not! They're not criminals at all. They—"

"The cops are after 'em. I shouldn't keep a secret like that. I could get in trouble, even." There was the hint of a smirk on Donnie's face, a twisted twinkle in his eye. Donnie wasn't scared of getting in trouble. Ravani realized: If Donnie had wanted to tell, he already could have. He wanted something else. "For me to take a risk like that, it'd have to really be worth it."

"I . . . I'll pay you. Look, here." Ravani dug in his pocket and pulled out the quarter Hortense Wallenbach had just given him and held it out to Donnie.

Donnie sneered at the quarter and snorted. "A quarter? You want me to protect a bunch of fugitives from the law for a *quarter*?"

"I got more. A lot more." And he did, too. Ravani had been saving up for more birdhouses. He had a hidden stash of cash wadded up in an old pair of underwear in his dresser at home. "At home." He didn't mention the old underwear. "I'll give you that. And my newspaper money every day from now on."

"Every day?"

"Yeah, every day. All you gotta do is not tell."

Donnie looked him up and down. His glare stopped on the quarter shining in Ravani's outstretched palm. He took it with a sniff.

"The money's a start. But you owe me more than that, freak. I *own* you now. Got it?"

"Yeah. Thank you. I got it." Ravani was stammering, almost weak with relief.

"From now on, any time I ask you for something, you do it. You make me mad, I swear I'll call the cops and turn in your little creep friend."

"Okay, Donnie. You won't have to. I promise."

Donnie's gloating face was practically shining. His was a soul, after all, that needed to feel powerful.

"Now get out of here, freak."

As Ravani walked home, his heart and stomach were in full riot.

"*This is bad, this is bad, this is bad,*" he mumbled to himself.

He knew what he had to do. The *right* thing. He needed to tell Virginia. The Ragabonds needed to know that their fate hung in the meaty hands of Donnie Carter.

But he also knew that if he did the right thing, they would do the smart thing. And then he would never see his comrade again.

Ravani had a choice to make.

He turned the corner onto Offal Road.

Saw his house up ahead. Quiet, as always.

Saw theirs, across the street.

Winnie and Benjamin and Annabel were playing some imaginary game on their front lawn, laughing and rolling in the grass. Colt was perched on the porch railing, watching. Virginia sat in a chair in the shade of the porch, reading a book. They all looked so happy. As though they felt, perhaps, safe.

Ravani could not bear the thought of saying goodbye to them. But, even more, he could not bear the thought of anything bad happening to them. He had to do the right thing.

Virginia, seeing him coming, set down her book and walked out to meet him in the street. His belly twisted and flopped as she approached. His trembling heart broke into a thousand little pieces.

"I need . . . ," he said, his voice as fragile as a chickadee. Cleared his throat. "I need—"

"I was hoping you'd get home soon, comrade," that creepy friend of his said with her funny, Virginia Deering flatness. "I've been waiting for you. It's time to paint that coffin."

He looked into his friend's gray, waiting eyes. He made the choice.

"I need to put my bike away first," he said.

"All right. See you in a minute. Don't forget the paint, Freak." She gave him one of her small smiles and turned and walked back toward her house.

Ravani had decided to do the right thing. But then. *I was hoping you'd get home soon, comrade. I've been waiting for you.*

Those were not words that Ravani was used to hearing. They were not words that his soul was ready to stop hearing.

Donnie won't tell, Ravani whispered in his rattled mind as he walked his bike back to his house. *Not before tomorrow, at least. He wants that money. Their secret is safe for now. I'll tell her tomorrow.*

Sometimes, souls lie to themselves. And one of their favorite lies is that there will always be time to do the right thing later.

Chapter Twenty-One

In Which Ketchup Is Made

"Would you say that's more of a *bloody-axe-wound* red, or *blazing-house-fire* red?" Virginia asked.

The coffin sat in the sun, wet paint shining. They'd pulled it out from where they'd been stowing it in the brush by the creek and set it up on a couple of logs in the woods.

Ravani only had one can of paint big enough to cover a coffin: a bright, flaming red.

"Um. I was thinking *cherry*."

"Oh. Let's meet in the middle and call it *bloody cherry*, then."

They stood for a moment, staring at their boat.

"It's perfect," Ravani said.

"Almost. It's time for the finishing touch." Virginia opened the last two paint cans they had: a small black, and a small white, mostly empty. "What should we name her?"

"How about the Osprey?" Ravani suggested. "It's a bird of prey. Super fast."

"No," Virginia murmured, tapping two of Ravani's mother's little picture-painting brushes on her lips. "It's a bold boat. It needs a bold name."

"Well, it *is* a coffin. How about the . . . Flying Funeral? Or the, I don't know, Careening Corpse?"

Virginia shook her head thoughtfully, mouth puckered. But then her eyes sparkled, and one eyebrow rose wickedly.

"Sometimes, when the world throws a tomato at you, you duck," she said. "But sometimes, you catch it and make ketchup."

"I don't know what that means."

"Don't peek."

She crouched down at the front of the coffin, on the far side where Ravani couldn't see. She went to work with the brushes, tongue poking out, eyes narrowed in concentration.

Finally, she sat back on her heels, surveying her work. She nodded, satisfied.

"Nailed it. Come take a look."

Ravani hurried to see.

She'd painted the words in big curly white letters and outlined them in black so they popped out boldly against the garish red coffin.

Ravani blinked, taking it in.

"Well? It's perfect, right?"

Ravani blew out a breath.

"The . . . the *Creepy Freak*?"

"Yep. What do you think?"

Ravani grinned, in spite of himself. "I think you're the weirdest person I've ever met, Virginia Deering."

Virginia, his creepy and wonderful comrade, smiled back at him.

He felt another stabbing spike of nervous guilt try to rise up inside him, but he pushed it down.

He could do this. He could keep his friend, and he could keep her safe.

Chapter Twenty-Two

In Which a Voice Is Broken,
and a Plan Is Made

Ravani ran up the stairs of the Ragabonds' porch, heart racing, and pounded the door with his fist.

Then he remembered the family that lived in this house. Urgent knocking might make them more likely to dart out the back door than open the front one. There were, after all, Wolves in the world.

So, Ravani sucked in a breath, forced himself to knock softly, and called out as loudly as he dared, "It's me! Ravani! I'm alone! Please open the door!"

There was a moment's pause, and then the door opened wide enough to show Colt's curious face. He glanced at Ravani, then looked out over his shoulder.

"Howdy, Frog Master. What's up?"

"My parents!" Ravani gasped out. "They're coming! Over here! Right now!"

Without hesitation, Colt swung the door wide, revealing that he was wearing nothing but a pair of baggy underwear. He grabbed Ravani's shirt and yanked him inside, then slammed the door behind him.

"How much time we got?"

Ravani shrugged, still trying to catch his breath.

"I don't know! My mother's just wrapping up a loaf of banana bread to bring over. A couple minutes at most!"

Colt's eyebrows shot up.

"That's great news."

"Why is that great?!"

"I love banana bread." He bit his lip. "Couple of minutes, though? This could be tight." He turned and cupped his hands over his mouth and did the same owl call that Ravani had heard Tristan do. "All hands! All hands!" he shouted.

From upstairs came the sound of doors opening, and then the thunder of feet on the floor. Beth came out from the kitchen, wiping her hands on a towel, Winnie and Benjamin behind her.

"Where's Tristan?" Colt asked.

"In town looking for a job," Beth answered. "What's going on?"

Virginia and Annabel came jogging down the stairs. Virginia looked serious, of course. Annabel looked scared. Virginia shot Ravani a questioning look, but Colt jumped in and took charge of the explaining.

"Rav's parents are on their way over. We only got a couple minutes."

Benjamin rolled his eyes.

"Is that all? Mom's got a headache, Dad's out of town, easy-peasy."

Colt shook his head.

"Used those last time, little brother. Rule of Repeating, remember?"

"Plus, it's been a week," Beth said. "It's time for them to meet our parents. We've got plenty of time to pull this together.

Benjamin, take lookout." Benjamin hurried to the narrow window beside the door and peeked out at the street.

"Coast is clear. I'll keep you posted."

Meet our parents? Ravani opened his mouth, confused. The Ragabonds were all business, though, and they moved on before he could ask a question.

"We'll do the Montgomery," Beth said crisply, looking around at the group. "Through the kitchen door. Virginia, seat them in the dining room, not the parlor."

"What about Dad?" Winnie asked. "Tristan isn't here."

Beth looked to Colt. "You've been practicing, right? Let's hear it."

Colt cleared his throat. "Hello, Mr. and Mrs. Foster." His voice started low and strong, but cracked and broke into an adolescent warble at the end.

Beth cocked an eyebrow. "Seriously?"

"It's better loud," Colt insisted. Then he yelled, "Hello, Mr. and Mrs. Foster!" He kept his voice deep and unbroken, but at a shout he could add some scratchy gravel to it and a little sharp rasp. He put a dollop of southern flavor on it, too. Ravani was impressed. It was good. Really good.

"Not bad," Beth admitted. "Through a door, that'll work. But keep it to hello and goodbye. I'll handle the rest." She spoke to each Ragabond in turn, eyes serious and words fast. "Annabel, I want you listening from upstairs. You haven't had enough practice. Benjamin and Winnie, you're doing Playtime. Virginia will have to lead. We can do this. If they look suspicious, we'll fall back to the Memphis Shakedown. You all remember that?" The circle of heads nodded.

Ravani's head snapped around, trying to follow the conversation. The Ragabonds had a whole language, a whole *world* of their own.

"Okay, places, everyone!" Beth clapped her hands three times.

"Um," Ravani said, raising his hand. "What do I do?"

Beth blinked at him like she'd forgotten he was there. "You don't have to do anything. Just keep your mouth shut and follow our lead."

"What about our Curtain Call?" Virginia asked. "This is a drop-in, not a pick-up."

"Hmmm," Beth said thoughtfully. "What do you guys think? Remember our practices?"

"Uh . . . Fire Drill?" Winnie suggested.

"No way, not in a Montgomery. They'll want to help. Come on, guys, think."

Colt snapped his fingers. "Sick Day!" He looked to Benjamin. "Did you eat enough breakfast to throw up, buddy?"

"Yeah," Benjamin replied with a sigh.

"Sick Day could work," Beth agreed. "But we're talking about a mother here. She might pull a Samaritan. Anyone?"

"Family Emergency," Virginia said.

"That'll work," Beth said. She turned to Ravani. "After a few minutes, you'll need to excuse yourself to go to the bathroom. Hop out the window and call us from your house, then run back and sneak back in. Got it?"

Ravani's neck hurt from trying to follow the rapid-fire conversation snapping around the room. "Why would I call you?"

"You won't be *you*," Beth said in an isn't-this-obvious tone.

"You'll be my sister. Giving me some upsetting family news that'll cut your parents' visit short. Get it?"

"I . . . I . . . I can't do a woman's voice!"

Beth gave him a barely patient smile. "I know, Rav. It doesn't matter. You'll be talking to *me*, remember?"

"Okay? But what if they, like, see me when I leave? Through a window or something?"

"Make sure they don't," Colt said, tousling Ravani's hair. "And if they do, just say you had diarrhea and you were embarrassed to go at your friend's house. This stuff's hard at first, but you'll be fine."

"They're outside!" Benjamin announced. "Heading our way." He squinted to look closer, then peeked over his shoulder at Ravani. "Is your mom bringing food?" he asked hopefully.

"Places, everyone," Beth said before Ravani could answer. "Keep it loose and easy. Benjamin, be ready to vomit if things take a turn. You remember the code word?"

"Yeah, yeah."

"Okay, go!"

There was a blur of rushing around, a hushed trample of feet and bodies without a word being spoken. And then, in what felt like one breath to Ravani, it was just him and Virginia, standing at the foot of the stairs. From above, Ravani heard what must have been Annabel's door closing. The kitchen door was still swinging shut from Colt and Beth's exit. Benjamin and Winnie were lying on their stomachs on the parlor floor, playing cards like it was nothing, like they'd been doing it all morning.

It was, to Ravani, a certain kind of amazing. It felt, for a second, like it was nearly fun, perhaps. Like a game.

But he remembered that it wasn't when he saw Virginia's face. There was a tightness in her jaw and dark clouds in her gray eyes. "I hate this," she said, her voice a wounded sort of sad. "I hate lying."

"I . . . I . . . I'm sorry," Ravani said. "I tried to stop her, but . . ."

From outside, they both heard the murmur of a voice, coming up the walk.

"*It's okay,*" she said. "*I can do it, so we get to stay here. Can you, Rav?*"

"*I . . . I'll try,*" he whispered back.

Virginia nodded, brow furrowed pensively. "*I know you will.*"

She put on a small smile that didn't make it to her eyes. And she turned and opened the door.

Chapter Twenty-Three

In Which a Turkey Is Stuffed, and a Stomach Is Emptied

"Hello, Mrs. Foster," Virginia said, moving aside to let them in. "Pleased to meet you, Mr. Foster," she added, solemnly holding out her hand. "Virginia Deering."

"Oh," Ravani's father said, then took it, his beefy hand swallowing hers completely. He looked vaguely like a grizzly bear trying to hold a teacup. "Thank you, uh, for having us."

"Goodness, Ravani," Mrs. Foster said, "you sure raced over here."

"Um," Ravani mumbled, his mouth suddenly dry. "I . . . had diarrhea."

Luckily, most of what he'd said had been covered by the sound of the door closing.

"What, dear?" his mother asked, frowning.

"Ravani's right," Virginia said quickly. "He knew my parents are *dying to meetcha*. Please, take a seat." She guided them toward the dining room, zapping a fairly frigid look at Ravani.

"Mrs. Foster, is that you?" a voice called out through the kitchen door. Ravani blinked in surprise. It actually took him a moment to realize it was Beth. Her voice was deeper, more formal. It didn't just sound *different* from Beth's voice . . . it sounded nothing like it. It was like when Fred did his exotic voices, but even *more* convincing. Not like acting at all. Like *magic*, perhaps.

"Oh . . . yes, it is!" Mrs. Foster answered, raising her voice. "And my husband, too!"

"Well, isn't this a surprise?" Mrs. Deering let a noticeable irritation creep into her voice. "Virginia, dear, why don't you bring our *unexpected* guests some water to drink?"

Ravani's parents exchanged a slightly uncomfortable look.

Virginia obediently pushed the kitchen door open. Ravani stiffened, thinking she'd just given the whole ruse away.

The door opened just wide and long enough, though, to give a quick glimpse of a sliver of the kitchen, including a woman standing at the sink with her back to them. No . . . it wasn't a woman. It was Beth, her hair pulled out of its ponytail, wearing a dark housedress instead of the jeans she'd been wearing before. With the sun shining in the window, all they could really see was her silhouette. She was definitely taller, too; Ravani suspected she was standing on something underneath that floor-length dress. He did his best to hide his smile.

The Ragabonds knew what they were doing.

"I'm . . . sorry to come over unannounced like this," his mother called out. "We were so eager to finally welcome you to the neighborhood. I hope this isn't a bad time?"

"Ha ha." Mrs. Deering laughed stiffly. "Is there ever a *good* time for uninvited guests?"

Ravani's parents exchanged a *very* uncomfortable look.

Virginia reemerged and handed glasses of water to Mr. and Mrs. Foster.

"I'm sorry to shout through the door like this. I'm stuffing tonight's turkey and I'm wrist-deep in the bird at the moment."

"Oh! Let me help you with that," Mrs. Foster said, jumping up and marching toward the kitchen door.

Ravani opened his mouth to shout, but he didn't know what to say.

"Absolutely not!" Beth shouted back, as Virginia practically dove in front of Ravani's mother. "Virginia, dear, could you explain our unfortunate situation to them?"

"We had a pipe burst in the bathroom," Virginia said breathlessly, standing before the kitchen door with her arms spread to block it, "and the plumber hasn't come yet. In the meantime, we're all taking turns bathing in a big washtub we dragged into the kitchen. My father's in there now."

"Hello, Mr. and Mrs. Foster!" Colt's voice hollered out, muffled by the door.

Ravani's eyebrows went up. Colt's voice was nearly perfect.

"Hello!" Mrs. Foster called uncertainly, then widened her eyes at Mr. Foster as she returned to her chair. He straightened up quickly and cleared his throat and offered, "Hello there!"

Ravani glanced at Virginia and saw that she was giving him an urgent look. He jerked to attention, suddenly remembering that he had a part to play, too.

He jumped to his feet, scurried quickly to the door . . . and then realized that he probably should say something before he left.

"I . . . have to go to the bathroom," he said. His voice sounded higher and more frantic than he was intending. His mind raced with what he had to do: get into the bathroom, escape through the window, run across the street, call the Deerings' house, run *back* across the street, and sneak back into the Deerings' house. And, he supposed, flush the toilet. "It's . . . uh . . . it's gonna be a while."

Ravani's parents looked at each other.

"Okay, dear," his mother said, mouth caught somewhere between a frown and a smile. "Thank you for letting us know."

"I wish we had known you were coming," Beth griped theatrically through the door as Ravani made his exit.

Then, a blur; into the bathroom, slamming the door, sliding the window open—his heart nearly stopping when it wouldn't open at first, before he remembered to undo the latch—then stepping onto the toilet and crawling out through the window frame. In his haste, his foot caught the sill and he tumbled headfirst into the bush beneath the window. He jumped up and ran, ducking low below the windows, then sprinted across the lawn toward his home.

He burst into his house and ran to the phone in the hallway. His trembling finger hovered, ready to dial the number.

His brain sputtered. Then died. His mouth hung open. His heaving lungs stopped.

Ravani Foster didn't know the Deerings' phone number.

He had one job. They were counting on him. At that very moment they were stalling his parents, waiting for the phone to ring. It all played out in his mind: the Ragabonds' secret revealed, them being led away in handcuffs, Virginia casting him one farewell look of hurt and betrayal.

He shook his head. No.

His eyes dropped to his mother's address book, sitting on the little table by the phone. His sweaty fingers thumbed desperately through the pages until they found the Cs. He scanned down, then saw it: *Croward, Arthur.* Their old neighbor's name, with the phone number in his mother's handwriting beside it. Heart racing, he punched the number in.

The phone rang once. Twice. Ravani held his breath. Had the number changed, had he dialed it wrong, was—

"Hello?" Beth's grown-up voice said through the receiver.

"It's me," Ravani gasped.

"Why hello! It's lovely to . . . what's that?"

"I didn't say anything."

"Oh goodness! Is it serious?" Beth's voice rose in alarm.

"Is what serious?" Ravani asked.

"*Hang up and come back*," Beth whispered into the phone. He was pretty sure her teeth were gritted.

"Oh! Right! Sorry!"

"That's just awful!" Beth was saying as Rav hung up. He took two gulps of air. And then he bolted.

Down the hall, out the door, off the porch, across the street.

He scuttled, bent over and wheezing, around the corner of the Deerings' house and up to the bush beneath the bathroom window. He launched himself over the sill and through the window, bouncing off the toilet and sprawling with a wind-sucking *thud* onto the linoleum floor. He lay there a second, praying that his landing hadn't been as loud in the rest of the house as it had sounded in the bathroom. Then he jumped up, ran toward the door, slid to a stop, ran back and flushed the toilet, and then swung open the bathroom door.

Down the hall, he heard the front door opening.

"Again, I'm so sorry to have come at such an inconvenient time," his mother was saying.

"Yes, well, a call ahead is always considered polite," Beth answered from the kitchen. "Now, I really must be getting back to my sister . . ."

"I'll be praying for your father. If there's anything I can do to help, with the children or something, or . . ."

"Oh, just respecting our privacy would be more than enough, Thank you. Goodbye now!"

"Goodbye, Fosters!" Colt barked out in his Mr. Deering voice.

Ravani hurried out to where Virginia and his mother stood by the front door. His father was already out on the porch.

"Oh, good," his mother said when she saw him. "We're leaving, dear . . . My, why are you so out of breath?"

"Oh," Ravani said, lungs gasping. "Um. It . . . it was a tough one," he said, pointing with his thumb over his shoulder toward the bathroom.

His mother's eyebrows went up. Virginia's went down.

"I . . . see. Well, we better get going. Mrs. Deering's father is being rushed to the hospital, I'm afraid."

"Actually, Mrs. Foster, could Ravani stay?" Virginia asked. "My mother will just be on the phone all afternoon with my aunt. It's not the first time Grandpa's gone to the hospital."

His mother frowned, considering, then her face brightened.

"Well, it *is* wonderful that he has a new friend in the neighborhood." Ravani's face burned, knowing what she really meant was it was wonderful that Ravani had any friend at all. "Don't overstay your welcome, though, dear, all right?"

"Okay," he agreed quickly.

His mother gave him one more tight smile, then stepped out onto the porch. Virginia closed the door behind her.

The house hung in silence. Virginia leaned forward and pressed her ear to the door. Ravani tiptoed up and joined her. Mrs. Foster's voice murmured from outside, just barely audible.

"Well, they aren't the *nicest* people I've ever met."

"Mm-hmm" was his father's low answer.

Footsteps, receding away down the steps.

"I can't believe it worked," Ravani said with a small grin.

"I know."

Ravani shook his head, still a little out of breath. "That was almost a *disaster*," he said just as Benjamin walked up.

Benjamin's eyes went wide. He bent over, heaved, and threw up on the floor.

Virginia looked at the puddle of vomit, then at Benjamin, her face expressionless. "Why did you do that, brother? They already left."

Benjamin scowled and shrugged, wiping his mouth. "Just doing my job, sis. *He* said the password." He pointed at Ravani.

Colt came walking out of the dining room, chewing on an apple. "That went well," he said, then saw the chunky puddle on the floor. "Oops. Accidental discharge, bud?"

"He said the password!" Benjamin repeated again angrily, then stomped off.

Colt watched him stalk away, then looked to Ravani. "Not bad for your first time. Solid bathroom performance. Really sounded like you had to go. You didn't wash your hands, though."

"I . . . didn't actually go to the bathroom."

"Still. You gotta commit to the scene, Frog Master," Colt said, squeezing Ravani's shoulder. "It's the little details that really sell it. The constipation was a nice touch, though."

He swallowed his bite of apple, then looked back down to the floor. "Hey! No one told me we had Cheerios!"

CHAPTER TWENTY-FOUR

In Which Things Are Shared, and Music Is Heard

*A*fter Benjamin's vomit was cleaned up, it was time for lunch. And lunch at the Ragabonds, Ravani learned, was a predictably chaotic affair.

"You can pour the milk," Colt told Ravani, handing him a bottle from the fridge. "No one gets to eat if they don't help."

The kitchen was a flurry of voices, elbows, and jostling bodies as the Deerings bustled, each doing their part. Annabel wiped the table with a wet rag; Benjamin got the bread and peanut butter out of the cupboard; Virginia stretched to get plates and handed them to Winnie; Beth started spreading peanut butter on the bread; Colt put eight plastic cups on the table. Ravani followed behind to add milk to each one.

Colt saw him fill the first cup generously. "*Just a bit,*" he murmured, and then picked up the cup and poured it out into the next three so that each had just an inch of milk at the bottom. Ravani remembered what Tristan had said the night they'd shared the secret with Ravani: *with so many mouths to feed, we never have much.*

"Right," Ravani mumbled back. "Sorry."

When the preparations were done, though, the Ragabonds didn't sit down. They each took an empty plate and then circled around the sandwiches stacked on the table. Virginia made a spot for Ravani.

"Who will be the hungry?" Beth asked.

There was a pause, and then Annabel's small voice spoke up. "I will."

Beth nodded at her.

All the others reached in and took a sandwich. Everyone except for Annabel and Ravani. He stood, uncertain. There was only one sandwich left. Virginia nudged him and nodded. "*Take it*," she said. Ravani looked at Annabel, who smiled and nodded, so he leaned in and took it.

"Who will share with the hungry?" Beth asked.

All the Ragabonds answered as one. "I will."

Annabel slid her empty plate into the middle of the table. One by one, all the other Ragabonds tore a piece off their own sandwich. And they put it on Annabel's plate. Ravani was the last one, but he added to her plate, too. After he did, Annabel's plate was full. She grinned around the circle.

"Thank you," she said, and everyone answered, "What's ours is yours."

Ravani didn't have to ask what it all meant. He knew it was part of their magic, part of that web the Ragabonds wove around themselves and between one another to stay safe, and to stay together.

And he was woven in now, too. It felt good, to be a part of something.

"Eat up!" Beth announced, and then in ones and twos the Ragabonds wandered off. Benjamin and Winnie ambled away toward the front porch, Annabel and Beth walked out to the dining room, and then it was just Ravani and Virginia and Colt standing in the kitchen alone.

Ravani looked at the torn edge of his sandwich. There was just a thin stripe of peanut butter between the slices of bread.

"Do you have any jelly?" he asked before thinking. He regretted it instantly. Virginia frowned a little, and Colt's forehead wrinkled.

"Peanut butter *and* jelly?" he said. "Geez, Rav, sorry we can't roll out the red carpet for you." He said it like a joke, but Ravani could hear a coldness in his voice. "Today is peanut butter day. Tomorrow we get jelly." And with that, he took his splash of milk and his torn peanut butter sandwich and headed out the back door.

Ravani's eyes darted to Virginia. "Gosh, I'm sorry, I—"

But Virginia just rolled her eyes. "It's not a big deal, Rav. Breaking news: we're not rich. Who is?"

Ravani moved toward the back door. "You want to eat out by the creek, too?"

"No. Colt's already there." She saw Ravani's confused look. "Colt eats alone. Always."

"Why?"

Virginia looked out toward where Colt sat chewing in the shadows.

"Colt's funny," she said. "He's always joking around. Pretends not to take anything serious. But he goes off by himself, every day. And, if you watch him, he's got just the saddest face. He thinks a lot, I think. And remembers. Bad stuff." Ravani looked at Colt, the boy with the loud laugh and the reckless smile and the sparkling eyes. He didn't look loud, or reckless, or sparkling at that moment. His shoulders were slumped, his back to them, looking quietly at the flowing waters of Carcass Creek, chewing on his sandwich.

"He's the saddest of us all, I think," Virginia said softly. "Maybe that's why he's always joking."

Souls are like that: they do what they have to. They put the darkness down deep, sometimes, so they can shine.

"Well. Come on. Let's go eat in my room."

Virginia's room was small and neat. It held a big bed with a scratched brass frame standing alone on the hardwood floor. There were no shelves, no dresser, not even a lamp. But on the floor were two suitcases, standing open, clothes folded up neat inside. They looked ready to go at a moment's notice, which Ravani knew was exactly what they were.

"I share with Beth. The bed came with the house, which is swell. At our last place, I slept on a mattress in the hallway."

"It's nice," Ravani said.

"It's perfect," Virginia said simply. "A real bed. A creek in the backyard. A cellar full of coffins. What more could a girl want?"

She sat down on the edge of the bed, balancing her plate on her knees, and Ravani settled in next to her. He peered out the window that was beside him.

"Both our bedrooms are on the second story," he said. "You can see my window, right there." He loved how it looked from there, surrounded by birdhouses.

"I know. I can see you getting dressed in the morning."

Ravani sputtered, his face growing red. One corner of Virginia's mouth went up, and both her nostrils flared. It was her version of a face-splitting grin.

"Holy spit you blush easy, Rav. Relax. I can only see your top half, which on you is mostly elbows and ribs. You're the ribsiest kid I ever saw. Like a xylophone. You should eat up."

Ravani laughed, face still burning. And he took a bite to hide his embarrassed smile.

It was strange, to Ravani, that Virginia could tease him and that it didn't sting. That you could sit with another soul and eat and joke and laugh.

He was still learning what having a friend felt like. He liked it. He felt fizzy as a cold soda.

"It's funny, the way we call the floors in a house 'stories,'" Virginia said.

"I guess."

"People would call this house a two-story house. Three if you count the coffin cellar. But, really, it's a seven-story house. Seven different stories, crowding in here together."

"Well," Ravani said, "maybe it's a *one*-story house, too. Because you're all a family, so you're all one story."

Virginia nodded, chewing. "Yeah. I like that. One story, together."

"How did you guys even find this place?" Ravani asked.

"An old Ragabond. He works as a nurse in the retirement home that Mr. Croward moved into. Mr. Croward's daughter was hoping to rent this house out. He said he had some family who were interested."

Ravani thought about it. A family of seven children, needing a big empty house. And a big empty house, needing a family. And Mr. Croward ending up at the same retirement home that a Ragabond worked at, at the same time that the Ragabonds were seeking a home. All those pieces, coming together.

"That's lucky."

"It's not luck, Rav. It's the magic. The magic made it happen. "

It didn't sound like magic to Rav. But perhaps the most powerful magic doesn't sparkle; perhaps it whispers. Or perhaps not.

He looked down to take a bite of his own sandwich and noticed something, white and wrinkly, sticking out from under the bed between his feet. A piece of paper, with lines and boxes drawn on it, black ink on white paper, in a familiar pattern.

"What's this?"

Virginia's brow wrinkled for a second, but then it smoothed and her eyes glowed with a little spark. She got down on her knees by the side of the bed and pulled the paper the rest of the way out.

The paper was long—really four or five pieces taped together. Drawn all the way down it, in ruler-perfect neatness, were piano keys. Pencil lines marked the ivory keys, black keys scribbled dark with black crayon.

"This is my practice piano," Virginia said, and she set it up on the bed. Ravani scooted to the side to make room. "I made it myself. For between lessons, so I can practice what your mother is teaching me. See, look. If I kneel here, it's at the perfect height." Her voice, for perhaps the first time since Ravani had met her, sounded excited. "It's *almost* as good as having a real piano." She closed her eyes and pressed her fingers to the keys. "And if no one bothers me," she said, her voice quieter than ever, "if it's *real* quiet, I can hear the notes. I can hear the songs."

Virginia's eyes stayed closed and Ravani saw her face go someplace far away. Ravani sat, still and silent. Her fingers moved across the drawn keys.

Then, she stopped playing. Her eyes blinked open. And she looked up at Ravani, her eyes shining, mouth half open.

There was something about that paper piano, about its careful lines and wrinkled edges, about the smudges on the keys where he could tell that she'd been playing it, about Virginia's glimmering eyes when she looked up at him, that made Ravani a sharp kind of sad.

He looked down at the shabby keyboard—with its crumpled corners, and smeared crayon, and flimsy tape holding it all together—so he didn't have to look in her eyes.

"It's swell, Virginia. Really swell." He said it just exactly like it was true.

But her mouth closed, slow. She blinked twice, fast. Her throat bobbed in a dry swallow.

"Liar," she said, her voice broken, like an eggshell.

"What? No," Ravani insisted. "I think it's great."

"You don't," she said, shaking her head. She breathed in, breathed out. "But that's your fault. You're looking at it all wrong. You're looking at it like Donnie Carter would. But you are not Donnie Carter, Ravani Foster. Come here." She patted the floor. Ravani slid down and knelt beside her. She leaned into him, so that their hips and shoulders touched. "Close your eyes. And *listen*."

Ravani watched Virginia close her eyes. He watched her breathe in, deep, and breathe out, long. And she raised her hands back to the paper piano. And she began to play.

Sometimes a soul has to go where another soul asks it to follow, even if it doesn't know why.

Ravani closed his eyes.

At first, there was nothing. Or, nearly nothing. He could

hear birds out the window. But, after a breath, his hearing went deeper. He heard Virginia's fingertips, rasping on the paper. Then, deeper: the sound of her breathing, steady and gentle.

And then.

His hearing went to an even deeper sort of deep. Or his *listening* did, perhaps.

And he heard it. A note, faint and distant. Then another. The warm, sonorous voice of a piano. Then, a song. Soft, and sad, and simple. A melody of single notes, played by gentle fingers.

And Ravani's sadness—and the pity that wormed from it—faded down to nothing as the music rose.

The dark world hadn't given Virginia a piano. So she had made her own. And Ravani felt, down to his trembling soul, the truth that there was nothing at all sad about Virginia hearing her own music and believing in it.

It was like making a wish, but believing in it so hard that it comes to life and you can feel it fluttering in your hand.

It was magic, and a very true kind of magic.

Perhaps music can be something you choose to hear. Just like a family is someone you choose to love. And a home is someplace you choose to stay. It is precisely the *choosing* that makes it real.

Ravani opened his eyes, and saw that Virginia had stopped playing and was looking at him.

"It's *wonderful*," he breathed at last.

Virginia nodded, and perhaps she even actually smiled. "Now *that's* the truth."

Ravani frowned. "How do you do that?"

"Do what?"

"The truth thing. It's like you can always tell when I'm lying."

"I can," Virginia answered, shrugging one shoulder. "It's my Special."

"Your . . . Special?"

"Yeah. It's part of the magic, Rav. Every Ragabond, when they join, gets a Special. A power, sort of."

"You mean . . . like a superpower?" Ravani tried and failed to keep the skepticism out of his voice.

"This isn't a comic book, Rav," she said, rolling her eyes. "Specials are smaller than that. Quiet. No flying, or invisibility, or anything. Just . . . a little ability. To help the family."

Ravani smelled a joke.

"Yeah, right," he snorted. "I don't believe you."

She nodded. "That's true." Her eyebrows raised. "Right? Go ahead. Try." She cleared her throat. "When's your birthday?"

Ravani licked his lips. "February twenty-fourth."

"Lie."

"It's March fourth."

"Also lie."

"May twenty-first."

"True."

Ravani frowned. Virginia was either lucky, or telling the truth.

"What's your favorite dessert?" she asked.

"Cheesecake."

"Lie."

"True. I hate cheesecake."

Virginia pulled her head back. "*True*. How can you hate cheesecake?"

"It's gross."

"Have you wet the bed in the last year?"

"What? No!"

One of Virginia's eyebrows inched up. A small smile spread on her face. "Lie?"

Ravani gulped. "Well . . . it was just once, and I drank a lot of milk before bed."

Her smile broadened enough to show her teeth. "Lie!" she said.

"Okay, twice! But that's it!"

"True," Virginia said, wrestling the smile off her face.

Ravani sat back on his feet, blinking and taking it in. He wasn't entirely sure that he entirely believed her, but he was at least partially unsure that he didn't entirely disbelieve her, either.

"Did you get to choose your . . . Special?"

"No. You kind of figure it out slowly. It comes to you over time. Annabel still hasn't found hers yet."

"What are everybody else's?"

"Winnie can throw things. With incredible accuracy."

Ravani thought back.

"That day," he said. "With Donnie and Stevie in the woods. Those rocks that hit his ear, his belt buckle, his hand."

Virginia nodded. "Beth can mimic sounds and voices."

"Like the mother voice, downstairs just now!"

"Um-hmm. Other sounds, too, though; birds, or trucks starting, whatever. And Benjamin's you already saw, of course."

"I did?"

She raised her eyebrows at him. He stared at her. Then it shot into his mind. Or, rather, splashed. "He can . . . throw up?"

"At will. Any biological function, actually. Vomit, burp, fart, cry, nose bleed. Poop."

"Why would . . . *pooping* at will ever be useful?"

"You'd be surprised at how many situations a kid pooping their pants can get you out of."

"Huh. What about Colt?" Ravani asked. "What's his Special?" With Colt's confidence and swagger, Ravani was sure his Special would be something extraordinary, like breathing underwater or X-ray vision.

"Paperwork," Virginia answered.

Ravani's face dropped. "Paperwork? That's . . ." Ravani trailed off.

"Incredibly helpful," Virginia finished for him. "He can fake signatures, forge forms, counterfeit documents. He makes us school records, birth certificates, whatever. The world runs on paperwork, Rav." She said it like it was true and, unfortunately, it was.

"Tristan?"

"He's the Shepherd. Once you're oldest, *that's* your Special."

"And . . . what power does the Shepherd have?"

"The magic talks to the Shepherd. The Shepherd knows when we should stay. And the Shepherd knows when we have to leave."

"Usually," Ravani said, remembering how they'd been caught, the last time.

"Always," Virginia said solemnly. "Tristan feels responsible for us getting caught. But I think the magic didn't tell Tristan to run because it didn't *want* us to run. If we wouldn't have gotten caught, we wouldn't have had to escape. Tristan wouldn't have called the old Ragabond at the retirement home. We never would have come here. And . . ." Virginia frowned and looked at her hands, choosing her words. "I feel like we're *supposed* to be here. I don't know why. But it's kind of like my Special, how I can *feel* if something is true or not? Well, here . . . this place, somehow, *feels* true. Like it's where we're supposed to be. At least for now."

It was the most Ravani had ever heard Virginia say at once.

Her eyes lifted back to his. She blew a brisk breath out through her nose.

"Or maybe not. It's hard to tell with magic. But, either way, at least I'm finally getting piano lessons." She slid the paper piano back under the bed.

"What is it with you and the piano, anyway?" Ravani asked. "Why do you like it so much?"

Virginia frowned. A little wrinkle grew between her eyes. *Mind your own business*, she seemed ready to say.

She pressed her lips together. And she made a different choice. "I'm going to tell you this once, and then we're never going to talk about it again, Rav."

"Okay."

"And I'm only telling you because you called my piano wonderful."

"Okay."

The corners of her mouth tucked down. She reached back under the bed, and this time pulled out the beat-up folder of piano music Ravani had seen her leaving her piano lesson with. When she spoke, her voice was even and steady and smooth.

"This was my mother's music," she said. "She played the piano, when she was younger. I never heard her play, because we never had the money for a piano. But she promised me that she'd teach me to play. Someday. Some *brighter* day, she said. That was our dream. And then she got sick. And then she got very sick." Virginia blinked. And then she blinked again. And again. "And then she was gone." A breath in, a breath out. And then, her voice wasn't quite so even, or quite so steady, or quite so smooth. "All that I have left of her is this music, and an old parasol. And that dream. I want to make it come true for us. For *her*."

Virginia's words hung between them, floating like fireflies.

Her eyes shone wetly, despite her blinking.

Ravani swallowed.

Sometimes, when one soul sees another soul's secret truth, it doesn't know what to do.

But sometimes it does. Sometimes it knows what to do, because another soul showed it.

Ravani leaned forward and wrapped Virginia in a hug. Strong at first. And then softer, and softer. Like the sun setting. Virginia didn't seem to know what to do, at first. But then, after a shaky breath, she wrapped her arms around him, too. And she squeezed him back.

Ravani was a good comrade, too.

And Ravani made a choice. He'd already made the choice before, twice, but that had been on accident. Standing there, hugging his comrade, Ravani made the same choice again, on purpose.

He wasn't going to tell Virginia about Donnie. Because then they'd leave. And she'd lose the place she felt like she belonged, and she'd lose her friend, and she'd lose this chance to learn her mother's music.

He held on to his comrade. And he made the choice to *keep* holding on to her.

It *felt* like the right thing to do.

Funny things, feelings.

Chapter Twenty-Five

In Which Blood Is Smelled,
and a Mouth Waters

The Hunter fingered the scrap of paper. Looked again, very closely, at the phone number written on it.

Two of the numbers were badly smudged. Unreadable.

There were ninety-nine possible combinations that those two missing numbers could be.

So the Hunter had been making a lot of phone calls.

The Hunter hated speaking on the telephone.

Luckily for him, most of the numbers he'd called had been dead ends: no such number.

One had been an elementary school, which was interesting. He'd written that one down.

One had been a travel agent's office. Also intriguing. Into his notebook it went.

Several had been homes, which he'd noted carefully.

There were many leads to chase down. Which was all right with the Hunter. He liked chasing.

He dialed the next number, pressing each number very precisely.

The earpiece rang.

There was a *click*, and then a voice spoke.

"Endless Days Retirement Home," it said cheerfully. "How can I help you?"

The Hunter didn't answer. The Hunter was thinking.

It didn't matter that the voice hadn't said something that he was expecting. Of course it hadn't. The Hunter almost never *expected* anything. The Hunter looked. And the Hunter listened. And the Hunter thought. And the Hunter hunted.

A very important thing for any hunter to have is *instinct*. And the Hunter had *very* good instincts. When the voice on the other end said those words, the Hunter didn't so much *feel* something as *smell* something.

The Hunter smelled blood.

"Hello? Is there someone you're trying to find?" the voice in the earpiece asked.

The Hunter's mouth watered.

"Yes," the Hunter said.

CHAPTER TWENTY-SIX

*In Which Cupcakes Are Eaten,
and Lips Are Sealed*

$\mathcal{A}$s he and Virginia bundled the papers in the *Slaughterville Spectator* office the next morning, Ravani was surprised to find a headline that actually interested him: FOURTH OF JULY FAIR READIES FOR OPENING.

"The fair opens tonight?" he asked.

"Yessirree." Hortense was crouched over, tapping away at her typewriter. "Pulled into town last night and they're already setting it up. Games of chance, hall of mirrors, funnel cakes, all the usual."

"Nothing . . . unusual?" Ravani asked Hortense. "You sure?"

Hortense paused her rapid typing and gave Ravani a wry smile, her eyes flashing between him and Virginia. "Well, I did hear an intriguing rumor about the fella who runs the haunted house. Psycho Sammy Sausage, they call him. A wanted serial murderer, with a knack for installing trapdoors. He sees someone who looks enticingly meaty, he pulls the lever, and *whoosh*. They end up in Sammy's food stall next door, and *not* as a customer, if you know what I mean. So, if I were you, I'd avoid the haunted house. And the corn dogs next door."

"Will do," Ravani said, grinning.

"Psycho Sammy Sausage?" Virginia said in her monotone. "Enticingly meaty? That's good writing."

"Thanks, kid," Hortense said, returning to her typewriter.

"What are you working on?" Ravani asked.

"Oh, nothing, probably," she answered, without looking up.

The rest of the route was uneventful. By the time Ravani and Virginia reached the end of town, crews were indeed setting up the carnival. The empty field that served as Slaughterville's fairgrounds was already crowded with colorful tents, half-erected booths, and carousels and whirling rides standing still and ready. A motley stew of smells wafted to Ravani and Virginia: sugar, diesel, manure, popcorn, and cigarettes. They stopped to watch the commotion.

"I've never been to a carnival," Virginia said. "Do they have caramel apples?"

"Sure. And elephant ears, and corn on the cob, and snow cones."

Her eyebrows rose with each item. "Dang." Her usually unimpressed eyes scanned the unfolding fair with longing. "I've always wanted to go to a carnival someday."

Ravani watched as a group of men heaved on a rope, pulling a red-and-white-striped tent up into the air. He looked at Virginia.

"You mean, someday when there's a carnival right in the town you live in?" he asked. She lowered one eyebrow. "You mean, someday when you have a comrade to go with?" He spread his arms. "Welcome to someday, Virginia. You're already here."

She rolled her eyes, but he could see her fighting a smile. "You think you're clever or something?"

Ravani grinned.

"Will you go to the carnival with me, Virginia Deering?"

She blew out a breath.

"Oh, fine."

Virginia, Colt, Winnie, and Annabel chattered around him as they walked through the darkness, but Ravani hardly noticed. He was so filled with nervous excitement, he was practically carbonated. Sure, he'd been to the carnival before. With his mother and father. But he'd never gone with friends before, or even comrades.

Tristan had to work, which had been good news to Ravani. Benjamin had stayed home—"afraid of clowns," Colt had said with a sad shake of his head—and Beth had stayed with him, so it was just the five of them. But five, when you're much more used to one, feels like a lot.

They could see the carnival from a mile down the road. The booths and rides and food stands were lit up, the carousel spinning, the Ferris wheel stretching tall into the night sky. As they got closer they could see the crowds milling among the attractions, smell the sweet and salty sizzling food, hear the festive *oompah oompah* of the music and the hiss and clank of the rides.

They were just walking into the glow of the lights when Ravani stopped cold.

"Shoot!" he said. "I didn't bring any money."

"We got it covered," Colt said. He dug into his pocket and held up one shiny nickel.

"You have . . . one nickel?"

Colt grinned.

"We have one nickel," he said, then put an arm around Winnie, "and we have her."

They wound past the food stands and the Tilt-A-Whirl until they got to the row of games.

First was a SHOW YOUR STRENGTH! sledgehammer swing. They kept walking.

Next up was a ring toss booth. At the back, a row of bottles was lined up. A sign read PAY A NICKEL, WIN FIVE!

"How's this work?" Colt asked the barker running the booth.

"Nickel gets you three throws," the man said, holding up a small red plastic ring. "You ring it on the top of a bottle, you win five nickels."

"Is it possible?" Colt asked, narrowing his eyes.

The man yawned. "Sure, it's possible, kid."

Colt looked to Virginia. She nodded. Colt handed over his nickel, and the man handed Colt three of the rings.

Colt leaned against the wooden rail, squinted in concentration, then tossed the first ring. It fell short, landing in the dirt before the bottles.

He was leaning forward, about to toss again, when he stopped.

"What do you say I let my little sister throw?" he asked.

"It's your nickel," the man grunted.

Winnie stepped forward, eyes wide and innocent.

Colt handed her a ring. She squinted at the row of bottles with one eye shut, her mouth twisted. Then, with a flick of her wrist, she flung the ring. It sailed through the air. With a little *ding* it rattled home around the neck of a bottle.

The carnival barker clenched his jaw and scowled.

Ravani raised his hands to cheer, but a quick look from Colt cut him off mid-hurrah.

"*We don't want to attract attention,*" Virginia murmured to him out of the side of her mouth.

The sour-faced barker started digging in his apron pocket for the nickels.

"Wait," Colt said. "We still have one more ring."

The man glared. "You think she's gonna get that lucky twice, kid?"

"No," Colt said, a small smile on his lips. "I don't think she's gonna get lucky twice. Let's make it interesting, though. If she misses, you keep the five we already won. But if she makes it, we get *twenty*."

The man looked Winnie up and down and smirked.

"You're on. Whenever you're ready, darling."

Winnie took the last ring from Colt. She kissed it, smiled at the surly barker, and then tossed it. A flight, a *ding*, a rattle, and the second ring settled around the bottle neck, coming to rest right atop her last one.

The barker's stubbly jaw dropped.

The children all traded quiet smiles.

Aha, Ravani thought. *So this is what magic looks like.*

They worked their way down the row of games. Winnie won ten more nickels throwing baseballs into peach baskets, five popping balloons with a dart, and another twenty knocking over stuffed clowns with a softball (including an extra ten for knocking the last one over left-handed).

Colt pulled the group into a circle between two tents at the end of the row. He held out a palm full of nickels.

"Fifty nickels," Colt said. "Not a bad haul, Winnie." Virginia and Annabel patted Winnie on the back. She smiled and blushed.

"Half goes to the family fund." He counted out twenty-five, picking them out of his hand and putting them in his pocket. "That leaves five nickels each. Go ahead and grab 'em."

They all did, except for Ravani, who felt suddenly awkward.

"You don't have to include me," Ravani said.

"'Course we do, bud," Colt said, then grabbed Ravani's hand and pressed five warm coins into it. He winked and tousled Rav's hair. "You're with us, Frog Master. What's ours is yours."

Ravani blinked fast and looked away, his face blushing redder than Winnie's.

Their loot divided, the group split up. Colt took Annabel and Winnie over toward the snack booths, each of his hands holding one of theirs. Virginia and Ravani set off on their own.

They rode the Ferris wheel first—it was fun to see the town from so high, and even though they couldn't quite see their houses on Offal Road, they could see the slaughterhouse, and Ravani pointed out to Virginia where the boat race would be the next day.

After the Ferris wheel, they followed their noses to the snack booths. All the usual booths were there, with one surprising new addition.

"Mr. Chin!" Ravani said. "You have a food booth this year?" Mr. Chin, baker at Bread & Butter, was sweeping behind the counter. His face lit up when he saw Ravani and Virginia.

"Indeed I do!" he said. He spread his hands to show the empty display case. "And I sold out!"

"You sold out of . . . bread?" Virginia asked, glancing around at the stands selling cotton candy, funnel cakes, and ice cream.

"No," Mr. Chin said with a sly smile. He leaned on the counter and raised his eyebrows at Virginia. "I sold out of *cupcakes*."

"Cupcakes?" Ravani asked.

"Yep. And I was hoping you'd come by. I saved one for my little inspiration here." He reached under the counter, and then held out a cupcake to Virginia. It was covered in a thick layer of rich light-brown frosting speckled with darker brown bits. "It's carrot cake. With ginger-maple frosting."

Virginia took the cupcake, smiling a true, honest-to-goodness smile.

"What are the sprinkly bits?" she asked.

"That's my own special touch. Those are bacon bits."

"Bacon bits?" Virginia's smile faltered, just a tad. She gave Ravani a sidelong look and murmured, *"What is it with this town and meat?"*

But then she took a bite of the cupcake.

Her eyes closed. She chewed. Her smile faded.

"Well?" Mr. Chin asked. "Is it good?"

Virginia was still chewing.

Slowly, her eyes opened.

"No," she said. "It's incredible." She took another bite, then handed it to Ravani. "Holy spit, mister. You're onto something with that bacon."

Ravani took a bite. His eyes rolled back. "Oh man. That's amazing, Mr. Chin."

"Thank you! You know, I always wanted to try to make something new and different, someday."

Ravani swallowed and grinned at Virginia.

"Welcome to someday, Mr. Chin," he said, doffing the cupcake toward him. "You're already here."

Bidding Mr. Chin a fond farewell, they wandered the carnival together, lost in the noise and the smells and the fun. Virginia bought a caramel apple, as she'd promised, and Ravani bought a corn dog, as he always did.

When they were down to their last two nickels, Virginia stopped them in front of the last attraction, at the very end of the carnival row. HAUNTED HOUSE OF HORORS was spelled in dripping, Gothic lettering on its plywood front, and all around the words were painted ghastly depictions of ghosts, zombies, and skeletal hands. An unshaven man stood before the closed door, the unlit stub of a cigar propped in his mouth.

"Hey," Virginia murmured. "Look at his name. What are the chances?"

Ravani squinted and saw the name sewed on to the man's stained overalls: *Sammy.*

"*You gotta be kidding me,*" he whispered nervously.

"Excuse me," Virginia said, stepping up to the man. "Do people ever call you 'Sausage'?"

"Whazzat?" the man growled around his soggy cigar.

"Never mind." She held their last two nickels out to him. "Two, please."

The man took the nickels and opened the door of the Haunted House of Horors. Behind it was a passageway that disappeared into pitch dark.

"You got five minutes," the man muttered. "No refunds. Don't touch nothing."

Without hesitation, Virginia stepped forward into the inky

blackness. Ravani stood outside. "Uh, Virginia?" he called after her. "I don't know if—"

"Come on," her voice floated out of the darkness.

Ravani looked up at the man, who was holding the door open impatiently. "Um," he started to say, but the man rolled his eyes, shoved Ravani roughly into the Haunted House of Horors, and slammed the door behind him.

Ravani's eyes gaped, lost in utter darkness. "*Virginia?*" he whispered, shuffling forward gingerly. "*Virginia?*"

"I'm right here," she said, practically in his ear.

"Gaaahh!" Ravani shrieked, jumping.

"Calm down. I'm not supposed to be the scary part." A hand grabbed his and tried to pull him forward.

"*That's* your *hand, right?!*" Ravani hissed, digging in his heels.

There was a distinctly Virginia kind of sigh. "This may have been a mistake. Come on."

Feeling with his other arm, Ravani followed timidly in Virginia's wake.

"Are you sure we should be doing this?" Ravani asked. "I mean, his name is *Sammy.*"

"No one would ever call you 'enticingly meaty,' so I think you're safe either way."

There was an abrupt buzzing sound and a light flashed on next to Ravani. He squeaked and jerked away. The light was coming through a grimy window in the wall. In a little nook on the other side of the glass, a skeleton stood, draped with cottony spiderwebs, below a sign that read CURSED SKELETUN. Ravani backed away against the other wall.

"Hey. It looks like you with your shirt off," Virginia said.

"Very funny. Is it . . . *real*?" Ravani breathed. Virginia leaned forward for a closer look.

"If it is, the deceased was made in China," Virginia answered, clearly unimpressed. "It better get scarier than this. I'm starting to understand the 'no refunds' policy. The only thing scary so far is their spelling."

The light sputtered out, and Virginia pulled him farther along.

They passed another lighted case, this time containing something that was labeled as a 100% REAL WHEREWOLF, but looked more like a sloppily taxidermied wolverine to Ravani. Next was a shelf bearing jars of snakes and spiders pickled in formaldehyde, some questionable-looking shrunken heads, and, mysteriously, a stuffed chicken.

They turned a corner, where a speaker on the ceiling was choking out some scratchy organ music. A red lightbulb shone down on a chair, in which slumped a black-robed figure in a wide-brimmed, pointy hat, a broom across its lap, face lost in shadow.

"Oh no," Virginia said blandly, walking toward it. "A witch."

"Don't get too close," Ravani whispered.

"Geez, Rav. It's a dummy."

"You sure?"

"Of course. Look how it's all propped up and leaned over. Go ahead, sit in its lap."

Ravani looked at her doubtfully.

"I dare you."

He looked at the lifeless mannequin.

"Fine," he said, walking up to the witch. He turned around to face Virginia. "Happy?" he said, plopping down on its lap. "Now can we—"

Ravani's words were cut off when the witch suddenly lurched into motion, screeching "Grahhh!"

Ravani shrieked and shot away like he'd been launched from a catapult, slamming into the opposite wall where he stuck, gasping and whimpering.

"Holy living saints!" the witch exclaimed, clutching her chest. "You gave me a heart attack! I was sound asleep!" She took a couple recovering breaths, then banged angrily on the wall next to her with her fist. "You're supposed to knock when you send 'em in, Sammy!"

The witch settled back into her chair, still breathing hard. "Is he okay?" she asked, looking nervously at Ravani, panting and plastered to the wall.

"He's fine," Virginia answered. "Just a little jumpy. Come on, Rav. Sorry for startling you, ma'am."

Virginia grabbed Ravani's hand and pulled him farther along. The passage ended at a rickety metal staircase leading up. As they climbed it, Ravani finally got his lungs under control.

At the top of the stairs, they found themselves in one large, dimly red-lit room. A sign announced the room as the GREWSOME GALLERY. A mummy stood against one wall—Ravani wouldn't move until Virginia poked it, proving that this one *was* a dummy—and the rest of the space was decorated with a jumbled mix of morbid decor. There were some headstones, a few stuffed crows and black cats, a bubbling cauldron, some chains, and an empty coffin leaning against the wall. In the far corner, an EXIT sign glowed over a curtained doorway.

Ravani moved as quickly as he could toward the exit, walking wide around anything that might wake up and attack. Virginia walked over to look at the coffin.

"Not as good as ours," she said, pressing her hands into the lining and checking the joints. "Might be okay for burying, but I wouldn't want to race in it."

"Let's go, Virginia," Ravani said, hand on the exit curtain. "We should—"

"Wait." Ravani turned and saw that Virginia was standing in the middle of the room, eyes serious. "Come here for a second, Rav."

Ravani reluctantly released the curtain and walked to stand before her. "What is it?"

"I'm going to ask you something, and I don't want you to freak out."

"Okay."

Virginia frowned and furrowed her brow. "Ravani Foster, I want you to kiss me."

Ravani's heart, still racing from the witch, stopped altogether. The Haunted House of Horors suddenly seemed much, much scarier.

"What?" he said, or thought he said, or wanted to say, or tried to say. He wasn't sure if any sound actually came out.

"Relax. This isn't romantic. It's practical."

Ravani's mouth was dry, his stomach swirling.

"Practical?" he squeaked.

"Yes. You haven't kissed anyone yet, have you?"

"No," Ravani said quick, shaking his head.

"Me neither. But think about it. At some point, I'm going to be ready for my first kiss. I don't know when that's gonna be, or where I'm gonna be. And a first kiss should be with someone special. Someone you trust." She took a step closer to him. "I don't know if someone like that is going to be around when I'm ready. But I trust you, Rav."

Ravani gulped. "Am I . . . special to you?" he asked breathlessly. It was, perhaps, an embarrassing question to ask. A *needy* question. But sometimes souls *are* needy. Sometimes souls need to *know* something, not just hope it.

Virginia rolled her eyes and sighed. "Of course. Aren't I special to you?"

Ravani nodded, a small smile on his lips.

"Good. And this is the perfect place."

Ravani looked right, to the open coffin. Left, to the tilting tombstones.

"It is?" he asked.

She reached out and grabbed both Ravani's shoulders and pulled him to her so that they were nearly nose to nose. He looked into her solemn, serious eyes.

"Will you be my first kiss, Ravani Foster?"

He tried to take a breath.

"I'll be yours if you'll be mine, Virginia Deering."

Virginia leaned forward. Ravani stretched his neck to meet her.

Their lips touched.

They held them there for a breathless breath. Or two, perhaps. Then she stepped back.

They looked at each other. Ravani looked confused. Virginia just looked thoughtful.

"Huh," she said.

"Yeah," Ravani said.

"I'm not sure what all the fuss is about. Honestly, the cupcake was way better. No offense."

"None taken."

Virginia licked her lips. "You taste like corn dog."

Ravani licked his own. "You taste like caramel apple."

"Could be worse."

With that, she walked over to the exit and pulled the curtain to the side.

"Let's hope this doesn't lead to Sammy's corn dog stand," she said, then slipped out of sight.

Ravani paused for a moment, looking back into the Grewsome Gallery. He hadn't ever thought about his first kiss, but if he had, it isn't likely he would have imagined it taking place in a haunted house. It did seem like an absolutely appropriate place to kiss a girl like Virginia Deering, though. She was, after all, both a ghost and a creep.

He smiled.

It wouldn't be true to say that he felt like an entirely different person after having his first kiss. But it wouldn't be true to say he felt entirely the same, either. Kissing can be confusing.

At that moment, in that place, with that girl, Ravani liked the story that he was in. He liked it very much.

Life, though, does not always stick to the story that we like, and it does not always stick to the story that we expect, and it certainly does not always stick to the story that we want.

Chapter Twenty-Seven

In Which There Is Hide,
and Seek, and Found

The window slid open soundlessly beneath the Hunter's fingers. The window was always locked, but it hadn't been this night. Which, of course, was no coincidence. The window had been open during the day, to let in the breeze. And, while it had been open, someone with very sharp nails and very steady fingers had slipped a small bit of clay into the window's lock housing. A very small bit. Unnoticeable. But big enough to keep the latch from catching when the nurse at the Endless Days Retirement Home had closed it after dinner. Very small things can be very important.

The Hunter climbed through the window. Like a cat. Velvet paws.

He stopped and listened. There were no footsteps, no alarms. Someone coughing, but far away, down a hall and behind a door. The Hunter did not care about the person coughing. Not in any sense, and not at all.

There was a desk in the room, and two chairs, and a clock, and several plants. The Hunter didn't care about any of it. Because in the corner of the room there was a filing cabinet. And that is where the Hunter moved to, with silent steps.

Most people, if they were hunting children, and if they had found a scrap of paper that held a phone number, and if they'd then discovered that the phone number connected to a retirement home, would have thought it to be a dead end. Because, for most people, it would have been.

Not for the Hunter, though, of course.

He had found the retirement home's address, and then he had driven to the retirement home, and then he had watched the retirement home. He had seen that the retirement home had several cars, but no trucks, and that the tires on the cars did not match the treads that had been left on the old dirt road in the forest by Madame Murdosas Home for Wastrels Foundlings & Orphans.

But that was not a dead end, either.

Because the Hunter had hunted this prey before, these seven children who were alone together. And he knew they were different from all the other souls he'd hunted before. He knew they would stay together, and he knew that they would not return to where he had caught them before, and he knew that they would need a place to hide. A house. A large house. A large house that was empty. And the Hunter knew that there were several reasons a large house might become empty.

Including people who move because they are too old to care for a large house. They might move, perhaps, to a retirement home.

The Hunter pulled a small flashlight from his pocket. He clicked it on. Its light was red and dim. Just enough for him to see, but not enough to shine out windows, or under doors, or catch anyone's eye. He shone the light on the file cabinet and scanned, very carefully, the labels on each drawer. The Hunter took some files out of the drawer, carried them over to the desk, sat down, and began to read.

Each file contained information on one of the residents of the Endless Days Retirement Home, arranged in alphabetical order. Almost all of the information in the files was uninteresting. Alma Aguilar had a peanut allergy, which was unimportant to the Hunter (but probably very important to Alma Aguilar). Eugene Bergenstein needed to take his heart medicine three times a day, which was three times more than the Hunter cared about. Gladys Breckenridge had *Skydiving* listed under her hobbies, which was actually *very* interesting, but not to the Hunter.

The Hunter looked at all this information, because the Hunter looked at everything. But there was one part of the form that he was most interested in. It was labeled PREVIOUS ADDRESS.

The Hunter took a small notepad and pen out of his pocket. He held the bloodred flashlight in his very sharp teeth. And he wrote down the previous address of each of the Endless Days Retirement Home residents.

Alma Aguilar had moved from Millburg. Her address went into the Hunter's notepad. Eugene Bergenstein's address in Fort Oyster went below it. Gladys Breckenridge had lived on Sewage Street, in Forge City. It was an atrocious name for a street, but the Hunter wrote it down without judgment.

But, then. In the fourth file. The one labeled CROWARD, ARTHUR. Right there, beneath where it listed *Undertaker* under previous occupation, was the space for previous address.

But Arthur Croward didn't have an address listed. Or, rather, he'd *had* an address listed, but it had been crossed out darkly with a thick black marker. It was unreadable. It was hidden.

"*Very*," the Hunter breathed in a whisper, "*interesting*."

There was no reason why a retired undertaker's address would be hidden. Well. There was at least *one* reason, the Hunter knew. Often, if something is hiding, it's because it is being sought. If there is *hide*, there is almost always *seek*.

The Hunter bent closer, narrowing his eyes. The address was indeed lost in thick black ink. At least, the street name and number were. The town, though. The Hunter could just see, sticking out from the black scribble that sought to hide it, the top round curve of an *S* at the beginning. And he could see, many letters later, the tall stems of two lowercase *T*s, or perhaps *L*s, near (but not quite at) the end.

A few minutes later, his notepad full of addresses, the Hunter carefully placed all the files back in the cabinet. He picked the bit of clay out of the window latch and put it in his pocket before he left. The Endless Days Retirement Home director, when she arrived to work the next day, wouldn't have the slightest clue that he had ever been there. Because the Hunter knew that prey is most easily caught when it doesn't know it's being hunted.

An hour later, the Hunter was sitting at the table in his very quiet, very small, and very tidy home. A map was spread out before him. His eyes searched it, spiraling out in widening circles from the Endless Days Retirement Home.

His eyes stopped their circling. They stayed, focused and unblinking, on the small black dot of a town he'd never been to before. It started with a capital *S*, and it had two lowercase *L*s toward its end. SLAUGHTERVILLE, the dot was labeled.

"Ah," the Hunter said, "ha."

Chapter Twenty-Eight

In Which a Name Is Forged,
and a Toilet Is Cleaned

On the morning of the big race, Ravani grinned at the sunlight shining in his window. It was race day. He, Ravani Foster, was going to finally, actually, be one of the Slaughterville children splashing and laughing in the Red River Raft Race *with his friend.*

Welcome to someday, indeed.

He threw back his blankets and leaped into the day.

He was heading down for breakfast when he noticed a form, just where he'd left it on his desk, with his own name and age filled out. His grin died, though, when he noticed the bold words, right at the top: *Teams Must Be Registered to Participate.*

His heart plummeted into his stomach.

He raced back down the stairs, stopped quick at the table so his mother could scribble her name under parent signature, and then he was out the front door at a run and across the street and then hammering on the Deerings' door.

Virginia answered the door sweaty-faced, with her hair pulled back in a ponytail and her hands in rubber gloves, a bucket in her hand.

"Hey," she said. "It's cleaning morning. You here to help?"

"No!" Ravani panted out. He held up the registration form. "I forgot to sign us up for the race! We need to—"

Virginia held up a hand, halting his panicked outburst. "Got it. Colt!" she said over her shoulder. "Get out here."

A minute later, Colt joined them on the front porch.

"This better be better than scrubbing a toilet," he said. "I was just getting into my rhythm."

"We're on a schedule here. Quit flapping your lips and work your magic on the form, brother."

Colt *hmm*ed his lips. "Is that how you ask for a favor?"

"Yes. That is exactly how I ask for a favor."

"Don't I know it. Fine, beloved sister, since you asked so nice."

Colt took the pen from Ravani and got to work. "I'll just do all the parent parts. You do the other stuff. Makes it look more convincing to have two styles. What's our dear mother's Slaughterville name again?"

"Florence," Virginia answered.

"Right."

Colt signed in flowing, graceful cursive: *Florence Deering.* Ravani blinked in disbelief. It was uncanny. The name looked nothing like a thirteen-year-old boy's handwriting. Just like Beth's voice through the kitchen door, Colt's flowery writing was amazingly, unquestionably grown-up.

"There you go, darling," Colt said, but then pulled the form back when Virginia reached for it. "Aren't you gonna say 'Thank you'?"

"Isn't there a toilet you should be getting back to?" Virginia said.

Colt *tsk*ed his tongue.

"Is that any way to talk to your mother?" he asked, but handed the paper to Ravani.

"You're amazing," Ravani said, looking at the flawless fake signature.

"Don't encourage him," Virginia said. "Off you go. See you later, comrade."

Ravani hopped down the porch steps. And then he stopped. And he made a choice. A *small* choice, he thought.

Lives—and stories—are shaped by choices, big and small. Sometimes, though, a soul makes a choice and doesn't even realize it. Or, it doesn't realize that the small choice it made will have very large consequences.

It would be faster to cut through the woods rather than travel through town. And more pleasant, perhaps, to walk with the trees and the birds. So he chose to walk around the Ragabonds' house and down to the creek, past the *Creepy Freak*, and down through the trees along the bank.

Ah, choices.

Chapter Twenty-Nine

In Which There Is a Hammer,
but No Nails

Ravani was approaching the bridge, the race form in his hand, when he heard them.

There was hammering, and some sloshing, and voices.

It was, of course, Donnie. It was always Donnie.

Ravani bent down, peeking through the bushes.

Donnie and Stevie were standing in the mud on the creek shore, under the bridge, shirtless and muddy. Behind them was their boat: a jumble of boards and plywood nailed and roped together on top of some old car tire inner tubes.

They hadn't seen him yet.

He looked around. There was a hopscotch of rocks in the creek where he stood. He could cross there, sneak up around through the woods, and Donnie and Stevie would never know about his close call.

It was a good plan. He began his tottering, silent escape.

It was the last rock that got him. It always is, isn't it?

The rock wobbled; Ravani teetered; he swung his free leg wildly and cartwheeled his hands; and then he fell. He landed off-balance in the calf-deep creek and took two splashing steps to stay upright.

"What was that?" Donnie's voice carried up the creek.

"You think it's a bear?" Stevie asked quickly. Bears seemed to be a frequent concern for Stevie Mueller.

"Let's find out," Donnie answered.

Ravani ran without thinking.

"It's a kid!" Stevie's voice shouted. "I saw a shirt!"

Ravani squeezed more speed out of his skinny legs. Or tried to. They just didn't have that much juice to begin with.

"It's Ravioli!" Donnie panted, his voice breathless and triumphant. Then it dropped down to meaningful menace. "You better stop, Ravioli!"

It was the *better* that was the worst. Because Ravani, of course, knew what Donnie meant. Donnie didn't have to say the *or else* out loud.

Ravani stopped running. And he turned to face Donnie and Stevie.

They came up, sweating and smirking.

Ravani steeled himself for what was to come. He would be teased, possibly shoved, certainly humiliated. Nothing new, he was sure.

But then Donnie's eye caught the paper in Ravani's hand. "Whatcha got there?"

Ravani's mouth went dry. "Nothing."

"That ain't nothing. Hand it over."

"It's mine," Ravani said, but even as the words left his mouth Donnie was snatching the paper out of his hand.

"You gotta be kidding me," Donnie said with a snort, reading the paper. "You think *you're* doing the boat race?"

Stevie cackled. "What?! Who'd ever race with *him*?"

Donnie squinted at the form, then at Ravani. "Who the heck is Virginia Deering?"

Ravani blinked miserably and bit his lip. Donnie's eyes widened knowingly.

"Ah. She's that creep, right? *Pfft.*" He held the paper out toward Ravani, but lifted it out of reach when Ravani grabbed at it. "Uh-uh," he said, holding the paper up in both hands. "*This* ain't happening, Ravioli." With sadistic slowness, he ripped the entry form in half. Then in half again. And again. "The race ain't for babies. Or creeps. Or freaks."

Ravani gulped down the pain in his throat. He didn't want to give Donnie the satisfaction of seeing him cry. But all the world was blurry.

"You ain't racing, are you, Ravioli?" Donnie asked, throwing the paper scraps in his direction. Ravani, blinking through the blur, saw Donnie's raised eyebrow, heard the warning in his voice. Ravani hesitated for a breath, perhaps two. Virginia was counting on him to do the race. But all the Ragabonds were counting on him to keep their secret.

"I . . . couldn't I . . . ," Ravani mumbled.

"*You ain't racing, are you, Ravioli?*" Donnie repeated, his voice dropping to an even lower seethe.

Throat tight, Ravani shook his head.

"I wanna hear you say it, loser," Donnie growled.

Ravani swallowed. "I'm not racing." His voice was a sparrow with a broken wing.

"That's right. Or else you know what I'll do, don't you?"

Ravani nodded.

"What? What'll you do, Donnie?" Stevie asked breathlessly.

"Shut up, Stevie," Donnie growled. "None of your business."

"Hey," Stevie said abruptly, peering up at the trees. "What's all that junk?"

Donnie's eyes looked up. His brow wrinkled in confusion.

Ravani looked up, too. And then silently cursed.

His fleeing feet, by habit or accident, had led him to the one place he didn't want Donnie to follow him.

"It's . . . *birdhouses*," Donnie said. An unpleasant smile bloomed on his face and his eyes dropped to Ravani. "You made all these, didn't you, freak?"

Ravani looked up at Haven Hollow: the sloped roofs, the carefully carved holes, the perches and porches, the reds and blues and greens. All the little homes he'd crafted and hung. For a moment, he saw it all through Donnie's eyes. Shabby and silly and senseless. Like a paper piano.

But, no. Virginia had been right, that day in her bedroom. He couldn't look at the world through Donnie's eyes.

He looked back to Donnie. He lifted his chin. "Yeah," he said. "I built them, and I hung them up. Like a little town. Some of them are for finches, and some are for sparrows, and some—"

"I don't *care*," Donnie spat. "It's stupid."

Ravani shook his head and looked Donnie right in his eyes.

"It's not," he said, his voice soft but firm. "It's wonderful."

His voice felt different in his throat. Like it was trying on new shoes. Shoes that finally fit, shoes that were at last big enough. His skin hummed. He was gold.

Donnie's jaw tightened. His eyes glittered like shark teeth.

"I don't know what's gotten into you, Ravioli. Actually, I do. It's *her*, ain't it? You think that because someone is stupid enough to not see what a loser you are, that changes anything? Well, guess what?" Donnie leaned in, his sweaty cheeks flushed red. "It. Don't. Change. Nothing. You're the same little freak you've always been. And you always will be."

Ravani shook his head. "I'm not, though. And you're not the boss of me."

Donnie breathed through flared nostrils. "You. Are. And. I. Am."

He held his hand out to Stevie. And Stevie handed Donnie something, something that Ravani hadn't noticed he'd been holding until that moment.

A hammer.

Donnie took the hammer by the dull iron of its head and held the wooden handle out toward Ravani.

"Every one of them," he said.

Ravani's breath stopped when he realized what Donnie meant. All his heroic tingling faded to shivers. All his gold flaked off.

He shook his head. "No, Donnie, *please*. They're homes. There's *nests* in them. You can't—"

"*I'm* not gonna do anything. You are."

Ravani shook his head harder. "I won't. *Please*, Donnie."

"It's your choice, Ravioli. Do it. Or I blab your little secret."

"What secret?" Stevie asked.

"Shut up, Stevie," Donnie and Ravani said together.

In the trees around them, birds chirped merrily. Wings flapped as feathered bodies flitted from branch to branch, and from home to home.

Ravani looked at the hammer, waiting for his hand.

He had thought he could keep them safe. He had thought he could have a friend. He had thought he could *be* a friend. He had thought, for a moment, that he could be something more than he'd always been. The funny thing about moments, though, is that they don't last long.

Sometimes a soul dreams. Yes. But sometimes, also, a soul wakes up.

"Your," Donnie repeated, "choice."

Chapter Thirty

In Which Words Are Said,
and Things Are Broken

Ravani walked up Offal Road toward his house. He was going to lock himself in his room and not come out. Ever, possibly, but at least for the rest of the day. He couldn't face Virginia.

Alas, though. None of Ravani's plans were working out that day.

"Hey, Ravani," Virginia's voice called out from her porch. A rug was hung over the railing and she was standing sweaty next to it, a stick in her hand. He waved and quickened his step.

"Did you turn in the form?" she asked, dropping the stick and hopping over the railing. Ravani kept walking. "Hey! Where you going?"

Ravani stopped and turned around. He was going to have to face her eventually.

"We're not racing," he said, and he said it surly.

Her frown deepened.

"What do you mean? Why not?"

Ravani didn't want to say. So he didn't. Instead, he told the truth that he'd finally realized in the woods with Donnie.

"You're gonna leave, Virginia," he said.

Her eyes slid to his porch and back, making sure no one was listening. "Yep. Someday."

Welcome to someday, Ravani wanted to say. *You're already here.* But he didn't. "That's not exactly breaking news. What's that got to do with the race?"

"When you run away, I'm still gonna be stuck here. Alone. And Donnie's still gonna be here. And . . . and it'll be worse—" His voice broke off, not sure what he was going to say. *It'll be worse being lonely after knowing how wonderful it is to have a friend,* perhaps.

Virginia clicked her tongue. "Oh. You ran into Donnie, huh? He tell you not to race or something?" She rolled her eyes. "Get over it, Rav."

Ravani's anger flared hot.

"Get over it?" He spat the words furiously. He was mad at Donnie, mad at himself, mad at Virginia for her rolling eyes and bored voice when it felt like his whole world was falling apart. Now was the time. The time to tell her the truth. Time to let her know the danger she was in, the danger that he'd been fighting to protect her from. He took one breath to steady his shaking voice.

"Listen. Donnie Carter knows—"

But Virginia rolled her eyes again and cut him off. "Ugh, stop worrying about dumb ol' Donnie Carter. You can't keep letting him boss you around, Rav."

Ravani sputtered, his terrible secret forgotten. "*Let* him? You think I *let* him?"

Virginia flared her nostrils. And when she spoke, she actually had a little fire in her voice, too. "Yeah, kind of. The Donnies of the world are always gonna try and tell you you're worthless. It's your choice whether you believe them or not."

Ravani swallowed a painful lump in his throat, his eyes

burning. "What do you know? You guys just run away when things get tough."

Virginia's shoulders rose and fell in a steadying breath. Her eyes were getting colder by the second.

"I know plenty," she said. "And I know that choosing who *you* want to be is a lot better than letting someone else choose. You wanna race, then race. Are you gonna just go back to being a scaredy-cat when I leave, hiding in your house?"

Tears boiled into Ravani's eyes. "I was fine before you showed up," he said. "I wish you'd never come."

They were cruel words. The cruelest words he could say, he thought. He was wrong.

But Virginia didn't gasp, or cry, or shoot cruel words back.

Her face kept the thoughtful seriousness it always had. But her eyes shone with a new, held-back wetness.

They weren't tears. But only because Virginia wouldn't let them be.

"We're supposed to be comrades," she said.

Ravani's soul shivered in shame. But anger is a great way to keep warm.

"What does that even mean?" Ravani scoffed. "You always call everyone else a liar. But *you're* the liar. Telling me I was, what, *gold*? I tried. And it was stupid. I'm not anything you thought I was. I'm not your stupid paper piano." The words almost took his own breath away. He kept going even though he hated everything he was saying. Souls are like that, sometimes. "And I'm not Annabel's stupid broken binoculars. You can't make something be something it's not, just with wishes and lies and make-believe. There ain't no magic, Virginia. I don't believe you anymore."

Virginia's eyes, when he got the nerve to look in them, were clear. The almost-tears were gone.

"Okay," she said. Her voice was flat. Her face stony. It was the voice and face of a stranger, not a friend. "We both made choices. I guess we both chose wrong." She shook her head. "I can't believe I wasted my kiss on you."

And then Virginia turned and walked away. She didn't stomp, or sniffle, or clench her hands into fists. Just walking, like Ravani didn't even exist, like she'd already forgotten he was there.

Ravani had thought that nothing cut deeper than cruel words from an enemy. He'd had his share, after all, and they had cut deep. But he'd been wrong.

Cruel words from a friend cut far, far deeper . . . whether you were the one hearing them, or the one saying them.

CHAPTER THIRTY-ONE

In Which There Is Bleeding, and Mending

Ravani Foster could find no peace for all the rest of that race-less race day.

He tried hiding in his bedroom. But his bedroom had a window that looked out across the street, toward a two-story house that held seven stories and one golden-haired girl who, perhaps, hated him.

He tried going downstairs, but downstairs was too full of quiet fathers home from work and mothers with sharp eyes and probing questions. The funny thing about a broken heart is that for something held so deep inside, it's surprisingly hard to hide.

Finally, he decided to try leaving the house. The front yard was out of the question, of course. So Ravani made his way out the back door and into the garage. It was shadowy and spidery and silent, so it was a good match for his soul.

Grainy, early-evening light seeped in through the dusty window onto the workbench. The tools hung quiet in their places on the pegboard. Cans of paint stood in the corner.

Sitting on the workbench was a half-done birdhouse he'd started a couple of weeks before.

It might feel nice, he supposed, to build something. To put something together, instead of tearing something apart.

He pulled the hammer down and grabbed the board that was

to be the back of the birdhouse and lined it up with the two pieces already joined. Propped it steady against a two-by-four. Carefully tapped a nail in until it was rooted straight, then buried it home. Picked up another. Did the same. Two more, and the back of the birdhouse was attached. It'd make a fine addition to his village.

Ravani eyes went blurry. He rubbed them clear. Picked up the next cut board.

He imagined himself hanging the birdhouse, then stepping back to admire it. The sun shining down through the branches, perhaps. It would be wonderful, wouldn't it? Wouldn't it?

He rubbed his eyes again. Cleared his throat.

It, suddenly, wasn't a happy thought. Himself, standing alone there in the woods, with his birdhouses.

Just like a boy, standing alone in a midnight window. And a boy, standing alone in a musty garage.

This wasn't how stories were supposed to go. Once upon a time, he had been a lonely and friendless boy, and then he wasn't, and now he was again, and he didn't think that a soul's *once upon a time* was supposed to match its *ever after*. Things were supposed to get better, he thought.

Perhaps, though, that was just for heroes.

He sniffed.

Held another nail. Swung the hammer.

His eyes weren't focused, though, and the hammer hit the nail crooked and bent it and sheared off and then slammed with a meaty *thud* into his thumb and pain flashed up his arm and he flinched and the board broke loose and clattered free. He swore and dropped the hammer and stuck his throbbing thumb in his mouth and just stood there, tasting blood and hurting.

He heard a sound, and realized it was a sob, and then realized it was his. Another one came, then another.

He wasn't crying over his thumb. Although it did, to be honest, hurt a whole awful lot.

Everything was a mess. He wanted to blame Donnie for all of it. But he found that he couldn't. Donnie had made choices, yes. Ugly ones. But Ravani had made choices, too. And Ravani had seen how Donnie's father treated him, had heard whispers about the man's meanness and roughness. Donnie, perhaps, wasn't where the ugliness started. It had been given to him, and he was just passing it along to Ravani. Who, after all, would want to hold on to it? And then he, Ravani, had passed it along to Virginia.

Choices.

Ravani wiped at his cheeks with his sleeve. Tried to breathe in through his clogged nose.

He was startled by a sound at his back. The door swinging open on its rusty hinges, a cautious footstep. *Virginia!* he thought, turning around.

But it was his father. His bulky shape barely fitting in the doorway.

"Oh," his father rumbled, "sorry. Didn't know you were in here." He started to back out, but then his eyes rose to Ravani's tear-soaked face and he stopped, one hand on the doorknob. "Oh. Are you . . . mmm . . . are you . . . okay?"

Yes, Ravani opened his mouth to say, *I'm fine*. Because, usually, that's what he would say, whether it was true or not. It was easier that way. Easier to hold some truths down deep. And, besides, he and his father didn't talk. Because Ravani was birds, and his father was baseball.

Sometimes, though, when a soul is lost in darkness, there is a reaching out.

So, "No," Ravani chose to say instead. "I'm not."

His father opened his mouth. Ravani didn't know it, but his father opened his mouth to say, *Oh, all right, I'll get your mother.* Because, usually, that's what he would say. It was easier that way. Because his son was birds, and he was baseball.

Sometimes, though, a soul realizes that what it's always done isn't necessarily what it always should do. Sometimes, when one soul reaches out, another reaches back. Even if it isn't sure how.

So his father swallowed, and stepped through the doorway, and walked over to Ravani.

Choices.

"What's wrong?"

Ravani didn't know what to say. It's hard, when the true answer was *everything.* So he ducked his head at the birdhouse.

"I broke it," he said.

"Oh." His father picked up the pieces of the birdhouse. Turned them in his hands to look at them. "We can fix this," he murmured.

"I . . . I broke everything."

His father pursed his lips. "Ah," he said. He breathed in deep, let it out. "Donnie?"

Ravani nodded.

"Virginia?"

Ravani nodded again.

His father cleared his throat. Opened his mouth. Closed it. Frowned.

"You can't fix Donnie," he said.

Ravani sighed. "I know."

"But Virginia . . ."

His father pointed at the bent nail sticking out of the board. "First, you gotta take back what you got wrong." He slid the hammer toward Ravani and handed him the board. Ravani picked up the hammer and turned it around and pried out the ruined nail.

"Mm-hmm." His father pulled a tube of wood glue out of a drawer. "Now, you gotta mend the damage you did." He pointed with his blunt, calloused finger at the splintery holes left behind. Ravani squinted and held his hands steady and squirted the wood glue into the holes, and then along the edge of the boards. His father reached and held the two boards together.

"Then, you make it right."

Ravani held the hammer in one hand and picked up a fresh nail with the other. Pressed its point into the hole. Carefully, holding his breath, tapped it home. Picked up another nail, did the same. Then three more, one by one, his father holding the wood steady.

He set down the hammer. His father did the same with the birdhouse, gently.

"There," he said. "See? Even better, now." His father had already been speaking softly, because he always did, but he lowered his head and dropped his voice even further. "Sometimes, when you break something, if you fix it right, it turns out even stronger than it was before."

Ravani sniffed. "I don't know if people are as easy, though."

His father shrugged. "Even easier, sometimes. 'Cause people, usually, want to be fixed."

Ravani shook his head. Beginning with a truck in the moonlight, his days and nights had been filled lately with the unexpected, good and bad. But nothing, perhaps, was as unexpected as all these words from his father.

"How . . . how do you know?" he asked.

"I been married for a while, son," he said. "I've broke my share of birdhouses."

Ravani looked at his father. His father who almost never spoke but who could fix things, and build things, and lift things, his father with the broad shoulders and thick arms and steady hands. His father who was never scared, never weak, never pushed around. His father who had a son who was none of the strong, sure things that he was.

Ravani's eyes filled again.

"I'm sorry," he said. "I'm sorry that I'm so—" His voice choked off. "I'm sorry that I'm not . . ." He took a shaky breath. "I'm birds. And you're baseball." He swallowed through the ache in his throat and finished, "I'm sorry that I'm not the son you want."

He said it like it was true. Because, of course, it was. To his soul it was true.

But our souls don't always know the truth, even when they think they do.

There was a moment. Two or three, perhaps. Of silence. Of Ravani, teary-eyed and red-faced, staring at the floor. Of his father, standing silent.

Then Ravani heard a rustle of clothes, a scrape on the concrete floor, a breath. He blinked away his tears and saw that his father was kneeling before him so that his face could look into his own.

"I don't know how to talk to you," his father said, his voice almost a whisper. "That's true. But that's my failing. Not yours." He licked his lips, looking for words. He found a question. "You know why I fell in love with your mama?"

Ravani blinked. "No."

His father chewed his lip for a second, then held up his hands. They were scarred, and big, and strong, with dull nails and hairy knuckles and blunt fingers like sausages.

"I'm good with these. Always have been. I can take things apart, put things together. My father was like me. My brothers, too. We don't sing, or write poems, or know the names of birds. We don't paint pretty pictures. We've got strong arms, and we work with our hands. And I'm proud of that. I'm good at it. It's honest." His eyebrows lifted, and a little sparkle of wonder kindled in his eyes. "But your mama was nothing like me. She could look at this . . . this *ugly* world, and see the pretty stuff. She could even look at this ugly man, with my bloody apron and my broken nose, and maybe see something pretty in *me*." His father cleared his throat. His face was a little red. But he took a breath and kept talking. "That's why I love your mama. 'Cause when I'm with her, I can . . . sometimes . . . see the prettiness, and the poems, and the birds." His father's rough hands reached down and took Ravani's. Ravani looked at his own hands, saw how small and soft they looked, lost in the great coarseness of his father's. "Listen, son. There's more'n enough baseball in the world. And bloody knuckles. What the world needs a little more of is birds, maybe. And boys like you." He squeezed Ravani's hands until Ravani looked up into his eyes.

"You are all the things I love about your mama. You are *exactly* the son I want. Even if I don't know how to say it."

You are exactly the son I want.

His father, it turned out, *did* know how to say it. Perhaps without realizing it, he had said exactly the words that his son had desperately needed to hear.

Ravani's soul shivered and shimmered.

His father stood up with a grunt. Scratched awkwardly at the back of his neck.

"So you . . . broke things with that girl, then?"

Ravani nodded miserably.

"Go fix it, then."

Ravani looked away, up and out the dusty window. The window where, once upon a time, he'd seen a trapped bird fly through to freedom.

Virginia was going to leave, someday. Someday soon, probably.

So perhaps, in the *ever after* that was right around the corner, he wasn't going to be a boy who was a good friend. But he could be, perhaps, a boy who *had* been a good friend, before his friend had left. At the very least, he could be a soul who had chosen to try.

He started to walk toward the door. Stopped, though, and looked back at his father.

There was something he ought to say. It's important to say things that ought to be said. Sometimes, though, it's even better to show them.

He took a quick step and wrapped his father in a tight hug from behind, his arms stretching around the man's muscly trunk. His father tensed for a moment. Then he blew out a deep breath, and his body eased into the hug. He patted Ravani's hand clumsily.

Ravani hadn't said it, but still his father had heard it. Souls are like that, sometimes.

"Me too, son," he said.

CHAPTER THIRTY-TWO

In Which Rocks Are Thrown, and Truths Are Spoken

Colt was sitting on a chair on the front porch when Ravani walked up. He didn't get up, or grin, or holler a howdy.

"Is Virginia home?"

"Who's asking?" Colt's voice was cold, his eyes colder.

"Um. Me."

Colt shook his head. "Then, nope."

Ravani got it. He was on the outside now. The Ragabonds were a family. They looked out for each other.

"I need to talk to her, Colt."

"Well she don't need to talk to you. And she don't want to."

Ravani stepped forward, braving the hostility in the older boy's eyes. "Look. I messed up. Bad. But . . ." He blew out a breath. It was time for truth. "I've never had a friend before. I've never *been* a friend before. So . . . so, I guess I'm still figuring out how to do it."

Colt's eyes didn't flicker or soften.

"It's like . . . it's like catching frogs," Ravani said desperately.

"Really," Colt said dully.

"Yeah. If you don't know what you're doing, you blow it. You get muddy. You make a mess. You chase the frog away. But you keep trying. Until you get it right. I gotta get this right, Colt."

"So in this equation, my sister is a frog?"

"Um. Kind of. But only, like, in the sense that—"

"No, no, I like that part." Colt stood up and walked to the front door, put his hand on the knob. "But you still gotta go."

"Wait! Colt, please. I'm sorry." He stepped up onto the porch's bottom stair so he could almost whisper and still be heard. "Maybe I don't deserve to be a friend. But Virginia deserves to have one. More than anyone I know. Don't you think?"

Colt let his hand fall off the doorknob. "Yeah," he said softly. His eyes found Ravani's. "'Course she does." He shook his head. "Still, I can't let you in," he said again, then narrowed his eyes. "She's in her bedroom."

Ravani's shoulders slumped. He'd failed.

"She's . . . in *her bedroom*," Colt repeated. He raised his eyebrows. And then Ravani got it. Colt wasn't giving him the door. But he was giving him a window.

Ravani dashed around to the side of the house and out into the yard a bit so he could see the side window to Virginia's room.

"Virginia," he called up to the window.

"Virginia!" Louder.

Colt stepped forward and leaned on one of the porch beams, watching. But the window stayed closed and empty.

Ravani shifted impatiently. The sun was close to setting. He didn't want the day to end with these words unsaid.

He looked down at the ground around his feet, picked a few pebbles out of the grass. He took aim, then threw the first one. It bounced off the gutter of the porch roof.

"You want me to throw one, or . . . ," Colt started to ask sympathetically.

"No! I can do it," Ravani hissed. He shook his head and started throwing faster. One hit the roof again. One missed completely and went rattling around the porch, making Colt duck. Two more dinged off the gutter. One hit the wall a few feet to the left of the window. He was panting by then, sweat dripping on his forehead.

He was down to one pebble. He cocked his arm back, taking aim. But then a voice stopped him. A flat, deadpan voice, scratchy at the bottom like the smell of a campfire.

"You are without a doubt the worst thrower I have ever seen."

Ravani spun.

Virginia was standing ten feet away, arms at her sides, half in sunlight and half in shadow. "I heard you talking to Colt. Came out the back door."

They stood there, the shadows long between them.

"Virginia, I'm sorry for what I—"

"I know you are," she cut in, her voice cool. "I'm not interested in your sorriness."

"Then . . . then why did you come out here?"

"Good question."

Ravani opened and closed his mouth. Virginia sighed.

"Three reasons, I guess. I heard what you said to Colt. That was nice. And you meant it. Second, all those awful things you said to me earlier? They were all lies, and I knew it. Which, in this case, is a point in your favor."

"Okay. What's the third reason?"

Virginia tucked in her lips. "I . . . I don't know how to be a friend, either. Or a comrade, I guess. I'm figuring it out, too. But

I'm pretty sure part of it is giving your comrade a chance to do the right thing. So, here you go. Say the right thing."

Ravani swallowed.

"Uh. What's the right thing to say?"

Virginia's eyes narrowed. "I'll know it when I hear it."

Ravani took a deep breath. He dug down, looking for all the words for all the truths his heart felt.

"I don't wish you'd never come here, Virginia. Not one little bit." Ravani took a steadying breath, his voice shaking. "Every day when I wake up, I'm glad that you're across the street and in my life, because if my heart could sing a song—"

"Oh for tripe's sake, Rav," Virginia interrupted with a scowl. "You want me to play a violin while you make this speech? Geez. You're trying too hard."

"Oh."

She took a step toward him. "Just say what I'm not. Then say what I am. And tell the truth."

Ravani nodded. He thought of his words from that morning. "You're not a liar. I don't know if I believe in the magic. But I believe in *you*, Virginia Deering. You're . . . you're my hero."

Virginia blinked.

"Better," she said, her voice uncharacteristically soft. "Now, say what you're not, and what you are."

That one was tougher. Ravani wasn't sure he knew who he was. He knew he didn't want to be who Donnie said he was. But was he really who Virginia said he was? Or was he something else he didn't know yet?

But perhaps it was okay not to know who you were supposed to be. As long as you were working on it. Perhaps being something better than you've been, or even just being who you think you oughta be, isn't really *a* choice. Maybe it's a thousand choices, and even more, over and over and over. Perhaps you have to keep choosing it again and again and again, every day.

"I'm not who I want to be, yet."

Virginia shrugged with one shoulder. "So what *are* you?"

Ravani looked up at the dusky pink clouds. Then back to Virginia.

"I'm . . . trying."

Virginia nodded. Then she smiled. Ravani smiled back.

"Good answer, comrade."

"I wanna be worth being your first kiss, Virginia."

"Wait . . . what now?" Colt's voice cut in from the porch. Ravani had completely forgotten he was standing there.

"Shut up, Colt," Virginia said without turning her head. "Inside, now."

There was a groan and a theatrical sigh and then the sound of a closing door.

Virginia took hold of Ravani's hand and looked into his eyes. "I'll be your creep, Ravani Foster, if you'll be my freak."

Ravani grinned and snorted. "Deal."

"Now, let's go race that coffin."

Ravani's grin faded. He let go of her hands.

"Oh. Right. Um. We still can't do the race, Virginia."

"Why in the world not?"

Ravani's mouth went dry. He'd just fixed it, and now he was gonna have to break it all again. It was time, though, to finally do the right thing.

"Donnie," he said. "Donnie knows." And then he told her

everything. How Donnie had overheard them under the bridge. The blackmail. The money. Other than her eyes getting a little wider with every revelation, she didn't react. Until he got to what had happened that morning, with the hammer in the woods, and the choice Donnie had given him.

"What'd you choose, Ravani?" she asked when he was done, her voice tight. Her eyes slid to look up the street. Was Sheriff Quigley already on her way?

Ravani held out his hands. Showed her the blisters from the hammer, the bloody scrapes and broken fingernails from smashing and prying apart an entire town of birdhouses.

"I had to choose between you or a bunch of birdhouses," he said. "It was easy. If I had to choose between you and just about anything, I'd choose you."

Virginia was frowning, her brow furrowed, looking first at Ravani's battered hands and then to the ground. She bit her lip pensively.

"This is bad," she murmured.

"I know. I'm sorry. You hate me."

Her eyes flashed to him. "I don't hate you. You definitely should've told me a long time ago. But you were trying to keep us safe. And you aren't the one who spilled the secret. That was Colt." She shook her head. "He's the dumbest smart person I know."

"But . . . we can't do the race. Donnie said so."

Virginia's eyebrows dropped.

"Donnie Carter doesn't get to choose what we do. We're racing."

"But—"

"I'll handle it. But first, we are racing that coffin, Rav." She swallowed and looked away, then repeated softly, "I'll handle the rest. After." She shook her head. "When does the race start?"

"A little after sunset."

"Then we better hurry."

Chapter Thirty-Three

In Which There Is a Pistol but No Bullet, and Smoke but No Fire

"Wow," Annabel said, looking down at the *Creepy Freak* in its hiding place by the creek.

"Yeah," Colt agreed with a whistle. "That's the fastest-looking coffin I ever saw."

"Thanks," Virginia said. "But we need less admiring and more carrying. Grab a handle, everyone."

Ravani and Colt each took a front handle, and Virginia and Annabel grabbed the ones at the back. There was quite a bit of grunting and groaning as they hoisted the vessel into the air between them and started off.

Down the creek, then across it. Stumbling and sweating, they made their way through the woods.

When they were almost to the bridge, Colt gave Ravani a sideways look and a smirk.

"So . . . you guys actually kissed?" He mumbled it soft, but apparently not soft enough.

"Drop it, Colt," Virginia growled.

But Colt's eyes were still on Ravani.

"It wasn't romantic," Ravani whispered, his face hot. "It was practical."

Colt's smirk grew. "That's a good line, Rav. I'm gonna borrow that someday."

"It wasn't my line. It was your sister's."

Colt's face dropped. "Oh. Gross."

They wrestled the boat up to the road. Ahead, Slaughterville was in full celebration mode. Banners were hung, the street was blocked off, children were running and chasing, and the salty smell of grilling meat wafted their way.

They made a bit of a scene once they got to the party. There wasn't time to go around, so they carried their flaming-red coffin right through the crowd. They got more than a few looks. "*Does that say . . . the* Creepy Freak?" Ravani heard someone whisper. It was a good thing that the Ragabonds were ready to be noticed, because they certainly were.

Up ahead Ravani saw the waterfront where the Red River Raft Race would take place. There was a churning mob of boisterous children and a jumble of boats lined up on a dock jutting out into the water. It looked like they'd made it just in time.

Ravani steered them toward a lady with a clipboard in her hands and a whistle around her neck. It was Mrs. Grunchly, the perpetually grouchy secretary at Slaughterville School (*Home of the Cleavers!*) and, apparently, race director.

The team she was talking to grunted their boat up onto their shoulders and hoisted it away toward the water. Mrs. Grunchly took a long drag off her cigarette and turned to them. Her eyes slid between them and she said, around her cigarette, "Just in the nick of time." She sounded more disappointed than relieved. "Last name?"

Ravani looked to Virginia, wide-eyed and frozen. Panicked realization washed over him.

Virginia squinted at him. "I don't think that's supposed to be a hard question," she said to him under her breath. "Your name is Foster."

"*I know that!*" Ravani hissed, "*but...*"

"Foster?" Mrs. Grunchly rasped, scanning her paperwork. "Hmmm. No Fosters registered. You sign up under your friend's name?" She blew out a cloud of white smoke through her nostrils.

"*I never signed us up!*" Ravani whispered urgently to Virginia. "*I never made—*"

"You ain't registered?" Mrs. Grunchly said. "Then you ain't racing, honey."

"I...I...I lost our sheet. But it was all filled out, and..."

Mrs. Grunchly rolled her eyes.

"I don't need a sad story, I need a...sweet Jesus, is that a *coffin?*"

Ravani gulped. "It *was* a coffin," Virginia deadpanned. "But now it's a boat."

"Huh," Mrs. Grunchly said, unimpressed. "That's a first." Her face hadn't been anything close to sweet before, but she managed to add even more sourness to it.

"Ma'am, I'm sorry we lost the paperwork," Virginia said, looking at the woman with her solemn version of puppy dog eyes. "But I *promise* it was all filled out proper, and if you'd just—"

"No form, no race," Mrs. Grunchly cut in with curt finality. She sucked in a lungful of smoke. "I wish I could help you, honey."

Virginia's eyes narrowed. "Liar."

"*Virginia!*" Ravani whispered.

Mrs. Grunchly's eyes narrowed right back. "Excuse me?"

"It's just a piece of paper," Virginia said, voice sullen. She seemed to have forgotten that paperwork made the world go round.

"Listen, kid," Mrs. Grunchly said, a bit of growl in the words. She pulled the cigarette from her mouth and pointed it at Virginia. "It ain't just a piece of paper. It's a legal requirement. Not that it's any of your business, but twenty years ago a boy named Tommy Wallace stood right where you are and entered this very race and then he fell out of his boat and he couldn't swim and he drowned. Body washed up three days later in Smelterville. His mama made a big fuss out of it on account of she'd never given her permission. We almost had to shut down the whole race." She took a long pull on her cigarette and blew out a cloud of bitter smoke. "And, honey, I ain't in the mood to deal with another Tommy Wallace headache."

Virginia blinked. She looked sideways at Ravani. "Lord, that got dark, didn't it?"

"Thank you, ma'am," Ravani said, tugging on Virginia's shirt. "Sorry to bother you."

Mrs. Grunchly just squinted at Virginia and blew one last cloud of smoke her way.

"Racers to the line!" she hollered, and slouched off toward the river without looking back.

"Rav!" Virginia spat, voice full of vinegar. "We can't just give up! We gotta—"

"Grab the boat," Ravani said, looking around at Colt and Virginia and Annabel. "Quick."

Ravani led them against the current of folks heading down to watch the race, and then turned them left to walk upriver. There was a walkway that ran along the river, and he shuffled them along it as fast as they could manage. Ravani had an idea. His stomach knotted. If it was just him, he wouldn't have considered it. But he had a comrade to think about.

"Pretty sure the race is that way, Frog Master," Colt said.

"We don't have that paper," Ravani grunted over his shoulder, not slowing down. "But we *do* have a boat, and we have a river. Just because we can't *enter* the race doesn't mean we can't *be* in the race. We just need our own starting line."

They cut down onto a rough path that led to an old, crumbling dock. It was rotten and missing boards here and there. It stretched crookedly out about thirty feet into the river, ending in a rough little shack where Ravani and his dad had spent a few awkward summer afternoons fishing.

He looked over toward the *real* dock with the *registered* racers. They were piling into their boats. There was laughing and shouting and splashing, and at least one boat had flipped over already. Mrs. Grunchly was pacing among them, barking orders. He prayed she wouldn't look their way anytime soon.

"Come on!"

They made their way out onto the dock. Panting, they set their boat down on the upriver side behind the shack. Ravani peeked through the shack's splintered walls. They were only about thirty yards from the real race.

"Let's get her in the water. We've gotta time this right."

With a heave, they sloshed the *Creepy Freak* into the river. She bobbed there, looking ready. Ravani grabbed the paddles and handed one to Virginia.

"You can swim, right, Rav?" she asked.

"Sure."

"Good. 'Cause I'm not really in the mood to deal with a Tommy Wallace headache, either."

From the other side of the shack, they heard a man shouting into a bullhorn. It was the mayor, giving his annual race kick-off speech.

"Get in," Rav said, his stomach suddenly a twisted knot of nerves. "It'll be any minute now." He and Colt held the *Creepy Freak* steady while Virginia carefully stepped in. She scooted up to the front and perched on her knees, paddle at the ready. Rav eased one foot in, holding tight to the sides. The coffin wobbled, and his heart pounded. The river was deep there, too deep to even see the bottom.

Downriver, he heard the chaos of the other racers at the starting line. Donnie was among them. He heard the hoots and voices of the crowd that had gathered to watch. The whole town, probably. He froze, one foot in the coffin.

Sometimes, when a soul is face-to-face with what it thought it wanted, it doesn't have the courage to make the leap. It's a big thing for a soul to jump from what has always been to what perhaps could be.

He swallowed his fear as best he could. Screwed on a smile to hold it down. Felt all his *somedays* line up and overlap and snap into the *one day* that he was right there in the middle of.

He stepped his other foot into the boat. Felt the boat rock, and sink lower, and settle steady. He lowered himself to his knees and grabbed his paddle from the dock.

Annabel was chewing her lip, brow furrowed. Colt eyed the boat dubiously.

"Don't lean or nothing. She'll tip for sure."

In the distance, the megaphone voice rose in both pitch and volume. The big moment was upon them.

"We gotta go," Ravani said. "Push us off, Colt."

Colt gave the bobbing coffin one more look, then grinned and shrugged. "All right. Well, uh, R.I.P., I guess, guys. Race in Peace."

With a little shove, he sent them gliding away from the dock.

"You paddle left, I'll paddle right," Virginia called back. "So we stay balanced."

It took them a few strokes to get the hang of it. They nearly capsized a couple of times, but stroke by stroke they found balance and dropped into a rhythm. By the time they came around the corner of the shack and into the main channel of the river, they were sailing smooth.

Colt and Annabel ran to the dock's end and *whoop*ed as they paddled by, picking up steam.

"Go get 'em, sis!"

The water swirled and sloshed around their oars as they dug them deep and pulled hard. The sky was on fire with pinks and purples and puffs of cloud like cannon fire. There was darkness at the edge, though. The world was fading from ripe peach to dark plum. Ravani Foster and that golden-haired girl charged their boat through the coming night, into battle.

Ahead of them, the other boats were all bunched at the starting rope, holding on. They were made from a motley assortment of junk and scrap: boards and pallets and barrels and washtubs and logs and tires and rope. No coffins, though.

Near the end, right over by the dock, Ravani saw Donnie and Stevie aboard their inner-tube raft.

They all had their backs to Ravani and Virginia and the *Creepy Freak*. Ravani scanned the crowd, saw the mayor with his bullhorn and Mrs. Grunchly with her clipboard. Neither of them was looking their way.

"Racers ready?" the mayor called. The kids clinging to their boats gave a holler. Virginia and Ravani paddled harder. The *Creepy Freak* was cruising, cutting through the water like a wooden torpedo. They were twenty yards back now.

"Racers set!"

The teams readied their paddles and oars, bodies tense and ready.

Ten yards back.

The mayor raised a starter's pistol into the air.

Ravani, squinting up between paddle strokes, saw Mrs. Grunchly turn her head. Right toward them. Her eyes went wide. Her eyebrows went angry.

Five yards.

Mrs. Grunchly's mouth curled open. Ready, Ravani was sure, to call foul. But whatever she had been going to say was lost in the *crack* of the pistol.

Just as they pulled even to the backs of the other boats, the rope went slack.

With a cheer, the boats churned into a wild melee of shouting and splashing and paddling and shouting and laughing, Virginia and Ravani and the *Creepy Freak* right in the middle of it all.

Chapter Thirty-Four

In Which There Are Fireworks and Water (and Then Even More Water)

The race was jostling, screaming, water-soaked chaos.

The boats bumped and rocked and knocked one another, a madhouse of tangled paddles and swinging arms and spraying water.

"Hey, watch it," Virginia growled to another boat when it veered into their path, but it wasn't their fault. Their boat was really just a bunch of barely lashed-together boards they were kneeling on top of, and after only twenty seconds of racing it was already coming apart. One of its passengers looked to Ravani, his eyes pleading, the water already a couple of inches up his legs. Ravani knew him from school, kind of. He was a nice enough kid.

"We're going down!" The kid's voice was a tremulous whisper.

"Can you swim?" Ravani asked.

The kid nodded. He reached out toward the *Creepy Freak*.

But, Ravani knew, life was tough . . . and there wasn't any room in his coffin. He frowned an apology and poked his paddle out, pushing the sinking ship away. The kid's mouth fell open in dismay as his boat slowly sank beneath him.

The *Creepy Freak* was a triumph, really. Slender and stream-lined, it glided smoothly past clumsier boats. They pulled clear of most of the mob and joined the pack at the front.

On the shore, the crowd was following along on the riverside walkway. Mothers and fathers were calling encouragement, little brothers and sisters were running and cheering. A few kids had sparklers crackling in their hands. Ravani had been among them, once upon a time, watching the excitement of the race. But now he was out in it, wet and dripping with it, just as he'd dreamed that someday he would be.

"Go, *Creepy Freak*, go!" Colt's holler rang out across the water.

"Yay, Virginia! Yay, Rav!" That voice was Annabel's. Ravani had someone cheering for him. For *him*. He paddled harder.

They were approaching the bend in the river, a big gentle curve to the left. Once they rounded that corner, the finish line would be in sight. Ravani put his head down and dug deep, ignoring the burn in his muscles, pulling them forward with everything that he had.

He snuck a sideways peek at the competition and got a shot of adrenaline: they were way ahead of almost everybody. There were only two boats up where they were, both to their left.

One of them was Donnie and Stevie's. Of course it was. They were rowing hard, eyes forward, faces red. Ravani gritted his teeth. Dug his paddle deeper. Pulled it back harder.

Virginia barked something but he couldn't hear her over the splashing and panting.

"What?"

She turned her head. "Turn the boat! You gotta steer us, Rav!"

Rav looked up. She was right. The river was turning, but they weren't. They were drifting wide, heading straight out into the middle instead of hugging the bank and following the curve like the other boats. The *Creepy Freak* was farther downriver, but the other boats were closer to the finish line.

Ravani stopped paddling and stabbed his oar down into the water on the right side of the boat. The water pulled at it and he gripped harder and braced his arms, and the nose of the *Creepy Freak* started to turn. Virginia was paddling for all she was worth and the bow drifted to the left and then they were heading the right way, cutting back across the river toward the other boats. He stopped steering and started paddling again and they surged forward.

A wild grin broke across Ravani's face.

Heading in the wrong direction can often be a fortunate accident in life. Their drift into the center of the river had been exactly that; the current was swifter there. The teams along the shore were thrashing and struggling through a lazy backwater that was scarcely moving at all. The *Creepy Freak*, on the other hand, was surging in moving water on a diagonal path that was going to pull them right into the lead.

"Faster!" Virginia grunted, but there wasn't any need; Ravani's heart was singing, his meager muscles straining, his lungs gulping . . . as were hers. Their boat pulled in front of Donnie's, cutting cross-river on an angle straight across his path, and they shot around the bend in the river in first place.

As they flew past, Ravani saw the moment when Donnie spotted them. His eyes widened and then narrowed. His jaw clenched and his arms started pumping double-time. His whole body was like a kicked hornets' nest. He locked eyes with Ravani and shook his head, lips snarling. *Don't you dare.*

Ravani just paddled harder and left Donnie's ugliness behind.

A hundred yards ahead, Ravani saw the dock that was the finish line.

The crowd running along the shore cheered louder as the boats splashed into the home stretch.

Somewhere, someone lit the fireworks. There was a series of ripping hisses as they rocketed into the sky, then pops and booms when they exploded. Bursts of light flashed and sparkled—red and blue and white, dancing in kaleidoscope reflections on the water. Like a million electric fireflies.

It didn't feel real to Ravani, for a breath or two. That moment, that life.

But then it did. Because it was. A smile broke out on his face, big and true.

He was soaking wet and there was water sloshing around his knees inside the boat from all the splashing. His muscles were on fire, his lungs desperate, his heart a hurricane.

"Don't . . . slow . . . down!" he gasped between breaths.

"Abso . . . lutely . . . not!" Virginia answered.

They were seventy yards from the finish. Ravani looked back. Donnie and Stevie were a good fifteen feet behind them and losing ground with every stroke. Triumph sizzled through him.

He dug harder with his paddle. Or tried to. He was struggling, suddenly. He could see Virginia battling, too, grunting and straining, like they were paddling through molasses instead of muddy river water. They were working twice as hard, but going half as fast. Ravani shifted, wiggling for better leverage, and felt water lapping around his knees.

He froze mid-paddle. Looked down.

When they'd passed Donnie, there'd been a little puddle of

water swirling around the coffin floor. From all the splashing and paddling, he'd thought. Now, though, he was kneeling in an inch of water. Perhaps two.

"Um, Virginia?" he said, trying to keep his voice calm. "We're going down."

"Are you kidding?" she groaned back, digging her oar deep. "We're a mile ahead!"

"No! We're actually *going down*. I think there's a leak. We're sinking!"

Just like a heart, a coffin can apparently race and sink at the same time.

Virginia lurched to a stop, paddle dripping high. Her head snapped down. She muttered a word that Ravani wasn't allowed to say.

"Funny story, Rav." Her voice sounded oddly tight. "I can't swim."

"You . . . you *what*?"

She looked back at him with one solemn eye. "Sorry to pull a Tommy Wallace on you." Gulped nervously, then shrugged. "But, if I drown, at least I'm already in a coffin. That's a time-saver." She looked toward the finish line. Dipped her oar back in the water. "Well. You scoop. I'll paddle."

And then she started paddling. Fiercely. Straight downriver, toward the finish line.

Ravani stared at her for a second.

Then he squeaked, "Are you crazy?" There was fifty yards of deep water between them and the finish line. The riverbank was only twenty yards away. "We gotta head to shore!"

"We . . . are . . . finishing . . . this . . . race," Virginia grunted, then shot him a one-eyed look. "Scoop, please, so I don't die."

Ravani chewed his lip for half a breath and then dropped his oar into the boat and started bailing out the water the best he could using cupped hands. Behind him, he heard the panting and sloshing of their competition catching up.

He was tossing water out as fast as he could but he knew it was a losing battle.

On the edge of his vision, a flurry of motion caught his eye.

Donnie Carter. And Stevie. Paddling like demons and nearly even with them, five feet to the left. Donnie's face was twisted with effort, but he still managed to shoot Ravani a triumphant sneer. Virginia saw them, too, and somehow picked up her pace.

The bow of Donnie's boat pulled even with Ravani. Then ahead. Stevie was in the front, plunging and pulling his paddle wildly. Stroke by stroke he inched up beside Ravani, then past him.

"Paddle, Rav!" Virginia growled.

"But . . . but the water. We'll—"

"Paddle! Now!"

Ravani looked to the safety of the shore, so close, and then at the dock, still forty yards away, then down at the water in the boat—over three inches now. His belly knotted and squirmed.

"*Give it up, loser!*"

The voice he knew so well slithered through all the splashing and panting and cheering. Donnie was even with him now, and gliding past. Ravani saw the gloating smirk on his face, lit an eerie red from the explosion of a firework overhead. Donnie's eyes said it all: this was exactly how he'd known it was going to turn out. Of course it was. Donnie winning. Ravani sinking. Like always.

Ravani grabbed his paddle.

He dug the blade into the water and pulled, hard, then swung and dug and pulled again. The *Creepy Freak* picked up speed. Again. And again. And again.

Someday, his paddle whispered with each stroke as it pulled them through the water. *Someday. Someday. Someday.*

Donnie's steady creep past them slowed. Then stopped. They were neck and neck.

Ravani threw his arms into it, his shoulders, his heart, his soul, his whole self.

Someday. Someday. Someday.

He tightened his grip. Snarled his lip.

Today. Today. Today.

"Faster, Stevie! Come on!" Donnie seethed through clenched teeth, a thin but unmistakable edge of surprise in his voice.

Ravani's and Virginia's strokes lined up for a second and Ravani saw how it made them jet forward.

They were better together.

"*Together!*" he hissed between paddles. "*It's ... faster ... if we ... paddle ... at the same time!*" Then he called it out, but as low as he could so that hopefully Donnie wouldn't hear and get the same idea. "*Stroke! Stroke! Stroke!*"

An inch at a time, then two inches, then three, they began to ease out in front of Donnie once more.

The crowd on the dock was screaming, hollering and whistling. It was a knuckle-biter of a race. The dock was twenty yards away. Donnie barked and spat at Stevie, commanding him to go faster, but it didn't matter.

Ravani and Virginia were going to win. In front of the whole town, he and his comrade were going to beat Donnie Carter. A reckless, joyful sort of song burst in Ravani's soul.

"*Yeah!*" he crowed, sinking his paddle deep and pulling harder. He let out a wild, wordless yell. It came from deep down in his lungs but really it came from his soul, from his heart, from all the things he'd never said, from all the times his soul hadn't been able to be what it wanted to be.

And he paddled. And he paddled. And he paddled.

But then Stevie slid past him. And still he paddled.

But then Donnie was beside him. And still he paddled.

The water around his knees was half a foot deep. Almost to the top of the boat. The river water was lapping at the edge, and sometimes even sloshing over inside.

Ravani and Virginia fought like heroes.

But, sometimes, that doesn't matter. Sometimes, even if a soul shines as bright as fireworks and fights as fierce as a falcon, it still loses. Not because it didn't try hard enough. But just because, sometimes, that is how the world turns out.

With ten yards to go, they were barely above water. But still they rowed, and rowed, and rowed. Ravani didn't see Virginia let up or slow down for one second, one breath, one stroke. He didn't, either.

Donnie and Stevie's boat hit the dock. There was a roar of cheers. They raised their arms in victory.

Ravani and Virginia had lost. Of course they had. Ravani's heart sank down to the dank mud of the river bottom.

Ravani had believed that, perhaps, that race in that boat with that girl would be his *someday*. And *someday* is indeed a powerful word. But so, unfortunately, is *nevertheless*.

The *Creepy Freak* had given up all dreams of forward motion, despite their frantic paddling. It gurgled and listed and turned sideways. Only a sliver of its sides showed above the water.

Ravani surrendered. He stopped paddling and slumped forward, panting. The dock and its cheering crowd and celebrating villains were still nine yards away. Virginia stopped, too, and twisted to look at him. Her eyes were wide.

"What do we do now?" he asked her, exhausted and heartbroken and defeated.

She was breathing hard through parted lips.

"Well, I think this is the part where you save my life."

A great bubble rose up from the *Creepy Freak* beneath them, and then that gallant casket could resist no more. It sank once and for all beneath them, disappearing down into the watery darkness.

Ravani lunged toward Virginia.

Most people who couldn't swim, if they found themselves suddenly plunged into deep water, would have thrashed and perhaps screamed. Virginia Deering, however, was not really the thrashing and screaming type. As the coffin sank, she sank silently with it. It was, to be honest, a fairly creepy thing to do. By the time he got to her, only her nose was above the water. By the time he'd snaked an arm under her armpits, both of their heads were below the surface.

It was quiet, down there. The noise of the crowd faded to a distant, dull chatter. Far off, he could hear the plunging of the paddles of the other teams, the wooden *thud*s of oars against boats.

He looked up as they sank down. The world above the water burst with a glittering galaxy of fireworks. It could have been beautiful, the way the lights danced on the water's surface. If he hadn't been drowning, anyway.

He kicked both legs like a frog and swept with his free arm and propelled them up toward the waiting world. They broke the surface together and sucked in its air. It tasted like river water and gunpowder and cotton candy.

Ravani kicked and kicked and kicked. But a sopping-wet Virginia, it turned out, was a heavy thing. He kept their noses above water. But barely, and only from time to time. They sputtered and coughed.

A splash sounded behind them, then another. Ravani heard breathing in his ear, then arms taking Virginia from him.

"Hey, sis," Colt panted, then, "I got her, Frog Master."

Ravani spun back toward the dock. He saw that the second splash had been Annabel, jumping in with Colt to save them. It was a sweet gesture, perhaps, but was something less than helpful because she could not, it turned out, swim.

Annabel, who in many ways was very unlike her older sister, immediately began to thrash and to scream. Which was, in fact, a completely reasonable thing to do.

There was a third splash. It was Lee Chin, jumping in beside Annabel. In a moment he had her in his grasp and was towing her back toward the dock. Ravani followed, his wet clothes slowing him down. Colt and Virginia were behind him.

One by one they pulled themselves up onto the dock with some helping hands from the crowd. There were a few concerned questions, and some slaps on their backs for a race well run. Other boats began to float up to the finish line and people's attention turned to them.

Ravani and Virginia and Colt and Annabel crawled to the other side of the dock and collapsed together in a soggy, panting pile.

"You all okay?" Mr. Chin asked, leaning over them with his hands on his knees. They all nodded, catching their breath.

"Thank you for saving my life," Annabel said cheerfully.

Mr. Chin laughed. "Yes, well, you're very welcome. But I'll promise you a free cupcake if you promise me you'll never jump in a river again until you learn to swim."

Annabel grinned broadly. "Deal."

The four children lay there, breathing big on the dock.

"Well," Colt said between breaths, "that went pretty well, all things considered."

"Yeah," Virginia agreed. She tipped her chin at Ravani and gave one of her small smiles. "Nice work, Freak."

Ravani looked at her.

"But . . . but we *lost*," he said, and his soul sighed sadly to hear the truth of the words out loud.

Virginia closed one eye skeptically at him. "Bullspit. Winning isn't always about who comes in first, Rav. We just raced down a river, under fireworks, in a floating coffin. *And* we didn't drown." She sniffed and rubbed a drip of water off her forehead. "If that isn't winning, comrade, I don't what is."

Ravani blinked at her words. Then he smiled. A big, true sort of smile. Because what she'd said was true. Of course it was.

"Well," he said. "It was a *sinking* coffin, technically."

She snorted a laugh at him. "Even better."

"You children did *wonderful!*" a warm voice enthused, and Ravani turned to see his mother and father elbowing out of the crowd. "What a race! And your boat was so . . . well, striking!" His mother wrapped Ravani in a hug, then did the same with Virginia.

"It was a fine race, son," Ravani's father murmured to him. He looked quietly into Ravani's eyes. "Well done."

"Thanks, Dad," Ravani said.

"Well, we were going to wander through the street fair if you children would like to join us," Mrs. Foster said.

"Thank you, ma'am, but I'm afraid we better get home. Our parents are expecting us," Colt said. He took Annabel's hand and led her away through the finish line commotion.

Virginia, though, lingered. She stepped close to Ravani and looked solemnly into his eyes.

"Thank you for saving my life," she said, so soft that only he could hear. "You've been a remarkable comrade."

"You too," Ravani whispered. "Do you think . . . we could just be friends now?"

Virginia frowned and cocked a wry eyebrow at him. A firework exploded, the reflection flashing and fading in her eyes.

"I got bad news for you, Freak. We've been friends for quite a while. Best friends, even. I blew it."

Ravani grinned. "Sorry," he said.

"Liar."

Then, she surprised him. She leaned forward and wrapped him in a tight hug.

"Goodbye, Ravani," she said, serious and quiet into his ear.

"Goodbye," he said, embarrassed. There were, after all, a lot of people around, some of whom were his parents. She let him go. "Paper route tomorrow?" he asked, clearing his throat. She looked at him, then gave a small smile.

"Sure."

Chapter Thirty-Five

In Which Someone Arrives, and Someone Flees

Ravani wandered through the festivities with his mother and his father, feeling a sort of happy that he'd never felt before. He walked between his parents, half listening to their conversation. His clothes were still damp from the river. His heart still singing from the race. And from Virginia's words. And from his father's words.

He remembered a question that Virginia had asked him, once upon a time, and he remembered his answer to it then, and he knew that, if she had asked it at that moment, his answer would have been different: *Yes*, he would have said, *I have felt like I was exactly where I belonged.* He smiled to himself. *Welcome to someday. You're already here.* This, he thought, this is the perfect ending to this story. This story about a lonely soul who finds a friend. This story about choices made, and families found, and secrets shared and secrets kept. It should end with fireworks, and splashing laughter, and a hug.

It was not the ending, though. Not at all. And, sometimes, after a soul finds something, it loses it.

There are moments when everything changes. Sometimes those moments are big, and loud, and dramatic. Sometimes, though, they come quietly and wear very casual clothes.

Ravani drifted ahead of his parents, who'd stopped to look

into a store window, and the everything-changing moment began like this: two children jostled past him. One of them said, "Hey, look! An ice cream truck!"

That was it. Nothing extraordinary at all.

But Ravani's eyes followed the child's pointing finger. He did, after all, enjoy ice cream. Who doesn't?

He saw the truck, and the drippy cone painted on its side.

He saw the man sitting inside it, behind the steering wheel. The window was rolled down. The man had very pale skin. And very short hair. And very straight teeth. And very clean glasses.

The man was talking out the window to Hortense Wallenbach.

"The old Croward house? Sure, I know where it is!" Hortense Wallenbach was saying. Ravani's blood turned colder than the winter water of Carcass Creek.

There are people who are looking for us. Wolves. Ravani had been told that once, by one of the souls living in the old Croward house. And Ravani knew, somehow, that the strange man in the ice cream truck was one of those people.

No! Ravani wanted to shout to Ms. Wallenbach. *Don't tell him!*

He never got the chance, though.

"It's on Offal Road, straight down that way," Hortense said, pointing. "First left after the bridge. Only house on the left—you can't miss it!"

Ravani's heart shuddered. His mouth dropped open. He stood on the sidewalk like a stone in the river, the crowd parting and streaming around him.

"Arthur Croward don't live there anymore, though," Hortense said. "You ain't looking for him, are you?"

"No," the man said, "not," he went on, "him."

Just as those words left the pale man's mouth, his cold eyes locked on Ravani, standing motionless and slack-jawed, staring back at him. The man's head cocked, just a bit. Like a hawk seeing a rabbit in the field below. The dangling lights of the café patio reflected on his glasses.

Ravani shriveled inside, snared in the man's probing eyes.

His mind screamed but his feet stayed as though rooted in the concrete.

A new voice, though, broke through his stunned shock, and through the stare that locked him and the stranger. A voice that was familiar, though he wished that it wasn't.

"Yes, ma'am. I'm telling you. No mom, no dad, no grown-ups at all. They're runaways. Wanted fugitives, hiding out in that house."

Both Ravani's and the strange man's heads snapped toward the voice upon hearing those words.

It was Donnie Carter. Of course it was. He was walking out of the café, talking earnestly to Sheriff Quigley, beady eyes shining.

Donnie looked up and saw Ravani. His lip curled in ugly triumph. He pointed a blunt finger toward Ravani.

"And *he's* been keeping 'em hidden!"

Sheriff Quigley's baffled face turned Ravani's way. So did the stranger's.

There was a moment. Ravani standing, paralyzed and panicked. The stranger, silent and intense as a cat on the prowl, eyes unblinking. The sheriff, squinting and already opening her mouth to call out to Ravani.

Quite a triangle, that. One a talon, one a beak, and him the prey.

Ravani, in that excruciating moment, wanted to do many

things. He wanted to disappear. He wanted to flee and hide. He wanted to burst into tears. He wanted to come clean and confess it all. He wanted, perhaps most of all, to run to his mother.

There's nothing wrong with that. All souls, sometimes, want to run to their mothers, no matter how old they are.

But stories, and the souls that shape them, are about choices. And Ravani, who was terrified, was also a comrade. So he made a choice.

Ravani turned. And he ran.

Not to hide, though.

To warn.

PART THREE

Chapter Thirty-Six

In Which There Is a Parasol, and a Telephone

avani bolted through the crowd.

He was in his second race of the day. And this one he *had* to win.

He charged past his parents, not even realizing it until he heard his mother's surprised voice.

"Ravani! Where are you . . ."

"Gotta go!" he shouted over his shoulder without slowing down. "Diarrhea!" Dozens of heads turned his way—as often happens when someone shouts "Diarrhea!" in a crowd—but Ravani neither slowed nor cared.

He broke free of the crowd and opened up his stride, sprinting into the darkness toward home, feet slapping the pavement as he raced down Skinister Street. He thought that perhaps he heard an engine start behind him. He had a horrible feeling of near certainty that it was the engine of an ice cream truck. Already going as fast as he thought was possible, he groaned and picked up his pace even more.

The slaughterhouse loomed and then receded as he passed it. As he crossed the bridge, twin headlights flared on the road behind him. He darted to the side, crashing through the trees and brush just as he had on his bike a few days before, when he had been hunted and mysterious children had saved him. Now *they* were being hunted . . . and he intended to do the saving.

He zigged and zagged along the faint trails dimly visible in the moonlight. Tears burned in his eyes, blurring his vision but not slowing his run. The tears dripped onto his face. Because, for a few moments or a few days, he had belonged to something. For a few moments, or for a few days, he hadn't been alone. For a few moments, or for a few days, he'd had a friend. And he'd been a friend.

But as he ran though the dark-shrouded woods, he knew that was all ending. If he didn't make it in time, she would be captured and carried away. If he did make it in time, she would leave and never come back.

He was going to lose her either way.

He wept as he ran, and the creek wept with him, and the forest closed in around to hold him, and the birds mourned in the trees, and then the house was there and he was running across the back lawn and then up the porch steps.

"Open up!" he shouted hoarsely. "Open up! It's me, Rav! You've got to open up!"

He drummed his hands on the door until they hit only air. He stopped, breathless. The door had swung open.

All the Ragabonds were standing there in the dark kitchen, in silence, looking at him.

Ravani opened his mouth to holler, to warn them about the Hunters heading their way. But his words died in his throat. Because his eyes picked out what he'd been too frantic at first to see.

The parasol over Virginia's shoulder.

The suitcases at each of their feet.

He'd meant to shout, *"You need to leave!"*

Instead, though, when his words came, they came different, and as a whisper.

"You're leaving?"

"We are," Tristan said. He was standing by the telephone.

"But . . . but . . . ," Ravani stuttered, still gasping from his run. "How . . . how did you know?"

"I told them," Virginia said.

"Like *you* should have," Tristan said. His face was hard, his voice stony. "We can't stay if a kid like Donnie knows our secret."

Realization washed over Ravani. They knew that Donnie knew. But they didn't truly know the danger they were in.

"No, you don't understand. You do have to leave. But *now*. There's someone in town. A man. Looking for you. He knows where you are. And he's on his way *here*."

Murmured whispers rippled through the Ragabonds. Annabel covered her mouth and leaned into Colt, who put his arm around her and pulled her in tight.

"What kind of man?" Tristan asked, and his voice was no longer cold. It was tight and tense.

"I . . . I don't know. He was in a truck. Glasses."

Tristan swallowed. "An ice cream truck?"

"Yes."

Tristan blinked. "It's him."

He grabbed the telephone and pressed it to his ear.

"*You don't have time!*" Ravani hissed. "*He's going to get here first!*"

Tristan shook his head.

"We'll still need a ride. I'll arrange to get picked up somewhere else. The church, maybe." He fixed Ravani with a glittering stare. "But you'll need to get us there."

CHAPTER THIRTY-SEVEN

In Which There Is a Good Reason for Bad Parking

The Hunter could move very quickly if he needed to. But the Hunter almost never hurried.

When he had seen the boy on the sidewalk, the boy with the open mouth and the wide eyes, the Hunter had known immediately. Even before the other bigger boy had arrived with his loud voice and pointing finger and given it all away. There's a sense that a soul gets when it has hunted enough. The wide-eyed boy had the look of prey about him. The Hunter could smell the fear on the boy, like a drop of blood to a shark.

The boy had run. And the Hunter had smiled.

"Thank," he'd said to the loud woman who'd given him directions, "you."

The Hunter had turned the keys in the ignition. And he'd pulled away from the curb, slowly, so as not to alarm the happy fairgoers. Had made his rumbling way down the street. Patient.

He'd driven down Skinister Street, out of the lights and noises of the downtown party. His gaze slid only briefly to a large, looming building he passed. SKINISTER QUALITY MEATS, the sign read. The Hunter had frowned. The Hunter was a vegetarian. Which was, perhaps, ironic.

Up ahead, he'd seen, just barely, the boy dash off the road

and into the trees. "*Hmmm,*" the Hunter had said. Taking to the woods had been smart of the boy. It wouldn't make a difference. But it was smart. The Hunter had smiled. It was so much more fun when they were smart. He was, after all, not simply a *catcher*. He was a Hunter.

The Hunter drove slowly past the spot where the boy had left the road. Noted the barely-there path. Kept driving.

He slowed the truck when he got to the turnoff for Offal Road. Peered down the street. Saw the two houses, dark and quiet. The dead-end road. His mouth watered.

He stopped the truck sideways in the middle of Offal Road, between the street sign and a telephone pole, blocking the road entirely. No one would be leaving—or escaping—Offal Road, until he said so. There would be no getaway trucks pulling up to the old Croward house. Not tonight.

The engine fell silent. The door opened, and it opened soundlessly . . . The Hunter always kept the hinges well-oiled. It closed nearly as soundlessly. He hoisted the large gray backpack onto his back. In addition to the various tools and implements he had packed inside, it now also held paperwork. Paperwork, after all, makes the world go round. Custody papers, signed by Madame Murdosa, granting him authority to detain and return the seven children listed.

He walked on quiet feet to the front of the truck and propped open the hood. Any passing motorist—even a nosy police officer, perhaps—who saw his truck would think it had broken down, and that the driver had gone for help.

The Hunter was ready, then, to close in on his prey. But he didn't, not right away. Instead, he climbed. One foot on the truck's back bumper, two hands onto the roof, and with a silent vault he was atop the truck. Reached over his shoulder, pulled a pair of wire cutters from the backpack. Leaned out toward the telephone pole. He had parked just close enough to it that he could reach it. Of course he had. The Hunter, after all, thought of everything.

He found the wire that snaked off from the pole toward the two houses of Offal Road. Reached up with his wire cutters.

CHAPTER THIRTY-EIGHT

In Which Words Aren't Said,
and Something Dies

"Can you do that?" Tristan asked Ravani. "Get us to the church without being seen? Can we trust you?"

"Yes," Ravani answered, already imagining the route through the woods, and backyards, and vacant lots.

Tristan nodded, then began keying in the telephone number.

As Tristan dialed the number, Ravani looked at Virginia. She was looking back at him. They didn't speak. They didn't smile, or frown, or wink, or raise their eyebrows. They just stood there, staring into each other's eyes. An awful lot can be said without saying anything at all. Things like *Thank you*, and things like *I'm sorry*. And things like *Goodbye*. And other things, too. Things that don't quite fit into words anyway, perhaps. There's a lot to be said when two souls find each other, and then when two souls lose each other.

"Hello?" Tristan said. He rattled the phone cradle. "Hello?"

Seven heads, Ravani's included, turned toward the telephone.

Tristan looked around at them. The whites of his eyes flashed in the dark kitchen.

"The line's dead. It's time to go. Out the back door. Now."

Chapter Thirty-Nine

In Which a Path Is Chosen

Back on the ground, the Hunter slipped the wire cutters into his pocket and began to walk. But not down Offal Road. No. He had hunted many times. And he knew this prey. They had escaped him before. And they had been caught by him before. Because of the wide-eyed skinny boy, they would know by now he was coming. They were too smart to march out the front door. So the Hunter walked back the way he had just driven, back up Skinister Street. He stepped off the road just before the bridge, following a barely-there path he'd seen a terrified child follow just minutes before. Darkness closed in around him. His feet made no sound on the pine needles, and his ears missed no sound. His eyes were wide and watchful. His arms and his fingers and his heart were flexed and ready. To throw. To grab. To snatch.

To hunt.

The Hunter was happy.

Very.

Chapter Forty

In Which a Road Is Not Taken
(and It Makes All the Difference)

"This is all wrong," Tristan said. His voice sounded different. On edge, which was nothing new, but something else as well: uncertain, and frightened.

"What do you mean?" asked Ravani.

"This kid, Donnie, he's known our secret for days now. And this . . . this hunter, on our tail, right in town." Tristan spoke in a tense whisper, so that his family on the back porch couldn't hear. "And the magic never warned me. It never told me to leave. Even now. With a Wolf at the door, and no cavalry coming . . . the magic isn't telling me to run."

"So . . . what does that mean?" Ravani asked.

Tristan took a shaky breath, and let a shaky breath out. "I think . . . I think the magic is broken."

Ravani wasn't sure if he'd ever believed in the magic. Virginia seemed to have a knack for knowing a lie, and Benjamin certainly had a touchy stomach, but it hadn't necessarily felt all that *magical* to him. But Tristan's words, and Tristan's voice when he said them, shook Ravani.

The man with the straight teeth was coming. They could use some magic.

But, then again, Ravani had made it back in time to warn

them. And Tristan had gotten them ready. And Ravani knew the path through the darkness. "Maybe, right now, we have to be our own magic."

Tristan's eyes narrowed. He nodded. "Let's go."

The other Ragabonds were waiting in the backyard, standing in a nervous clump.

"What's the plan?" Beth asked. They all looked to Tristan. He looked back at them, his face lost. He was, perhaps, listening for the magic. And, perhaps, not hearing it.

"We shouldn't take the road," Ravani said. "I know the way through the woods. We'll get to town. Find a phone. Then head to the church." He looked around at the faces of the Ragabonds. There was fear there, and doubt.

"I'm scared," Annabel said. She was holding tight to Colt's hand. Ravani wanted to say something comforting, something brave. But sometimes the most comforting and brave thing to say is the truth.

"Me too," he said. And he smiled at her. The smile didn't say *Everything is going to be all right*. It just said *I'm with you*. And, an awful lot of the time, that's all another soul really needs to know.

Annabel gave him a little smile back. Shaky, and gone quickly, but there. *Okay*, it said.

She looked up at Colt. "Will you carry me?"

"'Course I will, darling." Colt reached down to lift her.

"It's a long way," Ravani murmured. "And you'll move slower if—"

Colt straightened up, Annabel in his arms, her arms around his neck. "She wants me to carry her, I carry her," he said. "Lead the way, Frog Master."

Ravani bent down and picked up Annabel's and Colt's suitcases, since their hands were full of each other.

Colt would make a great Shepherd someday, he thought.

He looked to Virginia. She looked different. It took half a heartbeat for Ravani to realize what it was.

Virginia Deering looked scared.

She hadn't look scared in the graveyard moonlight, or facing down Donnie, or sitting in a sinking boat when she couldn't swim. But she looked scared then, with a parasol over her shoulder and a suitcase in her hand. But Ravani knew, down in his soul, that Virginia wasn't afraid of being caught. She was afraid of losing her family.

Well, Ravani thought to himself, *then I'll just have to make sure she doesn't.*

And then, taking a deep and bracing breath, Ravani led them into the forest, leaving most of the moonlight behind.

They worked their way downstream, along the bank, Ravani sticking to the easiest and quickest trails. Even if the strange man in the ice cream truck was pulling up to the house right at that moment, they would still have several minutes of a head start. And even if the man figured out where they'd gone and tried to follow, Ravani was confident that he could move through those woods faster.

Confidence, sometimes, is a shining light that pulls a soul forward. Sometimes, though, confidence is a blindfold.

"Okay," Ravani whispered to the Ragabonds. "We're gonna cross the creek at a spot up ahead."

Annabel gasped.

"It's okay," Ravani said. "It's not deep."

"No," Annabel said, backing up. "I forgot my binoculars!"

"It's too late," Tristan said. "We need—*Annabel!*" But it was, indeed, too late. Annabel had wiggled out of Colt's arms and spun and taken off running through the trees, back toward the house. Tristan spat out several appropriately inappropriate words. Then he said, "Colt, go get her. We'll go slow. Catch up quick."

Without a word, Colt sprinted off after Annabel.

Tristan shook his head, chewing his lip and breathing through his nose. "*This is all wrong,*" he said again, low, to himself. His black eyes found Ravani's. "Go. We'll follow. Now."

Ravani turned and started off again. The creek was just up ahead.

It's strange, sometimes, how we can know something before we know it, without even knowing *how* we know it.

After taking only perhaps ten more steps through the forest, Ravani *knew*, without knowing how, that they'd made a terrible mistake.

He stopped. Heard the others stop behind him, waiting.

There was a silence in the woods.

The hair on his arms rose.

It could have been described as an *eerie* silence, but that would have been redundant. Any true silence in a forest is an eerie silence. If one listens close, and all is well, there are always sounds: wings, scurries, little quiet scutterings of life. But, as Ravani stood frozen in the darkness, what he heard was true silence.

And there is never true silence in a forest.

Unless, of course, there is a hunter.

Ravani swung his head back toward the Ragabonds.

Something whirred through the night over his head. Like a bird. But not a bird.

Benjamin and Winnie, at the back of the line, cried out and fell to the ground. They writhed there, tangled in something that looked, impossibly, like a net.

Tristan spun and took two steps toward them. It was as far as he got.

There was another *swoosh*.

Tristan tumbled with a grunt, his legs wrapped tight at the ankles.

Beth bolted. And was brought down almost immediately, her legs bound like Tristan's.

Virginia took one running step toward Ravani. Once more, the sound of capture whistled through the shadows. She crashed to the dirt and pine needles at Ravani's feet.

She looked up at him through the holes of a net, gasping. "*Run!*"

Ravani stared down at her, his breath and his heart stopped.

"*Get away!*" she hissed at him desperately, eyes pleading.

Ravani shook his head. "I'm not leaving you."

She reached out. Or tried to. But her hand was stopped by the net.

He stretched his own arm out toward her.

From the darkness, another hand stretched out into the moonlight. A very pale, very careful hand.

There was a soft *click*, and Ravani felt the cool metal of a handcuff snap around his wrist.

"Got," a very cold, very calm voice said, "you."

Chapter Forty-One

In Which There Is Growling, and Handcuffs

The Hunter had guessed that he wouldn't have to net the last boy, the one who'd been leading the others. The Hunter had found that the last child or two almost always stayed once the others had been snared, shackled only by their loyalty. It was handy.

Quickly, smoothly, expertly, he cuffed the boy's wrist to the other. Then, on swift and silent feet, he went down the line. In a matter of breaths, all the children were free from their nets and bolos, but bound by the surer strength of handcuffs. The oldest boy—the one who had eluded the Hunter the last time—seethed and growled and tried to kick, but the Hunter was unsurprised and unbothered but not at all unprepared. For good measure, he handcuffed the older boy's ankles as well.

He stood them up. Frowned. He was one short.

No matter. The other might turn up. Or, if it came to that, the Hunter wouldn't mind in the slightest returning to complete the hunt. It would be like dessert. It's important to have something to look forward to.

He walked back to the front of the line.

Pulled the paperwork out of his backpack. He held it up in the moonlight so that the clump of frightened children could see it.

There were typed words, and swoopy signatures, and shiny seals. It looked very official, which it was.

"You're," he said, "in," he continued, "my," he added, "custody," he finished.

And with that he got them marching. The children did not beg, or whine, or even whimper. He did not have to bind them all together, or even watch them all that closely. They would not run.

These children would not leave each other behind.

The hunt was over.

Chapter Forty-Two

In Which a Mind Races,
and a Heart Breaks

It's no fun walking through a forest at night when you're wearing handcuffs.

Ravani shuffled along, his hands held tight in front of him.

He was trying very hard not to cry. And he was, for the most part, succeeding.

His stomach boiled. His hands dripped sweat like a leaky faucet.

He had spent an inordinately large share of his life scared, but he'd never been as scared as he was walking with that man, in those handcuffs. He was scared for himself. But, even more, he was scared for his friend, and for her family.

But a soul can be more than one thing at a time.

His feet stumbled, his legs lurched, but his mind raced.

He had to help the Ragabonds. He had to help his friends.

Ravani was frightened, yes, but he was also determined. And *determined* is nearly always a very good thing to be.

He thought of his parents, of the sheriff and Hortense and even Mr. Skinister, but what could they do, even if he could get word to them? The Ragabonds were, in fact, runaways. The strange man who'd caught them had paperwork. Paperwork makes the world go round.

What could he, Ravani Foster, do?

As he struggled desperately to come up with something, *any-thing* that he could do to help his friends, he knew that there was one thing he most definitely would *not* do: nothing. And deciding to not do nothing is in fact quite something of a decision to make.

Through the woods they tromped, through the darkness, through the night.

Then, far too soon, they reached the road.

There, up ahead, Ravani saw the waiting ice cream truck with its hood open, beneath the streetlight.

Soon, they would be inside it. Soon, they would be driven away.

Ravani's heart broke with every footstep. The truck grew nearer and nearer. When they reached it, all hope would be gone.

Ravani glared at the truck through tear-bleared eyes. He hated that truck, that truck that would tear his friend away. That truck that would roar to life and then roar away.

Ravani's breath caught in his throat.

His eyebrows shot up.

Ravani had a wonderful thing: an idea.

Ravani flexed his fingers.

Then, before his fear could whisper his courage away, Ravani ran.

Chapter Forty-Three

In Which There Is a Flee,
and a Plea

When the boy broke from the line and took off running, the Hunter didn't panic.

The boy was handcuffed. He wouldn't get far. And he was running down the road, toward the truck, not even into the cover of the trees.

The Hunter cocked his arm back. He'd kept one bolo in his hand, just in case. He watched the boy's trajectory for half a heartbeat, then swung his arm and let the bolo fly. It shot in whipping twirls through the air. Wrapped tightly around the boy's ankles and brought him crashing down in a skidding slide onto the asphalt, just short of the truck.

The boy, though, did not give up easily. Though he was now bound hand and foot, he still tried to squirm away, wiggling and grunting under the truck.

The Hunter did not even bother to walk faster. He kept his eyes on the other children, ready in case one of them decided to flee as well. They didn't. They knew better. They stared either hopelessly down at the ground, or angrily back at him.

By the time he reached the truck, the boy was completely beneath it. The Hunter knelt down and grabbed both his ankles. He did not jerk the boy from beneath the truck, or yank him.

That might hurt him, and there was no need for that. No, he took both the boy's bony legs in a hand and then firmly but gently pulled him out into the moonlight.

The boy, who had rolled onto his back, blinked up at him with frightened eyes. His shackled hands were clenched into fists on his chest.

"Nice," the Hunter said, "try."

The Hunter swung open the back doors of the truck, revealing an interior completely devoid of ice cream.

"In," the Hunter said, "you," he added, "go."

"Let him go," Tristan said sulkily, tipping his chin at Ravani. "He's not one of us. He's just a friend."

"I," the Hunter said, "don't," he continued, "care." And he didn't. That was not his job. Sometimes children got mixed up. Sometimes they lied. That was no concern of his. He would take them all back. And Madame Murdosa could figure it out.

And, one by one, they went inside.

They each sat down glumly on one of the benches along the side.

The Hunter took hold of the doors and was about to close them when the oldest girl spoke up.

"Please," she said. "Wait."

The Hunter did not care that she said *Please*, and he didn't care that she had asked him to wait. Hunters rarely grant favors to their prey. But, he thought, perhaps the girl would tell him where the missing child was.

"We aren't doing anyone any harm, sir," the girl said. "We just want to be together. That's all. We're a family. And if you take us back, they'll separate us. They'll tear us apart. Please, I beg of you, don't do this. Because if you do, we will lose the only thing that matters to us in this whole world: each other."

The girl's words hung in the air, a metallic echo in the stripped-bare truck.

The Hunter blinked at her. Looked from one child's pleading, hopeful, tear-stained face to the next.

"Boo," the Hunter said, "hoo."

Sometimes, a soul doesn't have a soul.

The Hunter closed the truck's doors. Pulled the padlock through the handles and clicked it closed. Gave it a pull to test that it had locked.

He walked around and closed the hood, then climbed into the driver's seat.

Pursed his thin, pale lips.

He was almost disappointed at how easy the hunt had gone.

He needn't have been.

Chapter Forty-Four

In Which There Is a Splash,
and a Scream

Ravani was sitting beside Virginia in the back of the truck, their shoulders pressed together, their cuffed hands in their laps.

Virginia was looking down, her face even graver than usual.

"It'll be fine," Ravani murmured to her.

Virginia cast her somber eyes on him, the corners of her mouth tucked down. "I know it'll be fine, Rav. He's not going to kill us. He's just going to return us to the orphanage. It will be . . . fine." Her shoulders rose and fell in a sigh. "But, for a while there, it was almost . . . *wonderful*."

"It'll be fine," Ravani repeated.

"It's over, Rav," Tristan said. He didn't sound angry. Just weary, like a grown-up explaining to a child why a blanket will never work as a parachute. "You'll be okay. They'll let you go, of course. At least Colt and Annabel got away. You'll have to hide them, Rav. And, listen . . . when they let you go, I'm going to need you to go and get the *Always and Forever*. It's hidden in the house, under the—"

"No, listen," Ravani said, raising his voice but only just a bit because he didn't want the strange, terrifying man to hear him. "I'm saying I think there's a chance—"

"Oh, Ravani," Beth exhaled, her head resting back against the side of the truck. "You just don't get it. We are handcuffed and locked in a truck that is going to take us away, no matter what we do. Things couldn't get any worse. It's a *disaster*."

In the darkness of the truck, there was a gag. And then a cough. And then a splash. And then a smell.

Things had, indeed, gotten worse.

"Benjamin!" several voices protested.

"What? You said the code word!"

The truck engine rumbled to life, quivering the benches beneath them. It lurched into motion. There were no windows in the back of the truck, but Ravani could tell that they were turning around at the dead end of Offal Road and heading back toward Skinister Street.

Ravani sat, listening. Waiting.

The truck paused again at the intersection. Then turned and pulled out onto Skinister Street, back toward town. The engine revved and hummed as the man shifted gears, gaining speed.

Ravani sat, listening. Waiting.

He guessed that they were approaching the bridge. Then crossing it. Driving toward the slaughterhouse. Nearly to it.

Ravani sat, listening. Waiting.

And then he heard it.

The engine shifted, bit by bit and then all at once, from purring to whining. Its rumble climbed higher, to a rattling sort of scream. A smell reached his nose: hot metal, and something nearly burning.

Abruptly, the truck slowed. It pulled swiftly to the side. Came to a stop. The driver cut the engine, dropping it to clicking silence.

"What's going on?" Winnie asked.

In the darkness, Ravani smiled.

He held out his fist, then opened his hand.

Showed the oily metal plug that he held in his palm.

"Told you," he said.

CHAPTER FORTY-FIVE

In Which Credit Is Given, and a Threat Is Made

By the time the Hunter had stopped the engine, he'd already figured out what had happened.

When the CHECK OIL light had first lit up red on the dashboard—just before he'd pulled out onto Skinister Street—he'd frowned, confused. He was sure that the truck had plenty of oil. The Hunter was very meticulous about vehicle maintenance.

But when the engine had begun to protest and grind, he'd known within a few seconds what must have happened. He remembered the boy's seemingly pointless dash toward the truck. How he'd crawled underneath on his stomach but how, when the Hunter had pulled him out, he'd been lying on his back.

The Hunter's eyes narrowed.

"Very," he whispered to himself in the silence of the truck cab, "clever."

The Hunter was many things, but *indecisive* was not one of them. He did not sigh, or slam his fists on the steering wheel, or even mutter a curse word. What good would that do? He had a problem. But when it came to solving problems, the Hunter's brain was as lethally efficient and effective as the slaughterhouse that he was at that moment parked in front of.

Less than a mile back, across the street from where the

children had been hiding, there was a house. A house with a garage, and a truck. That garage and that truck, he was sure, would have everything he needed.

He got out of the truck and closed the door and walked with a steady but unhurried stride back the way that he'd just driven. As he passed the back of the truck, he said three words to the souls that were locked up inside.

"I'll," he said, "be," he said, "back."

Chapter Forty-Six

In Which Many Things Are Not Found,
but One Thing Is

"What did you do?" Virginia asked. She saw the little cap in Ravani's hand, but she didn't know what it meant.

"He drained the oil," Tristan answered for him, his teeth flashing whitely in a smile.

Ravani nodded.

Once upon a time, Ravani's father had tried to teach him about cars, and fixing them. His father had meant well, of course, but it had been an awkward and unfortunate afternoon for both of them. Ravani, who could barely tie his shoes, had been a hopeless mechanic. All that he had really managed to learn was the first two steps of changing a car's oil.

It was very nearly the only thing that he remembered about engines. But it was also, it turned out, the only thing he *needed* to know about engines, at least at that moment. Because he knew that, just like a story cannot work without choices, an engine cannot run without oil.

"Way to go, Rav!" Winnie cheered.

"Nice work." Beth grinned.

Ravani smiled around at them.

"So . . . what now?" Tristan asked him.

"What do you mean?" Ravani said, still smiling.

"Well . . . what's the next step? How are we gonna escape?"

Ravani's smile faded. He looked around at the hopeful faces. "Oh. Um. I didn't really have a next step in mind."

Five hopeful faces dropped.

"Well," Virginia said flatly, "at least we get to spend more time with Benjamin's vomit."

"It was a good first step," Beth said, and gave Ravani an encouraging head nod. "Now we just need to keep thinking."

"True," Tristan agreed. "We were beaten before, but now we're just stuck. I'll take stuck over beaten any day."

He stood up and shook the doors of the truck. They rattled, but didn't budge. Virginia stood on the bench and peered through the narrow window to the cab of the truck. It was closed, though, and was far too small for any of them to fit through, anyway. Ravani got on his hands and knees—steering carefully clear of Benjamin's regurgitated supper—and felt along the side of the truck beneath the benches. Was there a panel that could be removed, perhaps, or a vent, or something, *anything*? But his hands felt only smooth, unyielding metal.

Beth was feeling along the floor as well, fingers fumbling in the dark.

Ravani gave up on his search, slumping back onto the bench. Tristan turned from the door, his jaw tight.

"We're stuck in here," he said.

"We're stuck in here," Virginia agreed.

"We're stuck in here." Ravani sighed.

"You guys stuck in there?" Annabel asked.

They all blinked at one another.

Annabel's voice had whispered, of course, from outside the truck.

"Brothers?" Colt's voice asked. "Sisters? Frog Master?"

"We're in here," Tristan said. "But you need to run. Hide."

"Obviously. But I'd rather y'all came with us," Colt answered. There was the sound of the lock jiggling. Lightly at first, then harder. "It sure seems like that fella intended you to stay, though."

"We're trapped," Beth said. "But you're not. Go, Colt. Take Annabel."

"Wait," Annabel's voice said. "Let me try."

"That's sweet, darling," Colt whispered back, "but it's pretty solid steel."

"Just give me a sec! I've . . . got a feeling."

"There's no time!" Tristan said tightly through the door crack. "Go hide in the woods. Rav will find you when they let him go, then—"

"Quiet!" Annabel's voice snapped. "I'm concentrating!"

"Listen, sister," Tristan said with forced calm. "There's a time to fight and there's a time to run, and right now is the time to—"

His words were cut off by a *snap*, and then a *click*, and then a *rattle*, and then the *creak* of the truck doors swinging open.

Annabel stood smiling widely in the moonlight, a hairpin held up in her hand.

"Guess what?" she said. "I think I found my Special!"

Chapter Forty-Seven

In Which a Warning Is Whispered,
and a Friend Is Found

"Well that's handy, sis," Colt said, patting Annabel on the shoulder.

"Handcuffs, quick," Tristan said, and they lined up at the truck's door and one by one held out their wrists. "Just do one cuff for now," Tristan said. "We need to move." Annabel stuck her tongue out in concentration and wielded her hairpin with magical quickness, clicking one side of each of their handcuffs open.

Colt peered past them into the back of the truck, licking his lips.

"Wait . . . isn't there any ice cream in there?" Colt asked.

"I'm afraid not, brother," Virginia replied.

"Dang. I was really hoping for some Rocky Road." He sniffed, and his eyes narrowed. "Ugh. Did someone say the code word?"

"Uh, guys?" Winnie said, pointing down the road. "Look!"

Their eyes followed her finger and saw him. The man with the very straight teeth and very cold voice and very accurate throwing arm. Running their way. He was running awkwardly, cradling several oil cans in his arms, but he was running nevertheless. And he was only a couple hundred yards away.

"This way! We can get help!" Ravani said, taking a few steps toward the distant lights of town.

"No," Tristan said quickly. "The law is on his side. We have to run." He looked around. There was town in one direction. There was the Hunter in the other. The slaughterhouse looming beside them. And there was the forest on either side. "Back to the woods."

Beth and Winnie and Benjamin darted off into the cover of the trees. Colt took Annabel's free hand and pulled her that way as well.

Tristan, Virginia, and Ravani sprinted after the others, who were waiting just inside the tree line. Together, they all scrambled away, ducking under branches and hopping over logs.

"Faster!" Tristan urged, helping Benjamin up when he stumbled, reaching back to give Virginia a hand and pull her over a log. Shoes thudded on roots, branches snapped.

"We need to hide," Ravani whispered breathlessly to Tristan. "We'll never outrun him."

Tristan growled, but he knew Ravani was right.

"There!" he said, pointing to a dense thicket up ahead. "Everyone, get in there! Quiet as you can!"

With heaving lungs but tiptoeing feet they all crept into the copse.

They cowered there, peeking out through the limbs and leaves.

Breath by breath, they stilled their lungs. The forest fell silent around them.

"*I think I hear him,*" Benjamin whispered. And, then, they all did. Quick, careful footsteps, the scraping of bushes, coming their way.

Virginia's hand found Ravani's and squeezed it. He looked at her and nodded and squeezed back.

Her eyes flickered up to his forehead. Her mouth tightened. Ravani felt a tickle where her eyes had gone. He grimaced.

"*Spider?*" he mouthed soundlessly. She nodded.

Ravani forced down the frantic freakout that flared inside him. Slowly, painstakingly, he raised his hand to his forehead. Flicked the eight-legged tickle away. Let out his breath.

"*Very good,*" Virginia whispered.

"*Sshhh!*" Colt breathed. "*I see him.*"

They all froze and looked to where Colt was staring.

And there, indeed, he was.

Backpack on. Oil cans abandoned. Treading soundlessly through the trees, eyes scanning the nighttime forest. A throwing net ready in one hand. Thirty yards away, perhaps, or less. Heading in their direction.

The children crouched lower.

There was a chance. His path wasn't on a direct line to where they hid, and it was dark, and they were well concealed. It was possible he would creep past without seeing them.

But then—and, sadly, there is nearly always a *but then* in these kinds of situations, especially with that kind of enemy—but then, their hope dissolved with one small *click.*

A flashlight flashed on in the man's hand. Its beam was white, and bright, and it cut through the darkness like a slaughterhouse blade through beef flesh.

It was only a matter of time.

At the end of the line of hiding children, Tristan leaned so that his ear was up against the ear of Beth. "*Be ready to run,*" he murmured, then nudged her. She leaned down to the child next to her. "*Be ready to run,*" she mouthed, then nudged. On down the line the warning went, from child to child until it reached Virginia.

Virginia pressed her lips to Ravani's ear when the message got to her.

"*Be ready to run,*" she said, and elbowed him. He nodded, then leaned toward the warm body beside him. He nudged it.

"*Be ready to run,*" he said, eyes still forward on the approaching menace.

A warm breath huffed on his face, enough to ruffle his hair.

Then something big, and tender, and moist slurped up the whole side of his face.

It was, he realized, a tongue. And a very large one. With a distinctly barnyard smell.

Ravani turned to look at who had just licked him.

He blinked. Then smiled.

"*Lucky,*" he said. A damp sigh blew out of Lucky's two nostrils into his face. "*You didn't die after all,*" he said, which was a rather obvious thing to say but also very true, and fairly relevant. His father had said that no cow had escaped . . . but that must've been because they'd never *realized* she'd escaped. He thought of Lucky, living these past days in the peace and freedom of the forest, and his smile broadened.

Ravani was brought back to his present reality, though, by the snap of a branch.

The flashlight beam stretched a bit farther, and then froze.

In its glare crouched Benjamin and Winnie, still as statues.

"Got," the man with the flashlight said calmly, "cha."

Winnie's arm was cocked back, a stone in her hand; Ravani knew that the stone, if thrown, would hit its target. But he also knew that a stone was too small to stop the monster that stalked them.

They needed something bigger.

He looked to Lucky.

Lucky's eyes were on the man whose eyes were on them. Her large bovine head looked from the man (lurking in the night), then to Ravani (crouching in fear), then back to the man, then back to Ravani.

Lucky had dealt with men before. Grown men, with large bodies, holding tools . . . like the man in the woods before her. They had poked her, and shouted at her, and shoved her roughly into trucks, and one by one bullied her herd-mates into a large building full of terrifying sounds from which they had never returned. And Lucky had dealt with the quiet boy before . . . the boy who had touched her nose tenderly, and looked into her eyes, and spoken with a kind voice, and led her to freedom.

Stories are about choices. It may not always be clear when a cow makes a choice. But, one can be certain that if Lucky had to choose between the man and the boy, she would choose the boy.

Lucky made a deep, guttural sound in her throat.

Before that moment, Ravani hadn't known that cows could growl. Perhaps they can't. Perhaps it was his imagination. Perhaps it was magic.

"*Go get him,*" Ravani said into his friend's large, round eyes.

Lucky's eyes narrowed.

Cows are, by nearly all measures, not particularly intelligent animals. They are, indeed, famous for it. But intelligence has nothing to do with worth, and certainly not with goodness.

Lucky was a friend, and she was a good one.

And, sometimes, one soul just understands what another soul needs. It's not important how.

Lucky snorted out one determined breath.

Then she charged.

Lucky was very large. She was very brown. She was very loud. She crashed like a truck through the brush and bushes and branches toward the man in the darkness.

An idea crashed just as loudly and abruptly into Ravani's brain. Inspired by, of all people, Stevie Mueller.

"*Bear!*" he screamed. "*Oh my God it's a BEAR!*"

CHAPTER FORTY-EIGHT

In Which There Are Trickles, and Thorns

When the Hunter found himself suddenly attacked by a bear, he very nearly wet his pants. In fact, the *very nearly* could more accurately be replaced by *only slightly*. There was, indeed, a trickle. It cannot be stated forcefully enough that, in all of his many hunts, the Hunter had never once before slightly or even very nearly wet his pants.

The Hunter jumped and stumbled backward, fumbling and dropping the flashlight. All that he managed to see before the world went dark was a flash of brown fur as the bear's enormous body rampaged toward him. A bear of that size and color, the Hunter knew, had to be a grizzly.

"GAAHHH," the Hunter said, "AAAGH!"

The Hunter tripped and fell and flopped once or twice and crawled for a bit and scrabbled his feet in the dirt and crashed his head into a tree and clawed at the ground and pulled himself to his feet and tripped once again and slithered over a log and lurched into a thorny blackberry bush and dragged his way through it and then got tangled in a vine and spun himself free and broke into a limping, staggering run.

The Hunter had become the Hunted.

He didn't care for it.

There was a terrified blur of running. Of branches hitting his face, and roots catching his feet, and thorns scratching at his hands. He wasn't sure when he managed to lose the bear, but eventually he emerged gasping and bleeding back onto the road, by his truck. He did not hear the bear behind him but he wasn't about to take any chances, so he jumped into the cab of his truck and slammed the door behind him.

Chapter Forty-Nine

In Which There Is Karma, and a Hero

Ravani and the others listened as the frantic sound of Lucky and the man's chase retreated farther and farther away.

Winnie slowly lowered her throwing hand.

Colt cleared his throat. "Was that a . . . cow?"

"Yeah," Ravani said. "She's a . . . friend of mine."

"Huh. Okay."

"That was kinda weird," Virginia said, and she was right. Being saved by a cow was pretty weird, if not entirely ridiculous. What would be next? Being saved by a goat?

But it wasn't quite as ridiculous as it may have seemed. Because stories, after all, are about choices. And not that long ago Ravani had made the generous but foolish choice to set another soul free. If a soul chooses to do the right thing, for the right reasons, it nearly always turns out well for them in the end.

The woods fell silent. There was neither the sound of a soulless orphan-catcher, nor a stout-hearted cowbear.

"We did it," Beth said.

"*Rav* did it," Annabel said.

"No," Tristan said. "Rav bought us time. But that's not the sort of man who gives up." Tristan was very, very right. "We need to get to a telephone. And fast."

Ravani led them away, sticking to the woods but moving toward town. He was creeping along the forest's edge when he looked out through the trees and saw something that stopped him where he stood.

The slaughterhouse.

Ravani knew what was inside the slaughterhouse. Blood and bones and entrails and blades and hoists and bolt guns and meat hooks and nightmares, yes. But also an office. An office with a telephone.

Ravani looked at the slaughterhouse looming in the darkness. There were no *hisses*, or *moos*, or *thuds*. But, still, the slaughterhouse was quite literally the last place on earth he wanted to go. He gulped.

It would take a hero, perhaps, for a soul to enter its own worst nightmare. Could Ravani be a hero?

Well, he thought, *if a cow can be a bear . . .*

"Follow me," he said, and darted from the forest and across the clearing toward the slaughterhouse.

CHAPTER FIFTY

In Which There Are Shrieks,
and Fangs

Ravani climbed through the fence around the feeding lot where, once upon a time, he had saved Lucky (who in turn had saved him). The rest followed him. He ran, hunched over, along the side of the slaughterhouse, toward the door to the killing floor.

"Annabel," Ravani called, and she ran up and he pointed at the lock. She got straight to work.

A moment later, the lock clicked and fell free. Tristan swung the door open.

Annabel scurried inside, followed by the rest. Ravani peeked one last time out at the woods, the feeding lot, the road, all standing silent and silver and shadowy.

There was no sign of the Hunter. No sound of tires on asphalt. He pressed the door closed as quickly and as quietly as he could.

He could hear, in the darkness behind him, the frightened breathing of the Ragabonds.

He could smell, in the air all around him, the unfortunately familiar smell of the insides of animals.

Ravani's eyes began to adjust to the slaughterhouse darkness. The narrow windows nearly three stories up were letting in just enough moonlight to cast a dim glow onto the killing floor, gruesome machinery, and huddled children below.

Tristan joined him at the door, his shoulder pressed against Ravani's. The older boy put his ear against the door.

"I think the coast is clear," he whispered.

Ravani nodded.

The door suddenly slammed against them. Ravani screamed. He tried to jump back, but the door had jammed over his toes, pinning him in place.

An arm shot through the opening. An oil-stained canvas sleeve, torn in places, ending in a very pale scratched hand clutching a throwing net.

The coast was not, after all, clear.

"*Aaaargh!*" Ravani shrieked.

The man on the other side of the door grunted and heaved against it. The arm that was attached to the man on the other side of the door dropped the throwing net and swiveled and grabbed and clawed at the door and the air and at Ravani's shirt.

Ravani batted at the horrible arm with both of his hands, slapping at it like a cat playing with a ball of yarn, shrieking all the while.

The screams of children echoed through the slaughterhouse.

Through his terror and pain, Ravani realized that, completely by accident, he'd done it. Or rather, his foot jammed in the door had. Whether he liked it or not, he'd stopped their pursuer. The Ragabonds could make the phone call, now, while Ravani bravely stood and shrieked.

"*GO!*" Ravani screeched between shrieks. The Ragabonds gaped at him and the rattling door and the flailing arm. No one moved. They were waiting for him. He pointed along the wall in the direction they should go, following the yellow line to the office and the telephone. "*LATER!*" he added, meaning that he would go after them when he could.

Colt, standing in front of Annabel, sprang into action.

"He wants us to go up that ladder!" he cried incorrectly. "Go, Beth!"

There was, apparently, a ladder.

Before he could shriek otherwise, Beth clambered up it. Benjamin followed. Then Annabel and Colt.

"*NO!*" Ravani screeched again.

"Don't worry!" Winnie declared, stepping forward. "We won't leave you, Rav!"

It was a steadfast, if mistaken, interpretation of Ravani's shriek.

Winnie didn't have a lot of options. She was too close to throw something and her hands were empty.

Sometimes a soul just has to work with what its got.

She leaped toward the arm, her teeth bared.

She sank her baby teeth fangs into the flesh just below the wrist. She sank them deep. Unlike the man connected to the arm, Winnie was *not* a vegetarian.

From the other side of the door, there was a shriek that was surprisingly similar to Ravani's. For a moment, they nearly harmonized.

Winnie growled and shook her head like a dog.

With a final, ragged scream the arm tore free from Winnie's bite and jerked back through the door.

They heard a few fumbled backpedaling footsteps, then a mucky *thud*.

Winnie pushed the door closed, sliding it off Ravani's foot.

He stood there, panting. Tristan had already followed the rest of them up the ladder. It was only Ravani and Winnie and Virginia left on the floor.

"We should probably go," Virginia said.

CHAPTER FIFTY-ONE

In Which There Is Snarling, and Decomposition

The Hunter lay on his back in the thick, squishy mud outside the slaughterhouse, breathing hard.

He looked at his arm. Fingered the deep, vicious fang marks.

Badger, he was pretty sure, based on the ferocity of the bite and spacing of the teeth. He'd had to contend with a larger share of the animal kingdom than he'd bargained for on this hunt.

And, sniffing warily, he was also *very* sure that what he was lying in was not, in fact, mud.

Bull manure.

The Hunter had very little patience for bull manure. And this night he'd had more than enough of it.

He pulled himself to his feet.

Did not bother trying to wipe himself off.

The Hunter did not smile or growl.

His lip *was* flickering in a bit of a snarl, but that was more of an involuntary twitch.

The Hunter had always been very proud of his composure. But he was, perhaps, beginning to lose his grip. He stood for a moment, ankle-deep in bull manure, and tried to recompose himself. He failed. One could say, in fact, that he actually *de*composed a bit. It was understandable. We all will eventually.

So, face twitching and arm throbbing and hands bleeding and clothes stinking, the Hunter set his jaw and marched toward the door.

Chapter Fifty-Two

In Which There Is a Calf,
and Blood

avani was only halfway up the ladder when the door was kicked open once again.

He wasn't sure why he was even climbing the ladder to begin with, to be honest. There was no telephone in the slaughterhouse rafters, as far as he knew.

But sometimes when a soul is scared, it doesn't think. It follows.

"Hurry!" he hissed to Virginia's feet, which were climbing the rungs in front of his face.

Behind him, the strange man stepped with slow determination into the dark slaughterhouse.

His head snapped toward the sound of frantic metallic climbing to his left.

Ravani was just pulling himself up onto the metal grate landing at the top of the ladder.

The Hunter leaped.

And fell promptly onto his face on the concrete floor.

He grunted and looked down at his feet. They were tangled in what had been a throwing net but was now a tripping net that he himself had dropped there. The Hunter's nostrils flared. He decomposed a bit more.

Ravani had reached the walkway and clattered along it to

join the others clustered a bit farther on. "Go!" he panted. But they didn't. And then he saw why. It wasn't a walkway so much as a platform. A rather small one. Fenced in by safety railings all around. A dead end. And with the Hunter standing at the bottom of the ladder that was the only way out.

They were like fish in a barrel. Or, even more so, like cows in a slaughterhouse.

"Why did you tell us to come up here, Rav?" Virginia asked, clearly unimpressed with their escape options.

"I . . . that's not what I . . . ," Ravani sputtered breathlessly. But then he saw it. A steel cable, running from the wall above them down and across the slaughterhouse floor. Ravani didn't know what its grisly purpose was during the day and he didn't care. Because it ended just above the door that led to Skinister's office. "There! We can slide down that!"

Tristan followed Ravani's pointing finger. "How?"

"The handcuffs!" Colt exclaimed. "Loop them over!"

Behind and beneath them, the Hunter yanked the net off himself and rose to his feet.

Tristan raised his shackled hand and tossed the dangling end of the handcuffs over the steel cable, then grabbed the empty end with his other hand. "Annabel," he said, "neck." Annabel jumped up and wrapped her arms tight around Tristan's neck and he kicked off and then slid away, picking up speed as they went, the handcuff chain zinging as they zipped down the cable.

"Wow," Colt said. "I didn't think that would actually work."

Behind them, the echoing *clang*s of boots on ladder rungs.

Colt helped Benjamin get up on the rail and loop his hand-cuffs over the cable.

"Okay if I hitch a ride, brother?" Colt asked.

"Fine by me."

Colt grabbed on to Benjamin's handcuff chain and off they whizzed.

Beth went next, then Winnie, and then Virginia. The Hunter's grunts and footsteps grew closer with each of Ravani's pounding heartbeats.

Ravani helped Virginia up onto the rail and she swung her shackle over and grabbed the end with the same hand. Ravani felt the platform vibrate beneath him and heard the unmistakable sound of stomping footsteps coming his way.

He gave Virginia a shove and jumped up on the rail. Whirled his handcuff chain over the cable. Grabbed the end. Nearly swooned when he saw how far down the concrete floor was. From this height, *killing* floor was probably an even more accurate label. There was no time for hesitation, however. He closed his eyes tight and kicked off from the railing and slid away down the steel . . . and then stopped.

Dangled there, far too far above far too hard of a floor. He was stuck, somehow. Looking back, he saw why: the very strange man—now also very dirty—was leaning out over the platform railing, holding Ravani's right shoe by the laces.

"Gaah!" Ravani screamed.

The man pulled, reeling him in like a wiggling fish. Closed his other hand around Ravani's calf.

Ravani's hands were busy clinging tight to the handcuffs, and his right foot was busy being clutched by a monster. Only his left foot was free. He raised his left knee to his chest, his leg coiled like a spring.

The man saw it. His manic eyes widened farther.

"Don't," he grunted, "you," he seethed, "dare," he finished.

Ravani dared.

His foot shot like a slaughterhouse bolt gun. His shoe connected with the man's furiously flaring nose.

Sometimes a sole is just what you need.

There was the gruesome *crack* of bone breaking. A gush of blood. A grunt.

Ravani broke free.

He sped through the darkness, the moonlight glinting in flashes off the slaughtering machines and blades below.

Chapter Fifty-Three

In Which There Is Gagging,
but No Gratitude

The Hunter, as he plummeted toward the concrete floor, had a brief thought about his own mortality.

He braced himself for what he was sure would be a very hard, and possibly fatal, landing.

Instead, though, he landed in something soft. Well, not *soft* so much as *soggy*.

Soggy is rarely a pleasant adjective. Especially in a slaughter-house.

He looked around. He was lying on his stomach. Surrounded snugly by four walls.

It was too dark to see what sort of soggy he was lying in. But it wasn't too dark to gag. Which he did.

If he could have seen the outside of the walls that were around him, he would have seen them painted with the words LUNG BUCKET. This was not really an accurate label, though. It was more of a bin.

The Hunter didn't know it, but in the Skinister Quality Meats Slaughterhouse, the lungs of the deceased beasts were collected separately from the other parts. The specifics of exactly *why* the lungs were collected separately were neither pleasant nor relevant.

What was relevant, though, is that lungs are very soft, and

that the Lung Bucket hadn't been emptied that day because the slaughterhouse had closed early for the holiday.

Lucky Hunter.

The Hunter should have been grateful for the Lung Bucket, perhaps. He wasn't.

Lungs don't smell. Noses do. But lungs stink.

Still gagging, the Hunter squirmed toward the nearest wall and pulled himself up and over the edge and dropped to the floor.

"Erk," the Hunter said, "grrrk."

He crawled away across the concrete floor, leaving a slimy trail of lung juice. Grunted himself up to standing. Using his very well-developed power of concentration, he managed to settle his gags down into something much more like whimpers. He attempted to clench his jaw and narrow his eyes into the intense look of a determined predator, but his facial twitch made that tricky. He looked more like a newly house-trained puppy who very much needed to be let outside.

The Hunter was many things, good and bad. And one of them was determined. Very.

Bravely holding down his stomach contents, he began to walk.

CHAPTER FIFTY-FOUR

In Which There Are Gasping Lungs, and Emptying Stomachs

Annabel was tinkering with the office doorknob when Ravani saw, yet again, the man approaching.

Ravani had thought, when he'd seen the man's very cold and very calm and very pitiless face in the forest, that it couldn't possibly be any scarier. But when he saw that same face twitching and scratched and splattered with cow blood, he realized he'd been wrong. Very.

He looked to Annabel, crouched by the door. Back to the man, trudging closer by the second. Even if the door opened at that moment, they wouldn't all get through in time.

"Quick," he heard Benjamin say. "Undo my cuff, sister." He held his manacled wrist toward Annabel.

"Not now," Tristan said. "She's got to—"

"*Lancaster Lockup*," Benjamin said, which made no sense to Ravani but seemed to make sense to Tristan.

"Oh. Okay," he said, eyeing their pursuer. "Be careful."

There was a *clatter* and *clink* and then Benjamin scurried off away into the darkness.

The man stopped about fifteen feet from them, between two silent slaughter machines.

The man slumped his backpack off his shoulders. Opened it. Pulled out a throwing net. Dropped the pack to the ground.

"Last," he said, "chance."

"Watch out," Virginia said, pointing at his feet.

"Nice," the man said, "try." It was a typical childish trick.

These, however, were not typical children.

There were two *clicks* at the man's feet. He looked down in time to see Benjamin leap onto his backpack, grab hold of it, and then roll away with it in his arms. The man lunged to grab him.

But didn't budge.

He looked down at his feet.

Light glinted off a pair of his handcuffs. One end was around his ankle. The other was around the iron leg of the very heavy, very gruesome industrial killing machine beside him.

The keys were in his backpack.

He looked up at the children who had led him through dark forests and musty garages and bear attacks and bull manure and bins of unmentionable entrails.

"You," the man growled.

"Win," Virginia finished for him. It wasn't what he was going to say.

Benjamin joined the rest of them at the door.

"Nice work, brother," Colt said. Benjamin shrugged.

"What's that stuck to his chest?" Beth asked.

The man lowered his head slowly to look down.

What was stuck to his chest was, in fact, a lung. With his own lungs, the Hunter gasped in a breath. The bovine lung glistened. The man, at that point, lost the long battle with his stomach.

"Erk," the man said, "grrrk," he continued, and then "huarah-hhhh," he finished. He hunched over, and the lung peeled slowly off his coveralls and *splatt*ed into the puddle he'd just made.

"Oh," Benjamin said. "Did someone say the code word?"

"No," seven voices answered immediately.

"Looks like someone ate corn for dinner," Colt said. Which was true.

"Shut up, Colt," several voices said.

The man straightened up. Wiped at his chin with a soiled sleeve. He turned and took hold of the monstrous apparatus he was shackled to. And then leaned back in a full-body tug.

Grunt-screeeechSCRAPE!

The machine moved. Just barely. A quarter of an inch, perhaps. Not very far.

But a quarter of an inch toward a grated trench in the floor. It was technically called a *blood gutter*, but that wasn't important. What *was* important was that, once the leg of the machine reached the blood gutter, the handcuff would be able to slide free.

"Man," Beth said. "This is getting a little old."

"It's almost inspiring," Virginia said.

Behind them, there was a cheerful, "Got it!"

Annabel straightened up from the doorknob, smiling.

"Lead the way, Frog Master," she said.

Chapter Fifty-Five

In Which There Is Mozart, and Metaphors

Mr. Skinister didn't like working late at the slaughterhouse. Truth be told, Mr. Skinister didn't like working at the slaughterhouse at all.

But, at the very least, when he worked late at the slaughterhouse, he could count on peace and quiet. Very few people just dropped by a slaughterhouse, after all.

So it's fair to say that he was surprised when Ravani burst into his office through the killing floor door.

He shouted and jumped back in his desk chair, knocking the needle of the record player out of its groove with a scratching snarl. Mozart, who'd been unknowingly covering the sound of a juvenile locksmith and a vomiting predator, fell silent. Mr. Skinister clutched at his chest, eyes nearly as wide as his mouth.

"Mr. Skinister!" Ravani exclaimed. "What are you doing here?"

Mr. Skinister sucked in a few huffing breaths. "Having a heart attack. Nearly, anyway. What are *you* doing here?" It was a very fair question.

Ravani stepped forward. Seven more children crowded through the door behind him.

Mr. Skinister's rapidly blinking eyes took them in. He made

an attempt to smile at Virginia when he recognized her. He recognized Colt as well.

"Roast beef," Mr. Skinister said with recognition, nodding at him.

"Pea soup," Colt answered.

"So . . . what are you doing here?" Mr. Skinister asked again.

"Um. Running away from a maniac with handcuffs," Ravani replied, pointing back toward the killing floor with a thumb.

"Really?"

"Pretty much."

Mr. Skinister looked at Ravani for half a breath. He'd known Ravani for several years now, but he'd never known him to be a liar. This is why it's wise to always tell the truth. A soul never knows when it's going to need another soul to believe an entirely true but completely ridiculous story.

Through the door came the sound of a very heavy killing machine scooting a quarter of an inch closer to a blood gutter.

Grunt-screeeechSCRAPE! It was every bit as chilling as the *hissmoooTHUDs* that usually echoed through the slaughterhouse.

"Well, then you better lock the door," Mr. Skinister said. Tristan pulled the door closed and clicked the lock.

"Does he mean to do you harm?" Mr. Skinister asked. Eight heads nodded.

"He put us in handcuffs," Winnie said, holding up her wrist.

"He chased us through the woods," Benjamin added.

"He threw nets on us," Beth said.

"He locked us in a truck," Annabel said.

"He lied about having ice cream," Colt spat. The other Ragabonds all looked at him. "Well, he did," Colt muttered sulkily. "Not out loud, maybe, but it was implied."

Mr. Skinister had heard enough. Mr. Skinister owned a killing factory, but he was not a violent man. He did not like people who handcuffed children, and he did not like people who threw children in trucks, and he outright *loathed* people who lied about having ice cream.

He reached for the phone on his desk. "I'll call the sheriff."

"No!" several voices said at once.

"Why not?"

"Because we're *also* running from the police," Colt said.

"Well, not *yet* technically. But we will be if you call them," Virginia added.

Mr. Skinister eyed them. "Have you broken any laws?"

"No," Ravani said.

Mr. Skinister shot a pointed look at their handcuffs.

"And yet . . ."

"It's a long story," Benjamin said.

"A long *secret* story," Annabel whispered.

"We just need to use your telephone," Tristan said, stepping forward.

Mr. Skinister kept his hand on his phone. "I can't let you use it unless I know the reason. I wouldn't forgive myself if something terrible happened to you children."

Tristan ran his fingers through his hair. He looked to Ravani. "You're in the book," he murmured. "And you know him. Can we trust him?"

Ravani swallowed. He thought of Mr. Skinister, of all the times he'd spoken to him, of his soft voice and kind words and his gentle sorrow about the work that he did. Mr. Skinister killed a lot of beasts, no doubt. But he was not a Wolf.

Grunt-screeeechSCRAPE!

"Yes," he said. "You can trust him. I think you have to."

And so they did. In hushed and hurried voices, taking turns, the Ragabonds told the owner of the slaughterhouse their secret. They told of lost parents, and lonely children, and orphanages, and midnight escapes, and hiding children . . . but most of all they told him about a family. *Their* family. A family without any parents, perhaps, but very much a family nonetheless. There were, at times, tears in Mr. Skinister's eyes. There was, always, a look of wonder on his face.

When they finished, there was a lingering moment of silence. Their story—their secret—echoed in the room around them.

"So you see," Ravani said, "they're not criminals. They're . . . they're . . ."

"Lambs," Mr. Skinister said quietly. Ravani nodded. He'd been going to say *birds just looking for a nest*, but sometimes different souls have different ways of saying the same thing.

"And through that door is . . . ," Ravani started to say, pointing toward where the man lay in wait.

"A slaughterhouse," Mr. Skinister croaked, and Ravani nodded again even though he'd planned on saying *a Hunter*.

Grunt-screeeechSCRAPE!

Mr. Skinister looked with wide eyes at the frightened family gathered around his desk.

Stories are about choices. Mr. Skinister made one.

He pushed the phone across the desk.

"Make your call," he said.

Seven pairs of shoulders sagged in relief. Not Ravani's, though.

Seven mouths stretched in grateful smiles. Not Ravani's, though.

Tristan lifted the phone receiver off its cradle. He put it to his ear. His finger reached for the call button.

"Wait," Ravani said. Tristan's eyes flashed to him.

Grunt-screeeechSCRAPE!

"We don't have time," Tristan said. "We need to go, and—"

"What if you don't, though?" Ravani interrupted. "What if you stay?"

Chapter Fifty-Six

In Which a Very Big Plan Is Pitched,
and a Very Small Dream Comes True

Eight pairs of eyes stared at Ravani.

"Listen, Rav," Beth said gently, "I know it's hard to say goodbye, and that you and Virginia are—"

"No, it's not about that." He looked at Virginia, who raised an eyebrow at him. "Well, okay, it's not *just* about that. But . . . what if you didn't need to hide anymore?"

"Listen, Rav," Tristan said again, "you're a good kid, but—"

"No, *you* listen," Ravani cut in. Tristan's eyebrows went up. "You yourself said that the magic wasn't telling you to leave. And it's still not, is it?"

Tristan frowned. "Well, I mean, I guess—"

"I'll take that as a no. And you," Ravani said, turning to Colt. "You said on the bridge that you're tired of always running and hiding, right?" He spun to Benjamin and Winnie. "On the night I found out your secret, you both said that you wanted to stay, that you liked it here." He looked to Annabel. "And you said this place was perfect. Your favorite place yet." Annabel smiled at him. He looked to Beth. "And you . . ." He trailed off, brow furrowed. "Well, I haven't talked to you that much. But I bet you'd stay if you could, too." Finally, he turned to Virginia.

"And you," Ravani said, his voice dropping. "You said that

you feel like you *belong* here. That it's the first place you've felt like you belonged, ever since . . ." He stopped. Took a little breath. "Ever since." He swallowed. "I think you belong here, too, Virginia. I think you deserve a friend. I think you deserve boat races, and carnivals, and piano lessons. You've got a family. A great one. But I think you deserve a home, too. I *know* you do."

It was possible that Virginia's eyes glistened. It was even possible that her chin quivered, just a bit. Or it could have just been the dim office lighting.

"It doesn't matter if we want to stay," Tristan's tired voice said behind him. "We've been found. That means we run. We're Ragabonds. It's what we've always done."

Ravani kept his eyes on Virginia, but spoke loud enough for Tristan to hear him.

"Things don't always have to be the way they've always been." His friend had told him that once. She'd been right. So was he. "And I think I know how you can stay. Safe and together."

And then he laid out his plan. Well, not a *plan*, perhaps, but an idea. An idea that had been slowly growing in his brain and in his heart for a few days.

The Ragabonds listened quietly. They were, perhaps, like birds. Trapped together in shadows. And he, perhaps, was trying to open a window. From time to time his words were punctuated by the sound of a monster in the next room, inching toward them.

"And *that*," he finished, "*that* is how you could stay. Maybe?"

Tristan's mouth was set in a hard line. His eyes were narrowed. He shook his head. "It's a . . . nice offer, Rav, but we can't—"

"I think we should do it." It was Annabel's small voice that had interrupted Tristan.

"You do?" Colt asked, looking at her. She nodded.

"I love being a Ragabond," she said. "But I'm tired of running away. I'm tired of being scared." Her voice shook, just a little.

"I know," Colt said softly, and took her hand. He looked at her for a moment more, then turned his eyes on Tristan. "Then I think we should do it, too, brother."

Winnie leaned to whisper in Benjamin's ear. He nodded, then whispered something back into hers.

"We think we should stay," they said together.

All eyes went to Beth. Her lips were pressed in a tense line. She shook her head.

"I don't know," Beth said to Tristan. She blew out a sigh. "But it might be worth a try."

"It's a yes from me, too," another voice said. They all looked at Mr. Skinister.

"I don't think you get a vote," Annabel whispered to him.

"Oh. Sorry."

Only Virginia remained. She had the worried little wrinkle between her eyes that she always got when she was really thinking about something.

"I want you to stay, Virginia," Ravani said softly to her.

"Obviously," she answered.

"But if you decide to leave, I'll be totally okay."

She looked at him with her serious face. Then, one corner of her mouth rose up.

"Liar," she said. She kept her eyes on Ravani, but raised her voice to speak to the room. "I think we should stay."

Tristan still had the phone in his hand. His jaw was clenched, his brow furrowed, his mouth tight. He didn't look angry, though. He looked scared.

"Being a Ragabond was never about running away," Virginia said, her voice gentle. "It's about staying together. You said so yourself."

"But what about the *Always and Forever*?" Tristan said. "It says, '*We'll wander and rescue, always and forever . . .*'"

"That's not the whole line, brother," Beth murmured. "It keeps going."

"'*We'll wander and rescue, always and forever,*'" Colt recited, "'*until we find where we belong.*'"

Tristan's throat bobbed in a swallow. His eyes blinked wetly. Then he looked to each of the others, one by one.

"We always wanted to find a home someday," Virginia said. "Welcome to someday, brother. Maybe we're already here."

Tristan's eyes narrowed. He looked, for a moment, off into the distance. Then his eyes drifted to Ravani.

"I hear it," he said, his voice hoarse.

"The magic?" Ravani asked. Tristan nodded. "What's it saying to do?"

Tristan blinked and blew out a breath.

He hung up the phone.

"Okay. How do we make this work?" he asked. Through the door came another *grunt-screeeechSCRAPE!* "We have to hurry."

"We have a phone call to make," Ravani said. "And . . . we'll need some help from you," he added, looking to Mr. Skinister.

Mr. Skinister shot him a dubious look.

"You need some livestock slaughtered and cut to order?"

"No," Ravani said quickly. "Definitely not. We don't need slaughterhouse owner help. We need local judge help." And then he outlined the sort of help he would need from the Honorable Judge Skinister.

"Hmmm," the man said. "It's . . . interesting. It's not *specifically* illegal, I suppose. And if something isn't specifically illegal, I suppose that makes it . . . vaguely legal?"

"Sounds good to me," Ravani said.

"But . . . ," Mr. Skinister trailed off.

"But what?" Virginia asked.

"It would take a lot of real tricky paperwork."

Colt straightened to attention. He flashed Ravani a quick look and took a bold step forward. He squinted heroically and cleared his throat.

"Lay it on me, old man," he said.

Ravani grinned.

Colt had been right, that day on the bridge.

The words *did* sound spectacularly nifty.

Chapter Fifty-Seven

In Which There Is a Strange Call, and Even Stranger Paperwork

While Colt rifled like a savant through the official forms and documents in Judge Skinister's file cabinets, Ravani made the phone call.

It was a strange phone call. He had a lot to explain. But no time to do it.

Luckily, the person he spoke to trusted him.

And so, just a few minutes later, his mother and father knocked on the slaughterhouse front door.

Ravani's parents looked around at the seven children, and their only son, and Mr. Skinister.

"All right," his mother said. "We're here. Now you have some explaining to do."

From the killing floor, a *grunt-screeeechSCRAPE!* sounded. Like the ticking of a clock, but far more sinister. Ravani did not have time for another lengthy explanation.

"They don't have parents," he said, pointing at the gathered Ragabonds.

"Yes they do," his mother replied with a frown. "I spoke to their mother."

"That was me, Mrs. Foster," Beth said, in her uncanny adult

woman voice. She cleared her throat. "I promise," she added in her normal voice.

"But we heard their father . . ."

"All me, neighbor!" Colt shouted gruffly with a wave, still sorting through Mr. Skinister's legal files.

"All they have is each other, and they're in trouble. Big trouble. There's a very bad man chasing them."

Ravani's mother blinked. Not quite a blink of *disbelief*, perhaps, but certainly one of at least *doubt*.

Ravani stepped to the killing floor door, unclicked the lock, and swung it open.

A bloodied, muddied man was framed in the doorway, half in slaughterhouse shadows. He paused mid-grunt, his face twisted and eyes wild and nostrils flared. He snarled at them and yanked the morbid machine harder. *Grunt-screeeechSCRAPE!*

"Oh dear," Ravani's mother said. Ravani slammed the door.

"They haven't done anything wrong," Ravani said. "They're just a family. And they need a home." Ravani took a deep breath. He looked into his mother's eyes. "I told them that maybe *we* could give them one."

Mrs. Foster's brow furrowed. "You mean . . . ?"

Ravani nodded.

Mrs. Foster frowned.

Virginia stepped forward. She looked at Mrs. Foster with her solemn eyes. "I'm sorry," she said. "For lying to you. And I know it's a lot to ask. It's okay if you don't want us."

Mrs. Foster shook her head. Ravani's heart sank. When she spoke, her voice was soft but firm.

"Ravani Foster, did you tell all these children that they could live with us?"

Ravani's heart sank even lower. A child should always ask their parents before taking the last cookie, or getting a kitten, or adopting seven new children into their family. Sometimes, though, there just isn't time.

He gulped. "Yes, Mother."

She looked at him closely for a quiet moment.

Then she smiled.

"Good boy," she said. Ravani's held breath whooshed out in relief. Virginia looked at him and her serious face smiled. Just a little bit. Ravani smiled back. "Of course we'll need some time to talk this over, and think about—"

"We don't have time," Ravani cut in.

"This guy ain't super patient," Benjamin said, pointing back toward the killing floor.

"And he has full legal right to take us," Beth added. "Probably with a cash reward."

Ravani's mother swallowed.

Mrs. Foster looked to Mr. Foster, who nodded, and then to Ravani, who nodded, too. She looked to Mr. Skinister. "Where do we sign?"

"I got you covered, Ms. Foster," Colt said, clearing a place on the desk and arranging the papers in piles. He turned to Mr. Skinister. "So, Your Honor, if you start by signing these three forms, and attach them to *this* one, I think that'll do."

Mr. Skinister squinted at the top form.

"Er . . . but this is the form for—"

"Listen," Colt cut in briskly, "none of these forms are *actually* what we need, but put together in the right way they do grant us temporary clerical legitimacy in the eyes of the law until we get our hands on the proper forms."

"They do?"

"More or less. It's like . . ." Colt screwed up his face, then shot a little smirk at Virginia and Ravani. ". . . like building a boat out of a coffin. It'll get us just far enough downriver." He turned to Mr. and Mrs. Foster, his face dropping back to business.

"Now, I'll need you two to fill out and sign these forms here. Nicest handwriting, please."

Mrs. Foster scanned the paperwork.

"This is a building permit for adding an addition to a house."

Colt blew out a breath, his patience clearly wearing thin. "Yes, I'm aware of that. Look closer, though, and you'll see it covers any additions, renovations, or *improvements*. That's us. With the possible exception of my sister." He dodged Virginia's kick.

There was a scribbling of pens and a whispering of paper. Colt looked over their work, pointed out a few places they'd forgotten to initial, and then with a flourish produced one more document.

"Now," he said dramatically. "The last one. We need all three of your signatures on this one."

Mrs. Foster took the pen and held it over the paper. She paused, then looked up at Colt and the rest of them.

"So if I sign here, we'll be legally adopting you all?"

"It is the way I do it." Colt shrugged.

Mrs. Foster's eyes found Ravani's.

"I always said I wanted a big family. Someday," she said with a smile. And then the pen scratched across the page in a loopy, triumphant signature.

Annabel cheered.

Winnie and Benjamin high-fived.

Ravani looked at Virginia. She wasn't smiling, but her eyes were shining. She looked scared, to be sure, but also *hopeful*.

"Well," Mrs. Foster said, sliding the paper toward Colt and raising her eyes toward the rest of them, "my goodness. I suppose I should—"

"Oh," Colt said, interrupting her. He shuffled through the paperwork, frowning. "Uh-oh."

"What is it?" Tristan asked.

"Well, we're not *quite* there yet. Looks like we really need one more signature."

"Okay," Beth said. "Whose?"

From under the closed door came another *grunt-screeeech-SCRAPE!*

"His," Colt said, tilting his head toward the killing floor.

Chapter Fifty-Eight

In Which There Is Some Fraud,
and a Flash

When the steel leg of the industrial bone grinder finally scraped over the empty blood gutter and the Hunter was able to slide the loop of his handcuff off and free, he fell back and sat for a brief moment to catch his breath.

He tried to collect himself, but there wasn't all that much left to collect. He was, by that point, very decomposed.

He marched—handcuffs clattering behind him on the concrete floor—to the door that the children had disappeared through. And then the Hunter walked into a scene he hadn't been at all expecting.

The children were arranged in a smiling cluster. They weren't running, or hiding, or begging, or siccing bears or badgers on him. There was a man and a woman standing with them, also smiling. The Hunter stopped.

"Come in, come in!" a beefy, mustachioed man called to him. The man was wearing a black robe and a white wig. "You're just in time for the ceremony!"

"I," the Hunter rasped, "am?"

"Yes! Step on over!"

The Hunter blinked and looked around. Besides the children and the man and the woman and the jovial judge, two other people were in the room. One of them was a police officer, who stepped toward him.

"Good evening, sir," the police officer said in a thick Irish brogue. "So glad you could make it. Please, take a seat," he said, gesturing toward a chair by the desk.

If the Hunter had been more composed, he may have noticed that the police officer's uniform was rather poorly tailored. And that the silver star pinned to it didn't read POLICE DEPARTMENT, but PROPS DEPARTMENT. The uniform was, in fact, from the local high school's drama department. And the person in the uniform was more of a local café owner with a theatrical flair for performance than a legal officer of the law. And he was fairly out of breath from hurrying over after receiving one of the strangest phone calls of his life. But the Hunter didn't notice that, either.

The Hunter took a seat.

One of the children moved to his side.

"Hiya," the kid said with a nod, then looked the Hunter up and down and lowered his voice. "Sorry about the, uh . . . well, everything." The Hunter's eye twitched. The kid clicked his tongue and pulled a piece of paper on the desk a little closer. "Right. We just need you to sign here." He held a pen out toward the Hunter.

The Hunter looked at the pen. "Why?" he said. It was a very fair question.

"Funny you should ask!" the other stranger in the room answered, springing forward. She had curly hair and sparkling eyes and held a large camera in her hands. "I'm Hortense Wallenbach, editor of the *Slaughterville Spectator*. And you are about to play an important role in a historic moment!" She smiled widely at the Hunter. The Hunter did not smile back. "Were you aware that these children recently escaped from an orphanage?"

"Yes," the Hunter replied, very truthfully.

"Do you know *why* they escaped?"

The Hunter looked at the woman without answering, his eye still twitching. It had never occurred to him to wonder why they had escaped, let alone to care.

"Well, I'll *tell* you why!" the woman exclaimed. And then she told him.

It was quite a story.

It involved a traveling circus act, and a family of acrobats and animal tamers, and a dramatic kidnapping by an evil ringmaster, and a years-long search that had nearly ended in hopelessness. But, then, that very night, there had been a miraculous and tearful reunion. The children's mother (a contortionist) and their father (a human cannonball), in town to perform in the carnival, had finally found their beloved offspring, who had been looking for them all along.

"And here they are," the woman finished with a flourish. "Their mother, the Astounding Astoria, and their father, Indigo the Indestructible!"

The woman and man gave a little wave.

"A family, together again at last!" The reporter beamed. "This is front-page stuff! And all we need you to do is just sign this little form right here to make it official."

The Hunter looked from face to face to face.

It actually, almost, made sense. He thought of the children, escaping from his bolted truck. Slipping out of his handcuffs. He thought of them flying through the slaughterhouse on a steel wire. He thought of all the animals that had attacked him since he'd arrived. The story he'd been told actually, almost, made the *most* sense to explain the night that he'd had. Except, perhaps, why *he* would need to sign anything.

"Why," he asked, "me?"

At that moment, the phone rang.

The judge picked it up. "Why, hello, Madame Murdosa, Thank you for returning my call. Yes, I have him right here." And then he handed the telephone to the Hunter. The Hunter, eye twitching harder than ever, held it to his ear.

"Good evening," Madame Murdosa's voice said through the receiver. "So sorry for this misunderstanding. Terrible to put you through all this for nothing. But I'm afraid you must sign the form and return these poor children to their rightful parents. Ta-ta."

The Hunter was very familiar with Madame Murdosa's voice, and the voice speaking to him was, no doubt, very much hers.

Yet the Hunter, because of his advanced state of decomposition, hadn't noticed that the oldest girl was missing from the crowd in the office. But missed details are often important. Very.

The boy held the pen out a little closer to him.

This was not the ending that the Hunter had had in mind. Not in his wildest dreams, as a matter of fact, would he have ever imagined an ending such as this, even if he'd been the type to have wild dreams (which he wasn't).

The Hunter did not want to sign the paperwork. He wanted to drive away with an ice cream truck full of firmly—but legally— restrained children.

A soul doesn't always get what it wants, though.

The Hunter took the pen.

He bent toward the paper.

The paperwork looked official, and it was signed by a judge.

The Hunter shrugged with one shoulder. It felt strange. He wasn't sure he'd ever actually shrugged before.

He signed the form.

"Smile!" the reporter said, dropping to her knee in a corner and pointing her camera.

Everyone around him smiled. The Hunter did not. There was a bright flash.

No one—not even a bitter orphanage madame—would ever be able to claim that the signature had been forged or that the children's custody hadn't been signed away by a legal representative.

"Okay, okay, off you go," the police officer said briskly, helping the Hunter to his feet aggressively. "Show's over, nothing more to see, time to hit the road, buddy."

The Hunter's backpack was pressed into his hands. Handcuffs were unlocked and returned. And then, before he could collect what few thoughts his exhausted brain had left, the Hunter was outside and the door closed behind him.

A few minutes later, he watched the lights of Slaughterville recede into the distance in his rearview mirror. He was very glad to be leaving. He was very determined to never return.

"Good," the Hunter said very sincerely, "riddance."

CHAPTER FIFTY-NINE

In Which There Is an Ending,
and a Beginning

A lot of people in Slaughterville were awake the night the children stayed. There was, after all, fireworks. And a boat race. And a car chase of sorts, and some sabotage, and a bovine rescue, and a slaughterhouse showdown, and a fraudulent phone call, and some dramatic paperwork. Those sorts of things tend to keep people awake.

And it ended with two souls (who had become friends) *not* saying goodbye. And it ended with a family finding a home. Each and every bird to a nest.

And, although no one saw it coming, those two souls and that one family hadn't just changed their own lives and their own stories. Stories overlap, after all. Indeed, nearly the whole town of Slaughterville was changed, in ways large and small, by that family of children that had arrived on one night, and stayed on another.

So it was, some weeks later, that the two souls at the heart of it all found themselves finishing a paper route in a town that was very different from what it had been not all that long before.

Their second-to-last stop was at Fred's Café, which was no longer a café and was in fact no longer even Fred's. It had a new name, painted on a new sign that hung above the door: SOME-PLACE SPECIAL. The sign had been hand-painted by the new owner. She was a superb painter, and a lovely piano player, and a wonderful mother. The food at Someplace Special was mostly vegetarian and entirely delicious. It was only open for breakfast, because the owner wanted the afternoons and evenings to spend with her family. She had, after all, eight children.

"Good morning, sweethearts," she said as they set the newspaper on one of the tables. They each got a hug, and they each gave one. Hugs are nice that way. When you give, you get. Like friendship.

"I got a letter from Fred this morning," Ravani's mother said.

"How's he doing?"

"Just fine. Still waiting tables. Hollywood is a tough place to make it. But he got a small part in a toothpaste commercial. He's voicing a French pirate with gingivitis, apparently?"

"That's unbelievable!" Sheriff Quigley exclaimed from her table.

"It sounds about right," Virginia said with a shrug.

"What? No! I mean today's newspaper! Skinister is developing a *fire-roasted* marinara sauce? Imagine that!"

The sheriff, truth be told, had not changed all that much.

Their last stop was the Bread & Butter Bakery. When they stepped inside, their noses were greeted by far more smells than three kinds of bread. Besides the usual loaves, the cases now also held three kinds of cookies and three kinds of cupcakes.

"Aha!" Mr. Chin shouted from behind the counter when he saw them. "Just who I wanted to see . . . my two best taste testers!" He emerged holding a dark brown square, wrapped in a napkin. "Try this. My newest idea. I call it 'Flaming Fudge.' A dark chocolate brownie with roasted red chiles."

Virginia shot Ravani a sideways look. "Sweet and . . . *spicy*?" she asked.

But Mr. Chin just nodded, beaming.

Virginia took a cautious bite and handed the brownie to Ravani, who did the same. They chewed. They frowned.

"Well?" Mr Chin asked.

"Surprising," Virginia mumbled through her mouthful. She grabbed the brownie from Ravani and took another bite.

"Unexpected," Ravani said, reaching to take the brownie back.

"And . . . ?" Mr. Chin looked back and forth between them.

"And," Ravani said, swallowing. Then he smiled. "Wonderful."

"True," Virginia agreed, wiping crumbs from her lips. "Make a big batch."

Mr. Chin grinned and rubbed his hands together. It was a lot more work, making all the new cookies and cupcakes as well as the breads. Luckily, business was booming. And, luckily, he had hired some new help.

"You hear that? They're a hit! We'll make double!" he shouted behind him.

Tristan looked up from the batter he was mixing. "You got it," he said, then winked at Ravani and Virginia. "Morning, sister. Morning, brother."

Hortense Wallenbach was at her desk when they stopped in the newspaper office to drop off the empty delivery bags, her fingers flying in a clicking blur over her typewriter keyboard.

"What's this one about?" Ravani asked.

"Well, it involves a jewel thief, a three-legged horse, and a shipwreck."

"Sounds interesting," Virginia said. "What happens?"

Hortense winked. "You'll have to read it to find out."

"Will it be in next month's issue?" Ms. Wallenbach had been

getting her stories published in the magazine *Tales of Mystery and Mayhem*.

"Nope," Ms. Wallenbach said, her eyes sparkling. "This one's gonna be a little longer, I think. A *lot* longer, maybe."

Ravani grinned. "A book?"

Hortense grinned back. "I'll have to write it to find out. See you tomorrow, kids."

The two friends began the walk home, their mouths still burning pleasantly with the sweet spice of Flaming Fudge. The birds were singing their autumn songs because time, as it always does, had turned the world from one season to the next.

They soon passed what had once been the Skinister slaughterhouse. It was still Skinister's, but it was no longer a slaughterhouse. The SKINISTER QUALITY MEATS sign had been taken down and replaced with a new one that proclaimed SKINISTER'S SCRUMPTIOUS SAUCES.

Ravani's father still worked there, and he still came home wearing a red-splattered apron . . . but now it was stained with tomato juice rather than blood. He had, in fact, gotten a promotion. It turned out that a large-scale slaughterhouse *could* be converted to a sauce factory, if you had a worker who was good at figuring things out and skilled at putting things together, two things that Mr. Foster just happened to be. A machine designed to slice the meat off bones, for instance, could be reconfigured to chop onions. Vats meant to boil down and render pork fat actually worked very well for simmering alfredo sauce. And, apparently, a machine built to dry beef into jerky *could* be tinkered to instead fire-roast tomatoes into marinara. Nothing—not souls, not stories, and not even industrial killing machines—has to be what it has always been.

The building still hummed and clattered with *hisses* and *thuds*, but there were no longer any hopeless *moos*. Ravani didn't avert his eyes when they walked past. Instead, he looked over and waved at Mr. Skinister. He was out in what had once been a pen for beef with a death sentence, but which was now a garden that grew tomatoes, onions, and garlic for some of Skinister's scrumptious sauces. Over the years of holding a constant parade of doomed animals, it had been *very* well fertilized. Mr. Skinister waved back. He was whistling, as he nearly always seemed to be these days.

They crossed the bridge, and stopped for a moment to look down at the water below. The bank beneath them was empty. No ogres lurked. Donnie was still around, of course. And, whenever they saw him, he was still unpleasant. Just the day before, he'd kicked Rav's chair out from under him at school. But Virginia had been there to help him back up.

They stopped when they got to the street they both lived on. Looked at the two houses, facing each other. The two houses had four stories between them—five if you count coffin cellars—but really the two homes had ten stories altogether. Ten stories that perhaps also add up to one.

One of the houses had a cow grazing in the front yard, a cow with a clover-shaped marking on its forehead. It was a friend, but it was also a watchcow. If danger came, they knew that the cow would do what it could to keep them safe.

Ravani lived in the house with the watchcow. He lived there, still, with his mother and his father, but also now with two of his sisters. It meant that he now had to wait a lot longer for a turn in the bathroom, but it was worth it. The sisters he shared a bathroom with still went by the names Virginia and Annabel.

Those were not the names they were born with, but they were the names they wanted to keep. There had been quite a lot of paperwork involved in officially changing their names.

But, luckily, they had a brother who was very good at that sort of thing. He lived across the street, with two other sisters, and two other brothers. There had not been room in one home for all of them, so just like they had turned two families into one, they turned two houses into one home. With Mr. Foster's promotion, and Mrs. Foster's Someplace Special, and with Ravani and Virginia's paper route, and with Tristan now working at the Bread & Butter, they'd been able to afford to keep paying the rent for the house that had once been called the Croward place.

But though they lived separately, they always ate dinner together, as one family. And Mrs. Foster walked across the street every evening, so that each and every child could be tucked in and kissed goodnight, if they wanted. Each bird to a nest.

A found family is every bit as beautiful as a born family. Even more so, perhaps. Stories are about choices, after all, and to *choose* to be a family is as wonderful a story as can be told.

Virginia sighed, looking at their two houses that were one home. "Man. Who'da thought, on that first night we saw each other, that we'd end up like this? Brother and sister."

"It's, uh . . . it's kind of weird that we kissed, now, isn't it?"

Virginia shrugged. "It was always weird that we kissed." She shook her head. "It almost seems ridiculous, though, doesn't it?"

"What does?"

"All of this. Ending up here. It's all just . . . too good. Too happy. To have such a happy ending, for everyone."

"Well, maybe sometimes what the world needs most is just a

happy ending. And they *do* happen, sometimes, to some people. Why not us? Don't we deserve one, at least for now?"

"It's a nice thought, Rav," Virginia said. "But it's wrong. This is a stupid ending, no doubt about it. But I got good news." She cocked an eyebrow at him. "This isn't really the ending of a story. It's the beginning. And stories *are* allowed to have happy beginnings."

Ravani and Virginia looked back toward town. Above the road, just before the bridge, was a new, big hand-painted welcome sign. It had been painted by the woman who ran the café, who also happened to be their mother. Around the words on the sign was a colorful mural of pine trees, and flowing water, and fireworks. And lots of birds.

The sign didn't read WELCOME TO SLAUGHTERVILLE, though. The town's name had been changed as well, and though there had been even more paperwork involved in that, it had been taken care of with almost magical skill.

"I'm gonna miss living in Slaughterville," Ravani said thoughtfully.

Virginia turned to look at him.

"Liar," she said, through a small smile. Ravani smiled back. She put her arm around his shoulder and gave him a squeeze. He did the same. They stood and looked at the town's new name, rolling in cheerful cursive across the sign.

WELCOME TO SOMEDAY, the sign read. YOU'RE ALREADY HERE.

THE END

ACKNOWLEDGMENTS

An immense amount of work, effort, and love went into making this book, and only a fraction of it was mine.

To Christian, whose patience, wisdom, and gentle hand were instrumental in making this story what it needed to be all along. My ideas and thoughts on this story were an unruly, scattered flock at best, and you were a perfect shepherd.

To Brian, who took the baton and ran with it in the best possible way. Thank you for your wonderful insight, care, and intelligence. Here's to many more.

To all the good folks at Macmillan/Holt, each of whom was essential to making this story a book worth reading: Carina Licon, Alexei Esikoff, Hayley Jozwiak, and Jessica White. Special thanks to Mallory Grigg and Matt Rockeller for making the book so beautiful to look at.

To my original family (Mom, Dad, and Erin). We were always on the move, but we were always together. I'm so glad that we still are.

To my home family (Karen, Eva, Ella, and Claire), who always cheer me on, and who were terribly kind about my rough draft, despite what a disaster it was. I couldn't do it without you, and wouldn't want to. And, just so you can see it in print: get off your screens!

To my chosen family as well. You know who you are. I picked you for a reason. Thanks for picking me back.

To every teacher and librarian who has supported me, and

handed my books to young readers. I owe you everything. Ditto for all you amazing indie booksellers . . . I'll be stopping by if I'm in your town!

And to every young reader. None of this matters if you don't pick up a book and read it. So no matter who you are, where you live, or how you got your hands on this book (or any book!): Thank you so very much. I hope you liked it.

If you think you should have been included in these acknowledgements and weren't, you're probably right. Thank you. Please don't mistake my absence of mind for an absence of gratitude.